C.

Cash. Eliminates. Opposition

A Novel By:

SHAAHIR

CASH IS KING PUBISHING LLC
Website: www.cashiskingpub.com

C.E.O.

C.E.O.

Published by: Cash Is King Publishing
Written by: Shaahir
Edited by: Jill Nail / jillbutterfly@yahoo.com
Cover Design by: Marion Designs / www.mariondesigns.com

For information on sales or book submission contact:
Cash Is King Publishing
P.O. Box 44434
Philadelphia, PA 19144
Website: www.cashiskingpub.com
Email: Cashiskingpublishing@yahoo.com
ISBN-13: # 978-0-9841348-0-9

DEDICATION

This is perhaps the easiest part of producing this title-something that requires the least amount of thought for me because it's that simple.

This and any other production I, Shaun 'Shaahir' Pettiway, am involved in is wholly and soley dedicated to the greatest accomplishment that I can endeavor to achieve…My diamonds and souls of my shell Zaahid and Asheeyaanah.

Words could never describe what you two mean to Daddy. I'm deeply sorrowed I wasn't there to see your progress in life, but know with surety that I have every intention on righting my wrong. I love you, and this entire production is in your name and a testament to your Abi's strength and things to come!

ACKNOWLEDGEMENT$

After thanking Allah Azza Wa Jal for teaching man by the pen, I want to thank all my haterz that motivated me to succeed at my dreams. It was your envious ways that made me go harder after the death of my freedom. I would also like to thank my sister, Nettie - Net, who by far has been my biggest supporter. Mountains could crumble, oceans could dry out, the stars could burn out their sizzle, and you will still be there as beautiful and loving as you are. Your children are a sign that Allah is Ar-Rahman, I love you baby.

To 'Khabeer' Dontay Pettiway, how we missed sharing the same womb is a mystery to me. You've always been my inspiration & motivation to prosper beyond life's adversity. You a real ass dude and made men don't come many these days. When I first said I wanted to start my own publishing company, you were the first person to cut the check, with as little as "It's done". I love you Tay, may Allah bless you and Artie, WE UP BABEE!

Mom, there's no way I can forget you. Only one word could truly describe the woman you are and what you did for me over the years…Amazing! Much love.

I can't count how many times I heard a nigga stamp himself with thoroughness and actually turn out to be a 'liz-zame'. In fact, the majority of niggas claim to be moving right and ain't moving at all; not B-Easy. My man, Brian Holt a bred for real. Niggas talk that money shit but they piss poor morally. When we discussed Cash Is King business, he met his end with my end and participation on

1,2,3. Much love dawg, you a real ass dude and I wish you millions and a speedy departure! Much love to the entire Holt family.

Gram-dukes, no words can ever describe how much it meant to me seeing you in the back of that federal courthouse in support of your grandbaby...Priceless. You have never dropped the ball and I appreciate it all.

To all my Cash Is King authors, "Muji" Keon Smith, "Tuffy" B Torrance, "Fly" Angel Serrano, and "Nino" Yusef Brown, I salute you all as kings amongst knights in this pen game.

They say if you love something you got to let it go, but if it comes back, then it means so much more. Ossheney, you'll always be my lady. Love you, Tink!

Reese cheese, it's never the setback, it's the get back. Dudes like you-they don't make no more. They all got fat while we were away, it's our turn!

A lot of assistance was rendered to see this project come to life. Expressing my gratitude would be an understatement. Rashayn, Q-deezy, Nettie-Net, Fly, K-B, and everybody else I bothered to death when reviewing this manuscript...Thank you. A very special thanks to Jill Butterfly.

To the rest that have been in my corner from day one: Pop-pop, Tee-lo, Pat the rat, Boo, Na'eemah Umm Ameerah, Diz, black ass Pig, whassup nigga? Bam, Yahya, Shaheed, Mink & Butter, Taylor, Eb, Monae, keep doing what you doing baby...I love you! Wanda, Mal, Kevin, Chanae Perry, Coco, my old head Sugar Wug, E-A from uptown, Markease from Aphillyation, thanks for the game, you a made nigga for real, dawg! Ghost aka New Jersey post-man, Rasheed, Sajad, Zakee, Hasan, Sideeq, A'qeel, Na'il, Trig, Maahir, Shaykh Saleem, Tawfeeq, may Allah bless y'all tremendously. Ameen wa salatu was salaamu alaa rasoolullah. The whole Uptown keep puttin' on, Philly, D-ware, D.C, Virginia, New Jersey, real niggas do real thangs...Whassup!

To everybody coppin up, allowing themselves to walk life with my characters, Big Ups!

I wouldn't end this without shitting on you scudbuckets that hate a nigga out. If I was a betting man, I'd put the crib on it that you bitches are fucked up right now: Ayanna, Ameenah, Latifah, Nee-nee, Haniyah, eat dust bitch, Maybach, lay-back, don't even talk to me!!!

Not out of respect, but out of space, I'll leave the rest of you hoes nameless.

Ya boy C.E.O., Shaahir!

PROLOGUE

"The world is yours!" Beanie exclaimed from an elevated platform in the spacious ballroom on Broad Street. Hundreds of gold and silver balloons fell from the ceiling with big face twenties bouncing within, while the spotlights skipped across faces and fabric's of celebrators, causing their diamonds and platinum jewelry to twinkle in the glaring flashes. Despite the chocolate, caramel, and ivory complexions that floated about, they all had two things in common; wearing white and biggin' up the C.E.O. of Cash Is King Entertainment. The release party was sure to be the dopest party the city of Philadelphia had ever seen. Every baller, bossy lady, and big willie in the tri-state was set to make an appearance. Bentleys, Jags, Benzs, and Ranges pulled into the parking lot one by one, until people had no choice but to park their hundred thousand dollar whips on the streets of north Philly, as this event was one nobody wanted to miss.

Since it all started here in these ruthless streets, Shiz wanted to bring the beat back to the city by having his release party in the heart of the district he used to roam. This way, no celebrity, musician, or reporter could misconstrue that he didn't always have major money. He had grinded his way up to the top!

The crowded ballroom roared slurs of self admiration. When Beanie gave them the world, each individually believed it was theirs; weighing their own success they had obtained in their minds. But, one knew it was his, Shiz.

"Every hood has a lot of niggas or dudes or whatever that came up bustin' their guns, trappin', robbin', whatever da fuck was needed to survive. But, only few make it out. My nigga, Shizzy Wiz, walked through that hood drama, and we all know how the city get down." The celebrators nodded, reflecting on their own past, as they stood attentively listening to Beanie's speech, enjoying the sparkle from his swinging diamond-crested S-P charm. Shiz and his murdering syndicates sat at a centered rectangular table, with some bad ass Brazilian arm pieces in all white Gucci. They were sipping vintage wine as they puffed away on Turkish cigars, staring on from Cartier frames which shielded them from the beaming spotlight focused on their table.

"But, what I personally want to say is, I know how hard it is to get some money, but still be you not lettin' the trips you taking, chic's you hittin', and whips you drivin' change you. This nigga is definitely one of the most thorough niggas you are ever gonna meet. And, the nigga filthy...So make sure you get a check before you leave." The crowd laughed along with Shiz, as someone added,

"Make my shit out to child support."

"Nah though. This night marks a new era, and I wish Cash Is King all the success in the world. Fill them glasses up, so we can big my man up and make this night the best release party that this company and city will ever have....And go buy his movie!" Beanie added as the Italian waiters began to spread out, filling the glasses of everyone with imported champagne. They especially gathered around Shiz's table to make sure all of his members were satisfied. This was for sure the best day of Shiz's life, and a long time coming, as could be determined by his frequent chuckles and free spirit. His people quietly bigged him up at his newly found success. They were all at ease. Beanie popped the cork on the champagne, allowing its bubbly suds to drip onto the stage.

"All you Go-Getters in here, put ya glasses up." The inhabitants raised them in Shiz's direction, as the low volume music came to a stop. Sitting to Shiz's left were his youngens, Bam and Dee, while on his right were his cousin Chantel and his right hand man, M.

"To my man, Shiz, and the Cash Is King family: I wish y'all a hundred years of success and multiple orgasms." The crowd laughed, as M noticed something strange on Bam's chest dancing around. He tapped Shiz's arm to alert him to its weirdness. Shiz saw the tiny red dots dancing about. Simultaneously, Bam noticed the same thing on M, and Chantel on Dee and Shiz, except Shiz's was on his head.

"So with no doubt...To that nigga, Shiz, and Cash Is King entertainment, rock the fuck out! Cash is King, babee!" The crowd returned "Cash is King" in unison, right before eight slugs tore through Dee's chest cavity, knockin' him completely out of his seat. Chantel pushed Shiz to the floor as their table underwent a barrage of deadly fire. Bam and two bodyguards weren't so fortunate. The raining bullets left them slumped over the table wearing their dinner. The ballroom occupants began scrambling to find safety. Screaming could be heard as panic erupted. The flaming shells not only found a nest in Shiz's deadly syndicates, but in plenty of innocent attendees as well. No one seemed to notice the over-staffed caterers miraculously diminish in numbers before the sudden gunfire.

Shiz regained his calm beneath the table with Chantel. M could be seen under a chair a few tables over, calling for his Mac-11 to be thrown to him by a shaken female near the DJ booth. Chantel lifted her dress to retrieve the twin forties she kept strapped to her inner thighs, eager to bring war as she cocked the irons, releasing death into the chamber. The slick backs continued gunning down Shiz's entourage, security, and employees. Most of the ballroom occupants tried desperately to reach the doors, but machine gunfire tore through them like human pinatas, splashing ounces of blood onto the floor, door, and hopeful attempters.

Shiz snatched his pistol grip gauge that had been attached to the table by his order, just as he heard some Italian slick backs get closer to his location.

"Channy, look. Go out that way, and I'ma get at these pussies from here," Shiz said windedly over the crackling gunfire, pointing toward the front part of the draped table.

"Say no more, baby. I'm all over these fucks," she spat, crawling toward the front.

Shiz raised the shotgun, dressed in all white Armani, taking the pasta-eating slick backs out of their shoes. BOOM! went the shotty, sending shell pellets crashing into the pale assassins knocking them over the seated tables. Click-Clack, BOOM! Click-Clack, BOOM! But the more he dropped, the faster they replenished their attackers.

M gave up on getting help from the frightened female covering her ears in a fetal position. He began snail crawling his way over, as wood and glass chips fell on him from the echoing slugs slamming against the decor. He had reached the gun and not a moment too soon. Shiz was under siege by three hitters who attacked his weak side.

The Mac ripped !

Chantel resurfaced at the end of the table where two hitters stood just feet away, holding Mac-90s with beams attached under the nozzles. She laid on her chest, causing her thirty-six C's to gather, pressing together through the V-neck Versace cocktail dress. They noticed the angelic facebearing a devilish grin, moments before her twin forties popped shells into their fleshy torsos.

"Fuck y'all niggas. Fuck y'all niggas!" M screamed from behind the spitting Mac, standing at the center of the dinner table pumping slick backs full of lead.

Chantel slivered onto the floor, after smearing some innocent woman's blood on her face and dress. She stopped motionless when nearing another slick back who paid her no mind, believing she was already dead until she pumped his body and head with five hollow tips sending his soulless shell collapsing.

"Joey, Joey. The fuckin' coon by the stage, ya idiot," Nikko tried to whisper Shiz's location.

"Yea, dickhead I'm right here, pussy!" Shiz spat, from behind the speaker. Click-Clack, BOOM! blowing an unreal hole through Joey...Lights out!

"Fuckin' Joey's dead, Vinny! That fuckin' nigger just shot Joey," Nikko said, ducking behind a table along with Vinny who was much older and more experienced than Nikko.

"Calm the fuck down, will ya? A'course he killed Joey. What the fuck ya think we doin' here? Now, shut ya mouth asshole, before I shoot ya myself."

M was painting the ballroom with Italian juices, as he reloaded the Mac to give up more heat. Screaming obscenities, he punched the clip in just as two slugs tore through his suit jacket, knocking him off the table. Blood began soaking his shirt, as it drooled from his mouth. He stood to his feet, squeezing rounds into the attacking assassins. Chantel slid up smoothly behind Nikko and Vinny after they stooped past her slumped body. With her hair unpinned and blood on her face, they turned to see a dead woman send them to hell, as she stood over their punctured bodies firing lead until the guns clicked.

Shiz could see M bleeding badly, firing an endless amount of rounds into the blood hungry Italian force. One by one they fell for the eternal snooze, spinning wildly into the walls, tables, and chairs, while smoking shell casings flipped from M's machine gun. It looked like it was all over, until two flaming shells split M's head open like a dropped pumpkin. With the look of shock filling his brows, M's bullet stricken body fell slumped to the floor. He was no more! Shiz ran across the room, witnessing the whole event as sorrow filled his heart. Click-Clack, BOOM. Click-Clack, BOOM. Click-Clack, BOOM. Click-Clack, BOOM. Click-Clack, CLICK. M's blood was revenged, but his presence would be truly missed. He was there from day one, and had paid a weighty cost in order to see this night along with his man Shiz. He stood over him with tears in his eyes and a throbbing heart.

At that moment, Shiz realized nobody was left standing. And more importantly, the countless amount of bodies that laid on the floor, with organs that normally nested their inside and kept them talking and walking hanging out. Cries of "Omigod" and terror could be heard clearly now that silence had finally befallen the spacious ballroom. Shiz noticed the bullet holes through his Cash Is king logo chipped out of ice. More seriously, he noticed his team, bloody and without life. One by one the surviving celebrators began to pick up their heads, canvassing the layout. Shiz recognized nobody he accompanied. As the crowd began seeking help for friends and loved ones, he searched for his. Ironically enough, Chantel was doing the exact same thing from the other end of the hall. Their eyes met through the injured partygoers.

Shiz began walking towards her, happy to at least see somebody that survived the hit. And, for it to be his lovely baby cousin was in fact relieving. As she neared him, he saw fear coat her face as tears welled her eyes. They had survived a gruesome attack that was designed to leave havoc. No one from Shiz's Cash Is King family remained alive. The Italians had finished them all off for no clear, apparent reason.

Shiz stretched his arms out to hug his cousin's feminine frame. Despite the chattering noise and screeching sirens, he heard clearly a Caucasian's voice chime:

"Da Don, send his greetings for Lou Maleano, YOU FUCKIN JIG!"

Chantel tried to warn him of the middle aged Italian standing behind him. Shiz's body froze hearing the iron cock inches from him, acknowledging the sound meant his run was up. It all was for nothing. The cars, company, murders, money, were for nothing. All of it would be left behind on his nearing trip. Chantel was so beautiful to him, as her eyes beckoned for him not to go and wished she could be in his place. His heartbeat quickened as his breathing slowed. It was time to lay down. He turned around swiftly, making an attempt to win life. But, there was no life left to win. It was his time. Bap, Bap, Bap, Bap, Bap! His body jumped.

"Oh shit! What da fuck, shit?!" Shiz spat with his heart kicking through his chest. By his breathing, you would have thought he ran a marathon. Sweating profusely, he leaned up to comb his eyes frantically over his surroundings. He was at mom's crib having another bad episode.

"Shit, fuck man." He breathed, sitting up rubbing his hand across his body, reassuring that all of his organs were still there. *A dream? Shit, these fuckin' nightmares, man*, he thought. Shiz checked the window, only to see M and Black schooling the youngens on getting money at three in the morning. This caused him to recall why he was at his mother's north Philly row home in the first place. He was waiting to re-up his block.

"Fuck it, let me go out there and see what's good," he mumbled, getting up to join his team and fearing more sleep meant more war with them spaghetti-eating slick backs; an event he wasn't ready to see just so soon.

CHAPTER 1

we Do us

"Hey mom, where my Prada jacket I left on the couch last night at?" Shiz screamed at the top of the staircase, drawing the irritation of his mother Ms. Pettiway. She was sitting on the edge of her bed directly under the ceiling fan, cooling herself with a half folded newspaper, in a pointless effort to stay cool from the sizzling summer heat.

"Noodles, what da hell I tell you about screaming in this house?" Ms.Pettiway shot back, her voice bearing an unfriendly tone.

"How you gonna tell me about screaming when you do it?" he spoke to himself.

"Whatcha say?" she retaliated, knowing her son too well. "I don't know why you stay down here so much anyway. Don't cha got your own place, boy?" she growled.

"Ma, what is you trippin' for? I didn't even say nothing." He knew how far to go before mom would be rapped out. Despite Shiz maintaining a 3-inch advantage over his mother's 5'7" frame, the extra 40 lbs. he gave to her in attitude was a world of difference when mom turned it up. See, mom was a wife of a hustler which helped develop the tough skin needed to raise a fatherless boy in North Philadelphia. Puddin had to shoulder it, after Shiz's father, Darren, was murdered in front of him. Ms. Pettiway had a plate-full being Shiz's mother & father in the heartless city the D.O.C. mostly raised. She did a wonderful job and to the best of her ability. Despite Shiz being grown now and on his own, paying her bills, she felt the need from time to time to show him she still had shit on lock.

"Noodles, your cousin's coming down here today so answer your cell when you leave this house, you hear me?" she said, unfastening the top part of her denim to add ventilation pouring from the dust infested fan above.

"Whatchu telling me for?" he returned.

"Because, you know damn well that girl only comes down here to be around you...and who ya talking to like that? Don't get smart!"

"Mannnn. Look." Shiz didn't understand why mom let Chantel come down there so much. It's not like they live in the Mount Airy section of the city. North Philly, Lehigh at that, was no place for a young girl to learn adolescence. Shiz swore that had Chantel's mom, Aunt Patricia, not been breaking mom off some of that case money she had won, mom would've never agreed to the temporary watch. Be it as it may, she was family, and he'd hold her down ever so tight while she visited. Shiz grabbed his Prada glasses that coordinated well with the white T, that matched the fresh air ones he just broke from the box. The navy blue Cavalli capris offset the outfit well. As he reached for the door to exit, he allowed his eyes to roll towards the ceiling, as if he almost forgot something. Shiz reached behind the worn out leather sofa and pulled his 10 shot 40 cal., tucked it into the front part of his capris, then exited with the world belonging to him, so dopeboy fresh!

No matter what time you came outside in North Philly, Seventh Street was always in full swing, with all the ingredients that made north, north…from the winos that stood motionless on abandoned stoops to the crackheads that wandered aimlessly up the block looking for opportunities to earn their next high. The blasting voice of Lil Wayne through the speakers of the sud-dripping Crown Victoria provided enough reason for the young hood girls hugging the corner to display the newest down south dances, much of it erotic.

> *"Shawty say the nigga that she wit ain't shit, shawty say the nigga that she wit can't hit, well shorty I'ma hit-it-hit it, like I can't miss, and he don't do this, and he don't do that…"*

Shiz reached the pavement where his '09' black Tahoe sat on chrome and black 24-inch Asante's, giving value to the block, which obviously screamed somebody gettin' that money around here.

"It's hot as fish grease out dis jawn," he spat, disarming the alarm, just as the crew of young wolves was calling for him at the top of the block directly in front of the deli.

"Ay Shiz, you ain't no baller nigga, fuck outta here," the distant voices grabbed his attention, just as he was grabbing the 'quarter bird' from his trunk. Shiz held up his index to silence the howling pack from the other end of the block.

"Hold up, Dawg!" he screamed, reactivating the alarm. Shiz began jogging cautiously up the block with his hands tucked under his shirt, holding the 40 cal. to prevent it from dropping. The moment he reached the corner, his cell rung with a message from his mom, alerting him that his cousin was on her way. Shiz wasted no time handing Black the package, as he stood sipping a Snapple while leaning against the brick store. Black was a big, fat cheeseburger-eating mutherfucka, and without the whiteness of his teeth and eyes, confusing him for a shadow was quite possible. He often had a problem following orders, as he felt like he should be running shit, but the amount of money and time spent on getting high would forever hinder that. He was the type to smoke until he blacked out, waking up wilding in jail, broke, and with a sore jaw. Without rap, Black grabbed the crack and stashed it under the light pole by the pay phone.

"What da fuck up, Shiz?" M asked.

"Ain't nothing M. What's up pimp?" he returned.

"Tryna get that MONEY up in here," M said quickly, with a raspiness in his voice.

"Cash is king, babee."

"Cash is king," M returned, looking distantly up the block. M, on the other hand, was totally opposite of Black...A bit of a pretty boy, high yellow with deep sea waves, medium built, and would let that cannon off in a heartbeat. His loyalty to Shiz was unquestionable. He valued the way Shiz used diplomacy in the streets, always knowing he would make the right move when it came to the clique.

"Ay Shiz, you fucked that bitch last night you had with cha?" M wanted to know.

"That chic ass is fatter than a muthafucka, please tell me the pussy good!"

"What bitch?" Black chimed.

"The bitch, Tracy, from Logan that used to fuck with that nigga Marv," M said.

"I ain't fuck," Shiz admitted.

"You ain't fuck?" M stared on confusingly.

"Hell naw. She start talking about 'you won't fuck me' then pass off like you'd be doing the rest of these trixs," Shiz imitated Tracy.

"Get da fuck outta here. That bitch trippin' like that?" M questioned, hoping his man had hit so he could go at her next. Truth is, Tracy was a freak, but before she was willing to jump on Shiz's dick, he had to pay what he weighed if he had any kind of thoughts of seeing that ass wiggle. Black's untimely interruption was well expected by Shiz and M, as he tossed his empty bottle into the dumpster next to him and Shiz filled M in on the events leading up to her refusal.

"That's the muthafuckin' problem witchu dudes. If y'all niggas just start telling these hoes up front we tryna party that ass, shit ah be smooth," Black shot, receiving the unconvinced look Shiz and M held silent on. The trio continued debating, as the neighborhood fiends poured in to purchase the beast trapped within the tiny ziplocks from the workers.

Forty-five minutes had passed Shiz easily, he seemed to totally forget about picking his cousin up from the subway. Without delay, he dapped his team, jumped in the husky four wheel drive, and peeled out of the cluttered block. When he arrived at Broad and Lehigh, he immediately noticed through the mass of pedestrians the face of Chantel's displeasure. And, at seventeen, she was as developed as a twenty-three year old fitness instructor. She had caramel skin and chinky hazel eyes that she repeatedly brushed her lengthy cinnamon strands from. Chantel had a deadly combination of educated ambition and heavenly allure, which basically meant, her milkshake bring all the boys to the yard. Even though Shiz wasn't that much older than she, he often carried her like he was her father, schooling her on the nut ass moves young bols played on, and always copping her the latest outfits and footwear that drew envy from all her haters. It was most likely this level of participation that had Shiz ready to split the wig of half the niggas he found in her face. The nigga that got that ass would for sure be a thoroughbred, capable of handling a born raised wife of a hustler.

When Chantel noticed her cousin's truck, she grabbed her Chanel travel bag sitting beside her and began tugging it toward the SUV. As Shiz hopped out, stopping traffic behind him, he noticed a gang of guys eye molesting Chantel's shapely thighs and bouncing ass, which rumbled in her Chanel skirt set.

"What da fuck y'all little niggas looking at, dawg?" Shiz screamed over the loud sidewalk, bearing fire in his eyes as Chantel beckoned him to get into the truck. He obliged her without releasing his eyes from the violators. Had somebody said something outta pocket, he would have put that twirk in with very little to consider. He didn't usually act that way. He was more of a thinker, but Shiz didn't play at all when it came to anything concerning Chantel.

"Why you always trippin' when I come through?" Chantel didn't hesitate as they pulled into traffic.

"Fuck dhat, what I tell you 'bout wearing them little ass skirts? You not gonna be happy 'til I take one of these niggas out there shoes, fuckin' with you."

Chantel wanted to reply smartly, but knew it was no use. Shiz was as bull-headed as they come, and he usually said what he meant. Plus, she realized she was the little cousin. So, she let it go. After the short altercation, Chantel struck Shiz in the back of the head.

"Do you know how long I was waiting on you, fathead?" She gave a stare that demanded a response.

"My bad, baby girl, I had to handle some B-I, my bad...Ay listen, you want me to take you to the crib or you gonna make this run with me right fast?" He inquired. She looked as if to say, *God damn right I'm going with you. I ain't sitting in that hot ass house all day with Aunt Puddin watching soaps all crazy.* Shiz picked up on the look and laughed deeply, while Chantel pondered how safe and cared for she was in her cousin's company. Plus, she enjoyed the jewels he dropped, and knew if they saw something hot while they were out, he would copp it for her.

$ $ $ $ $

Meanwhile, back on the block the cash flow was picking up something vicious. The two wolves along with their young bols, Dee and Bam, were tearing 7th street a new asshole. Shiz wasn't gone long and the workers already tore through three onions on the nick-dime tip. M never liked Black running shit, as bullshit was always on the verge of happening when he was in charge. M layed under the shade of the mini umbrella attached to the edge of the deli, peeping how their youngens moved. Black wiped the sweat from his forehead with the wetted terry cloth towel he was sporting around his neck, while he talked on his cellie to some brawd that topped him off the night before.

"My dick big, youngin'?' he spat through the phone, grabbing his manhood. "Yea, I wanna see you back it all the way up...Yea! that's what I'm talking about. So what's up for tonight then?" he said zealously. By the grin on Black's face you could tell it was on. He ended the call, just as Ms. Rosie was walking past. Despite her being twice their age, she was still, very much so, the brawd their old heads drooled over. Standing 5'6", she was cocoa brown, had dimples that your finger could get lost in, and with an ass that could sure enough give Buffie a run for her money... Which is why Black couldn't control himself, whenever she came to the corner store. Her husband had told Black before to stop disrespecting his wife. As she came gliding up the block, he could see the sides of her gigantic ass from the front. He licked his lips in wait of the feast. When she was passing him, he thought lustfully to himself, *Um, look at that shit swinging everywhere.* Without sense or consciousness, he squeezed it deeply, as if he could no longer resist the temptation. Of course,

Ms. Rosie launched a series of cusses and occasional swings at Black's head, to which Black simply responded,

"Go 'head, yo! You know you like that shit."

M proceeded to calm her down, but she wasn't tryna hear none of that shit. She stormed back down the block, citing she'll be back when her husband Dino got off from work and he was sure to kick his ass.

"Why you do that nut ass shit, dawg?" M spat to Black, not feeling his actions at all.

"Man, fuck dhat, bitch! She knows she like that shit."

"Still, that was some nut shit, dawg, straight up!" M restated, clearly agitated.

$ $ $ $ $

Shiz pulled the truck towards the curb. He hopped out while Chantel remained within the blinging truck, parked on Germantown and Erie. She watched as Shiz disappeared into one of the clothing stores.

"Salaamu Alaykum, Mu'min here," Shiz chanted, as he entered the shop.

"Naw, akh can I help ya wit something?" a dark skinned brother with a full beard spat.

"Yea dawg, I need some baggies."

Just outside, Chantel was applying the K.L.S. lip gloss in the passenger mirror, when she noticed a sharply dressed chocolate Puff look-alike with a chisel line-up and bread, staring hard at her applying the gloss. His intensity made her blush, as he leaned against the milky 750 IL with deep dish Giovanna's. Unaware that her face read she was completely attracted, he walked toward the truck, as her eyes now raced frantically to see if Shiz was emerging from the store.

"What's up, shawty?" he shot, pulling his cell from the waist clip to check the vibrating phone. She stared at the definition on his forearms and chest, which got the wheels turning on Chantel's coochie juices.

"What's ya name, gorgeous?" He wanted to know, laying his killa smile on her.

"Chantel," she sang.

"Well my name is Markease, sis. So, what agency do you work for?"

"Excuse me?" a confused Chantel asked.

"Nah, I just thought that you was probably a model. You have the type of face seen on the front of a kings Magazine," he sounded sincere.

"No photo shoot for me, but I'll take the compliment." The two flowed in conversation very easily, keeping it on a basic level. Markease couldn't help but notice how sexy Chantel's thighs were, and their thickness pressed against the cushion of the Tahoe. It literally made his dick hard. There was something in the exoticness of her look that made cement of his legs. He definitely wanted her on the team, as Chantel mildly flirted with the mid-twenties gentlemen by batting her luscious eyelashes, that accentuated the pearly whites she smiled. Chantel grabbed his cell from his hand and encoded her number.

"Get at me when you got some time, Markease," she said flatly, open to more conversation. To Markease, that was an indication the meeting was over, but he didn't really want to leave. However, the possibility struck him of her having a man, as her eyes kept darting behind him while they conversated. So, he disappeared in the ghostly white BM he pulled up in, banging some down south shit. He left Chantel considering how soon she'd allow him to talk to her.

In a startling manner, Shiz opened the driver side door to enter.

"Who da fuck was that, Channy?" he shot, breaking her daydream.

"How I supposed to know who that is? He was looking for you, but said he'll holla back 'cause you wasn't in the truck and he didn't have time to wait," she lied, but truly felt bad because she didn't like keeping secrets from Shiz. But, after the incident earlier, she knew Shiz would've rapped her head off for hours about how trifling niggas are. He seemed to have bought what she said, or she believed so, because of his lack of questioning. As he pulled into the congested avenue traffic, she did make a mental note, *no more lying*!

"Noodles, where we going now?"

"To the crib, I need to be getting back to the block."

"Can we make a quick stop?" she asked, cutely.

"Make a quick stop WHERE, Channy? I'm not going to no mall."

"No, I'm hungry. I just want to go to my favorite restaurant. Ya gonna take me, right?" Shiz stared at her briefly, urged to say no, but how could he refuse her. She was his heart. To Champs they went on Delaware Avenue.

During the quiet ride, Shiz found himself in heavy thought about the block and the amount of trouble Black seemed to always stir up while he was away. Some of the shit made him think that maybe he was deliberately tryna mess up his bread. At the end of the day, Shiz knew Black was a liability, rather than an asset. But, the two go back a long ways to when they used to grab off Fats from 13th Street. Most wouldn't know it, but Black used to have shit popping, hustling for Fats. The nigga stayed on the grind out there. That's how he met Shiz, out there grabbing up. Black used to see his face so much re-ing up, Black told Fats to give Shiz a shot because the nigga was bringing a lot of dough through there. He and Shiz would wind up getting close, real tight. They swore to be squad to the bitter end, which is why when Shiz got the half of bird fronted to him by Fats and some dope head crept 'em for the jawn, Black didn't hesitate to ride out with his man, even though Black's actions got 'em booted from the strip. Once the guns came out, Black bucked his gun alongside of his man. The sincerity Black showed throughout the war would never be forgotten by Shiz. After the war, the drug induced backward hustling allowed Shiz to far surpass Black in both status and money. Shiz would, however, let him run his block as a homage the old time friend earned. Over the years, Black's ass managed to cost Shiz tons of money, with his oversized ego and ruthless behavior. Quite frankly, Shiz didn't know how much more of Black's antics he could endure. But, with M on the scene, Shiz could trust things would go down how he wanted.

The restaurant was in normal attendance when Shiz and Chantel arrived, having their regular seats by the chef's window. The relaxing spot provided the usual laid back atmosphere, with all six big screen plasma's going along the wall and multiple channel selection. Central air made the wait pleasurable. Chantel ordered bruschetta as her appetizer, and fried salmon for Shiz's and her main course.

"Noodles, wait 'til ya taste the bruschetta here, it's so good."

"Ain't no black folks eating no stuff like that. You better stop letting ya mom fill ya head with that bullshit."

"Would you stop being so hood and try it. I bet ya like it," she enticed, noticing some unfriendly looks staring at her from across the dining room. She thought she was buggin' at first, until the ladies started pointing at her. Still, it was nothing to her feeling like a pimp. She brushed her shoulder off, as she was so used to being hated on. Now, it appeared to her that the ladies were heading over. They didn't get the response they wanted so they thought to deliver the message themselves, and that sure enough got Chantel's attention and an ass whoppin' on hold.

"Noodles, do you know these monkey dog ass bitches, 'cause I'm about to whup on that ass?" Chantel said softly, maintaining strong eye contact with the both of them. She sneakily took off her Jimmy Choo's under the table, saving enough time to arch one of her eyebrows as they arrived.

"Who?" Shiz didn't understand.

"Shiz, who is this?" Tracy shot in her most annoying hood voice possible.

"Maan, if you don't get the fuck outta here..."

"Don't worry 'bout who I am, better yet, ya rude ass shoulda found that out before you walked over here."

"And, why is that?" Tracy smartly replied.

" 'Cause ya silly ass woulda known, bitch, I'll punch ya in da mouth." Without warning, Chantel jumped up and threw a jab at Tracy that Shiz couldn't catch before it landed. Shiz began holding the ladies back, while trying to calm Chantel down. Tracy acted as if she wanted to retaliate, but the look Shiz shot at her made her rather swing on the pope before this lady friend of his. She did manage to squeeze out over the blood that coated her teeth, "You better control that dizzy ass bitch then." Tracy's screams clearly caused a scene in the restaurant. Saving herself some pride, she decided to leave, but knew she had to turn her game up if she wanted to compete with that pretty ass red bone. Shiz was her target first, and she refused to let somebody else take the bread she planned on getting out of him. Her plan was already devised before leaving the restaurant. She had to fuck him and good, too!

After the drama subsided, the food was delivered and tranquility was re-established.

"You need to stop messing with those kind of girlz," Chantel advised between bites.

"I don't mess with them. I just let 'em give me head." That response brought about a weird look from Chantel, as Shiz sipped from the drink before him.

"Yea, then you need to find better acting females to getcha..." Chantel rolled her eyes, not wanting to repeat her cousin's statement 'to getcha head from,' she choked out reluctantly.

"Why? You gonna knuckle up for ya cousin?" Shiz shot, wearing a smile.

"Boy, I woulda whupped that ass up in here."

"Watch ya mouth, girl."

"Oops! My bad. But, I'm serious! Ya not gonna have me out here acting a fool, cause you can't keep ya thing in ya pants."

"A'ight Channy, take it easy, baby."

Ironic enough, the rest of the afternoon was without incident, and the food was delicious. Shiz even tried some of that bruschetta. To his surprise, it was good. Chantel teased him all the way to the car about it.

On the way home, Chantel asked if they could go by Nieman Marcus to check out the newest Louie Vuitton jeans. She promised to be in and out, as she had no intentions of buying anything...Boy, was that true. Shiz knew that was game when she asked him to come with her. In and out turned into an hour and a half of shuffling outfits into the fitting room, which ultimately led to $7,000 in designer labels charged to her cousin's stash.

"I'ma put your ass on an allowance," Shiz shot, watching Chantel browse through clothes like a crazed woman possessed, just as he disconnected from the cell call.

"Why?" she asked, as if she didn't notice the price tags on the chosen item.

" 'Cause you spending bread like ya little red ass be standing out on the block with me getting this money." Chantel walked over to Shiz, opened her pocketbook, and gave him all of the currency contents.

"What's this for?" Shiz asked, eyeing the money his hand held.

"I don't want you sweatin' the money we spend up in here," she said flat out.

"Channy, if you don't cut it out. You know damn well I'ma hold ya down, but ya little ass definitely going on a budget." She sucked her teeth.

"How much then?"

"I don't know, but we gonna reduce our trips up in this mutherfucka," Shiz shot, as he began stuffing Chantel's money into his pants.

"I'll take this off ya tab though."

"Stop playing with me, Noodles. Betta give me my money back before I tell Aunt Puddin' on you," she whined, smiling.

"How? You the one pulling bread out like you big willie and shit. Dis be me, baller!" Shiz said, returning the same.

Despite their little conversation, Shiz loved providing for Chantel, and she truly appreciated all that Shiz had done for her. She planned to repay him when she graduated from college, and started her own business. She knew even at that time, Shiz would probably still be taking care of her. But, if he ever needed her, she'd be ready. Before they could finish checking out, Shiz's cell started blowing up with all sorts of nasty text messages from Tracy's thick ass, detailing how she wanted to get fucked. If nothing else could put an end to Chantel's afternoon with her cousin, some good 'ole fashion pussy could handle the task. Tracy was known to have some bomb ass wet-wet and thoughts of her backing that juicy ass up would have him run a few lights on the way back. Before dropping Chantel off, he decided to stop at the top of the block to check on his team.

"Yizzo, what's up?" Shiz shouted through the window of his Tahoe to the hustling crew. Black nodded, acknowledging Shiz's presence. He was obviously beat down from the mid day heat, and from the looks of him, he had already gotten the jump-start on the night, as the smell of haze lingered the air while he sat propped against the store on an empty milk crate. M approached the truck and handed Shiz a wad of money.

"A'ight. I see niggas is gettin' that bread," Shiz sang. M noticed Chantel in the shotgun with her legs crossed and hair pulled into a side ponytail.

"Damn, what's up Cee?" he addressed, stroking his chin hair.

"Hi M," she sang flirtatiously.

"Look at you, Cee, getting all big. Ay Shiz! I might have to wife your little cousin if she get any badder," he spat, nodding his head with a wicked grin.

"You don't wanna wife me, M," Chantel returned, flickering her eyelashes.

"And why is that?" he wanted to know.

"Because I'm already married," she said as if he knew.

"To who?" M didn't get that one.

"Niemen!" Chantel told him, receiving a confused look from M. She raised her bag from Niemen Marcus off the floor of the truck at head level so M could see. M began laughing hard when he caught on to the joke.

"Ha, ha, ha," Shiz chimed mockingly, shooting Chantel a look that snapped her back into reality from the open flirting with M in his presence.

"Look. I'm about to ride out. Everything good out here, right?" Shiz asked. M searched around then strutted as if shit was normal. Shiz passed M a black plastic bag, dapped his hand, "holla," he sang, pulling to the end of the block to eject Chantel, before spinning a left merging into traffic.

Tracy had hit Shiz and informed him to meet her at the Days Inn on Roosevelt Boulevard. She had gone too far with that restaurant scene, and needed to smooth things over with her potential donor. She already reserved the suite 206 which was her favorite. That room occupied a jacuzzi with floor to ceiling mirrors. Tracy figured how she planned to fuck the shit out of Shiz. She'd get the money for the room back that she charged to her Visa and more, as she admired her 5'5" frame that could bring a Coke bottle to shame in the mirror of a Logan apartment. She wanted to turn Shiz out so a hot outfit was well needed. After fumbling through a couple of looks, she found a one piece sheer stomachless by the Stacy Dash Collection, that hugged her in all the right places. She turned to gain a view of her sexy ass she was in tote of. Irresistible to herself, she smacked it, knowing full well Shiz would enjoy all that ass. She viewed him like most men when it came to her bodacious body. They couldn't wait to feel their dicks slide in between her humongous ass cheeks, while her sugar walls brought them lustful smiles. Tracy finished the touches on her hair and the look was tastefully complete. So without delay, in the Honda Accord she went to meet Shiz at the hotel.

Ms. Pettiway opened the door after hearing the knocks of Chantel from the exterior of the house.

"Hey Channy, get in here and give me a hug," she said, beckoning for an embrace. Chantel wrapped her arms, in tote of her Nieman Marcus bags, around the average frame of her Aunt Puddin.

"Aunt Puddin, why you don't call me no more?"

"Why I gotta call you? You can call me, and it's not like every time I turn around, you not down here."

"Well, I still like to hear from you because when I try to call you, nobody answers the phone."

"Alright, enough wit that. I see somebody still showing them legs," Ms. Pettiway added, viewing Chantel's get up that revealed her shapely thighs. Chantel twirled around to give her aunt a better view of her perfect body.

"Girllll, ya know you get all that ass from this side of the family, 'cause your mom and them don't have no ass at all. Your cousin didn't say nothing about your skirt, 'cause I can see ya ass print all in that piece. You know how he is when it comes to you."

"Yea, he said something," she spat, looking over her shoulder to view her ass.

"You keep it up, that boy gonna be killing somebody over you, watch!" she said, walking into the kitchen as Chantel briefly pondered her statement.

"You fly, though," Ms. Pettiway screamed from the kitchen, as Chantel went to get settled in her room up stairs.

"Thaaannnkkks!" Chantel cut back.

"And, where you get all those Nieman Marcus bags from?" Ms. Pettiway blurted to a faded Chantel. Despite all the bitching her son did about letting Chantel stay down there so much, she knew that her son loved the ground she walked on and was willing to do anything to protect and keep her as safe as possible, even at the expense of his money and blood.

CHAPTER

2

Back Dhat Shit Up!

Shiz pulled into the parking lot of the Days Inn and rolled up the haze he had gotten from Black. He sparked up and considered how he'd been hustling for some years now, and still really hadn't gotten where he would've liked. Sure the block money was good and kept food on his and the family table, but at the end of the day, that shit was table scraps. And he didn't want to still be pushing packages with the Feds indicting everything under the sun involving crack. Where would his way out come before the entire game closed up on him, he pondered nodding his head to Esco.

> *"Life a bitch then you die, that's why we get high, 'cause you never know when ya gonna go."*

The song blasted through the fifteens, as he turned the volume up a little more, feeling the throw back lyrics of Nas helping him coat his problems, as the smoke fog thickened encompassing the entire cockpit. In search of the Wine & Spirits bag, Shiz grabbed the Henny to continue his party with a waiting Tracy inside the hotel. There was an Indian man overly engaged in whatever was playing on the small black and white. Shiz rang the bell repeatedly before the bronze foreigner responded.

"Where's 206 at my man?" Shiz asked, to which the man pointed angrily, as if he wasn't hired to do just that. Shiz found the room without delay. When he arrived at the purple door, he noticed the scent of Jasmine penetrating the cracks. He knocked, and Tracy answered after peeping through the peephole, wearing her one piece with Monola stilettos revealing skin more reflective than diamonds under city lighting. Her right hand rested on her thick hip, as her hair wrapped cleverly around her almond face. Shiz knew that Tracy was alright, but who the fuck was this bitch?! The sex appeal Tracy displayed had Shiz questioning *why wasn't he, in fact, taking her more seriously?*

"Damn look at you, all sexy and shit. Fuck goin' on up in here?" Shiz shot, receiving a blush from Tracy.

"It's all about daddy," she sang, as she led Shiz to the bed by hand. He willfully followed, at which he centered in intensely on her ass, all of which was what Tracy wanted most from Shiz. After taking his shoes off, she poured him a shot of Henny and brought it to him subserviently. Taking a seat beside him on the bed allowing her thighs to spread, thereby gaining Shiz's attention at the same time, she began stroking his back lovingly.

"What da fuck goin' on Trase? Da-hell ya up to?" he asked, suspicious of her actions.

"Nothing, I just wanna please you. Plus, I was really rude earlier. Why? Is it a crime?" she asked.

"Nah. If that's what's poppin'..."

"Well it is." She stood before him watching him sip smoothly from the cup. Resting her knee between his legs on the edge of the bed and interrupting his guzzle, she grabbed the cup and finished the drink, licking her lips seductively upon completion. Tracy found her way to the stereo with her back facing Shiz as she hit play:

> *"Baby I see you working hard, I want to let you know I'm proud, let you know that I admire what you do. The more I need to reassure you my life would be purposeless without you..."*

Tracy slid into her best striptease, grinding her hips and resembling Alicia Keys' *No One* video, while the rhythmic sounds of Destiny's Child *Cater to You* enchanted the small suite. Shiz watched the performance attentively, feeling the warmth in his pants from the blood rush to his penis. He called for Tracy to join him at the bed. She could see lust in his eyes, as he eyed her full breast when she walked toward him.

"Shiz, do you really want to fuck me?" she asked alluringly, combing her hand over her hips.

"Is the sky blue, water wet? I'm tryna bust ya ass." Shiz tossed his phone and keys onto the table nearby. Tracy followed his actions by pushing him onto his back, immediately undressing his bottoms. Helping himself out of his shirt, Shiz attempted to kiss her luscious breasts. Tracy refused him, wanting to maintain total control of what was unfolding.

"So that's how we rockin'?" he asked.

"Yup!" Tracy responded. She would, however, plant wet kisses from his neck down. Unable to ignore any longer the bulge within Shiz's boxers, she wanted to know eagerly was it true? Did the boy really have an abnormal width? As she had heard hella-stories before about chic's scaling the wall, fucking with that green eyed nigga. The way he kissed, she knew his tongue game wasn't suspect at all. He could spin tornados on an average night. Given the right illegal substance, Shiz could bring reasonable doubt to a dike's sexual preference. Tracy could only hope she would be who he'd be spinning tonight. Snatching his boxers off only intensified those feelings. Ummm, I'ma fuck the shit outta this dick, she thought, eyeing her target's chubby friend. The doubt was removed. She had never seen a penis so fat and juicy before. It took all from within to avoid jumping right on for sexual ecstasy. She slowly slid his dick into her mouth until it began to disappear into her throat, deeply swallowing it whole as she had no gag reflex. Her neck game was the meanest! He began to moan at her warmth and intensity.

"You like it, daddy?" she moaned, receiving no response. He was overly into the pleasure. Without instruction, she found a rhythm in her technique, centralizing the tip and then going deep while fondling his balls. Tracy was hot! She began loving the way the young thug tasted in her mouth. She didn't even realize the amount of saliva she was using and the slurp was becoming obnoxious. She picked up the pace, as Shiz watched her slide down his shaft which ironic enough, turned him on more.

"Damn, Trace! Ya mouth good ass shit," he spat, with ecstasy in his voice, hoping her pussy was just as wet. Making her head a handle bar for the sexual ride he boarded, Shiz pushed deeper into Tracy's neck. Eating his dick caused her pussy to start juicing its way to being soaked, as she eyed his level of handsomeness and enjoyed his lollipop. The nigga had it, and I mean all of it; an unblemished complexion, dimples, green eyes, wavy dark hair, straight teeth, tight abs, tattoos, and a big fat fuckin' dick. Her pussy began to intensely throb. She had not experienced this before off a blowie! She could no longer hold out, which was opposite her plan to make him bust first, using her mouth only. Her thoughts became the voice her heart forbade.

"Fuck this shit; I want you to put it in. Put it in, Shiz, put it in!" she demanded, begging and massaging her pussy from behind. Stroking

Shiz's dick with desperation in her eyes, she was awaiting permission to proceed. Careless, she had lost the very game she sought to play. She needed to feel him within, to bring her hunger to satisfaction.

"Let's get it," Shiz grunted, allowing Tracy to board his rocket by grabbing her humongous ass, adding direction for the blast. His tip hit her wet spot.

"Oh shit!" Tracy moaned all the way down, feeling her vagina stretch. Shiz began coaxing Tracy by her fat ass to pick up the pace a bit. She obliged him, but the size of Shiz's dick, caused a pain that her pussy hadn't adjusted to yet. It had been a while since Tracy had last fucked. Feeling like Tracy was playing with the dick by her reluctance to go all the way down; he flipped her onto her back. With an intense look in his eye, he began delivering his male package like she had tipped him well. Tracy thought, why didn't I just troop it out.

"Ah shit. Wait. Ohh shit, Shiz. Fuck," she grunted.

"This that daddy dick Trase, dis that big dick shit!" With her legs pinned behind her head, there was no running from the dick she craved for. Shiz had now assumed total access into Tracy's swollen vagina, with every moment. Tracy didn't know whether to call the police or a wedding planner. As he dug deeper, he could feel the sporadic twitching of Tracy, breaking his rhythm periodically from the long dicking. Applying a much harder and deeper thrust to Tracy's soft spot, she had felt his dick hit something that no one proceeding touched. Her moaning intensified, as the pipe filled her completely. She wanted to push him off and break out the hotel asshole naked, but with the pain came a rush of sensation that she had only heard about.

"Oh shit, Shiz!....Shizzzz. Shit! Omigod...0ooh!" she moaned in lust, with her titties bouncing and pussy dripping. Tracy's juice box exploded into multiple orgasms. Shiz had her, and he knew he had her.

"Turn da fuck over!" he growled. Tracy happily obliged him, eyeing the swollen one eyed beast that had her pussy doing numbers. Tracy's ass seemed to take on double size when she positioned herself on all fours, with her back arched professionally. Tracy really had one of them Cherokee asses. Why she wasn't on the front of somebody's magazine beat the hell out him. He penetrated her warm, wet canal using every inch of blessed machinery. Shiz never fucked a brawd who described pound cake to the tee. Using the thin waist of Tracy for leverage, her ass cheeks punched jabs at Shiz's lower body, as he drilled his way closer to nuttin', enjoying the wiggle and clapping sound Tracy's ass made. He smacked her ass thunderously, as Tracy could feel her legs trembling, indicating she was about to cum again. But this time, Shiz would accompany her on the trip.

"Throw dhat shit back, bitch! You like it dirty don'tcha ...shit," Shiz slurred through clenched jaws, richly engrossed in pleasure. Tracy, approaching her climax, answered back throwing her round ass into the throbbing dick she had become adjusted to.

"Ohh! Fuck this ass. Shit yea...witcha big ol' dick," she shot back, feeling Shiz also nearing climax. She squeezed her vagina, grabbing his shaft to hasten the nut because her recent comments had Shiz punishing that ass. She knew she would pay dearly for the pleasure tomorrow.

"Yea, keep talking that shit. Dis my pussy, Trase. Who pussy is it?"

"Yes, Oh yes Shiz, this ya pussy."

"Whose?"

"It's ya ass, shit! Omigod, Omigod, Shizzz. I'm cumming, I'm cumming, Shiz." With tears in her eyes and Shiz in her ass, she came all over his dick, followed by his explosion that Tracy had the honor of dripping off her butt. Shiz sparked up the haze he had from the truck, while Tracy's ass too herself right on to sleep.

$ $ $ $ $

Chantel dropped her bags on the floor of her bedroom and removed her Chanel skirt set, revealing her Victoria Secret panties and bra combo. Chantel closed the door for some added privacy. She admired her curvaceous shape in the full-length mirror, inhaling her stomach to increase her already perfect bust size. The ripples in Chantel's abs were stunning to say the least. She only wished she never got her first's name tattooed slightly above her panty line. Regardless of such, Chantel knew she was bad, as her ass doubled in size since the summer before. Her chinky hazel eyes could seduce whoever she stared at. She was the type to cause problems in others' relationships unbeknownst to her. Her noticeable Naomi walk and diva attitude could do numbers against all in possession of a warm heart, which is why every older man that fell for the young sister disregarded the possibility of catching a case. Fortunate enough, Chantel had no desire to be out fucking, as she had only been spoiled once by her first boyfriend.

Since then, Chantel allowed her cousin's advice to soak her head concerning most men and their agendas, which are ass, money, and more ass. And, Chantel wasn't about to be nobody's jump off. Shiz schooled her on the best thing a hustler's wife could give to him was an unblemished record. The last thing he wanted to hear about his Shawty in the streets is how freaky she was, so and so fucked her in the ass, she had this dick and that dick in her mouth, and whatever else nut shit you can think about when idle niggas sat around rattling. So, she might flirt, kiss, and possibly let a bread winner brush across her ass once or twice, but let it not be fucked up, she wasn't giving no pussy up!

Satisfied with her reflection in the mirror, she hopped in the shower to brush the day's events away. She wondered if Shiz was home or out running the streets. He seemed to be in a rush when he departed from her, and that action worried her some.

After the shower, Chantel noticed she had a few missed calls from Markease on her Sidekick. *I wonder what he wants. That's him blowing me up like that? I hope that boy don't think he about to get some, 'cause it ain't even going down like that*, she thought to herself. She decided to hit him back, even though it was against her one week policy. Plus, she did give him her number, which means Markease had made a pretty good impression. After three rings, sounding sexy as ever, he answered in his baritone voice. Just then, she remembered why she had given him the number in the first place. He seemed to be distracted by the noise and commotion on his end. She could tell there was a gang of people swarming about asking him tons of questions about the smallest things. It was clear to Chantel, he was a busy man and the crew that surrounded him respected his opinion and authority. But, Chantel wasn't used to being second fiddle to anything. A little bothered by the distant attention, she wanted to 'bang'.

"Look, Markease...call me back when you have time to talk," she broke into Markease's ongoing conversation.

"Hold up y'all. What's up Chantel? Why you hanging up?" he asked.

"You seem busy, so just hit me back when you can holla," she said dryly. Even though he knew Chantel was bad, most girls fell over Markease, and stayed around just to hear him breathe, if they could. Chantel's unimpressed attitude caught Markease's attention. Realizing she was definitely worth his time and hating to miss an opportunity to get at her, he requested a minute to go outside to his BMW where the two could talk and discover what makes them tick. Chantel appreciated the gesture to say the least, so she decided to stay on the line and allow Markease to try at picking her brain.

$ $ $ $ $

Night had finally befallen the block. With it came some coolness, as the murderous air of Philadelphia swept through the infested city. Black ordered the troops to change clothes into something darker, as they had been a little more active than usual tonight. M had half his body bent into some young jawn's car, filling her head with lust and lies. Truthfully, the block couldn't have been more peaceful had you pressed mute, which is why the sudden appearance of Dino, Ms. Rosie's husband was overly due. He seemed to appear out of nowhere at the most perfect of times. Dee and Bam just left in search of some weed, while M was still around the corner shooting at the potential pussy donor. Black, using the pay phone, was completely overwhelmed by the startling voice of Dino's thick, rich, Jamaican accent.

"Fuck boy, how many times me tell ya 'bout fuckin' with de bitch, muthafucka." Black turned to see who the fuck was screaming behind him like that, but before his eyes could focus and serve a name with the blurry face, Dino stole the bullshit out of him! Black tried to rush him; however Dino's strength was too much for him. But, it wasn't until he was on the cement, that he realized it was a costly mistake. Dino continued punching Black in his face, until he noticed an unchained trash can nearby that would look pretty good wrapped around Black's head. The delay allowed Black time to get back to his feet. Black knew he didn't have a win and escape was his only card left to play, if he wanted to survive the attack. He wished his .45 was nearby, but he had given it to Dee to hold earlier and didn't get it back before they left for the weed run. Black must've only staggered a few paces from where Dino was smashing him at. Without awareness, Black felt the steel trash can slam into his back, stinging and causing him to crash into the ground, as well as leaving some memorable strawberries on his hands and knees. The sound of the rattling trash can caused M to look up when he heard the commotion a little clearer. The North Phillians began enclosing on the scene, as the hood could always smell blood. Dino stood literally trashing Black's beaten body. While M gave shorty the number to get at him once she got settled in, he noticed Bam and Dee coming up the street with a quicker pace than normal.

"Where da fuck y'all goin' at youngen'?" M shot at Dee.

"The young jawn, Tasha, said niggas around there fightin' on the strip. You ain't heard?" M didn't know what was going on, but knew that anything other than getting money out there was strictly forbidden. So, ceasing the activity was a must. Dino continued stomping Black into mashed potatoes while everybody watched. Surprisingly enough, Dino had plans on murdering Black in front of everybody, and nobody even seriously attempted to prevent him from doing so. The North Phillians 'ohhh'd and 'ahhh'd with every blow delivered to Black's beaten frame. He did manage to get a few "Aww...that's a shame" from some female onlookers.

"Muthafucka, mae told ya, mae told ya," Dino shouted over Black's bloody body. As the crowd parted, M emerged like a hooded villain stepping from the depths of the shadows. Accompanied by his chrome 44, he shut shit down! Firing a multiple of shots through the Jamaican copper body and frying everything it touched passing through, it sent his blood splashing onto the pavement and nosy bystanders. MOCK MOCK MOCK MOCK MOCK MOCK!!!! echoed in the slender block.

Chantel's entire body locked up hearing the loud cannon go off not far from her, causing her to drop the phone and disconnect from Markease.

"What da hell is goin' on?" she whispered. Not sure if there were more shells looking for a home to nest at, she laid on the floor totally in tune with the drill, as Ms. Pettiway screamed her name.

"Chaaaantellll!"

"I'm good Aunt Puddin," she returned.

"Stay on the floor, alright?"

"I am." She began checking her body for any missed hits. She was shaken but cool.

Chantel didn't agree to senseless killings, but understood the game well. Sometimes niggas went too far and needed to be dealt with, or at least that's what her cousin would say. And, she had met a few who seemed like their whole existence was on some 'make an example out of me'.

After gathering herself from the floor, she peeped out the window and saw M standing over a bloody corpse, as the bystanders scattered out trying to avoid a chauffeured ride to church this Sunday. M wasn't at all bothered by the screams and hysterical cries of most of the onlookers. He licked the blood splatter that shot on his lip. Standing like a lion over his conquered prey, M's eyes showed murder, cold and merciless. His heart pitiless watched the intestines push out of Dino's punctured stomach while he gagged on blood he coughed up, unable to stop the twitching leg that flopped like an un-killed fish washed to shore. M's 44 was still smoking from the six he put in him when he fired three more. MOCK MOCK MOCK! It brought a permanent halt to Dino's twitch. Scraping Black from the pavement was the toughest task M had yet.

"Ay, Dee, Bam, get this bol da fuck up." With the help of the youngens, Black was shoved into the back of the BM wagon, finally out of harm's grasp. He was driven away, staring at the stars questioning why he grabbed Ms. Rosie's ass in the first place.

Shiz lay asleep next to a nude Tracy, entangled in bed sheets. He turned up his ringer before crashing, so as not to miss anything important. He had been having another crazy ass dream. This time, Tracy started trippin', calling everyday, following him, and stating she was gonna kill herself if he didn't leave his wife. The bitch even shot at him! Awakened by the ringing of his cell, Shiz found himself sweating profusely, but feeling a sigh of relief that his nightmare was just that. He combed his eyes coldly over Tracy's nude body, as if the possibility really existed in her. Realizing the cell was still ringing, he retrieved it, seeing the display of the crew code for an emergency.

"Yo!" Shiz answered.

"Where you at, dawg?" M questioned, coasting the BMW on 95 north.

"I'm at the Days Inn with Tracy. What's good?"

"Ya man Black, man, ya man Black," Shiz knew this couldn't be good.

"Dis motherfuckin' nigga touched the bitch Rosie's ass. You know old head Ms. Rosie with the fat ass that fuck with Dino? This bol grabbed her ass earlier on some nut shit."

"Get da fuck outta here?" Shiz returned shockingly.

"Yeah dawg, now you already know that Jamaican ass Dino don't fuck wit that nigga like that from the last incident. Long story short, I'm screaming at the young bitch and I hear all this noise coming from the corner. Dis nigga airing Black da fuck out," M explained.

"Yeahhhh," Shiz squeezed in with amazement in his voice.

"Why dis nigga alllways got some nut shit going on?" Shiz continued.

"I don't know, dawg, but his fat ass is in the back now, all fucked up... (Silence) Ay Shiz... (Silence) A nigga had to put that twirk in, ya heard me?" M said, with the BM purring in the background.

"Damn," Shiz spat as the line grew stale, completely knowing the ramifications of the action.

"This gonna fuck up a lot of money, man," Shiz said disappointedly in deep thought. M mentioned they were heading for Delaware to lay for a minute, until the heat cooled down a bit. Shiz agreed with the move as his mind screamed that nigga has to go. So, he told M to leave that nigga down there. After ending the call, he noticed Tracy awoke from her sleep. She could see whatever he was informed of had him upset. In an attempt to ease his frustration, she stroked his back and kissed his neck.

"Baby, it'll be ok, watch," she mentioned sweetly, bearing a smile. Shiz flopped back on the pillow wondering how all this would affect his money. That block got him paid and with Patrol, Detectives, Homicide, and God knows who else buzzing around, shit was sure to be a lot slower. Tracy snuggled him like she was his chic, burying herself deeply under his muscular arm. Truth is, after the way Shiz slammed that ass, she began looking at him in a different light. She was ready to see what this could bring, how far it could go, and when trust could be given. Basically, she was ready to love again.

She was ready to love again.

CHAPTER

3

A Month and a Half Before

The spacious dorm room was completely empty, as you could hear the quiet motor of the desktops running. The usual scent of past due laundry and tennis shoes combed through the area, reeking the smell of a sweat shop. The school's game had the campus on fire. Everybody that was somebody attended to see Channey on its way to the chip. The over-publicized game had everybody rearranging their schedules to witness the historic moment. Everybody but Jay, that is, who utilized the time to play catch up on lovemaking while his roommates were cheering the home team onto victory.

Jarrell, who most referred to as Jay, had enjoyed a four year relationship with his girlfriend, Kelly. She had met Jay during her freshman year. The two decided to take a liberal arts class together after finding there was no more room left in their first selections. At first, she opted not to let anything come of it, citing the fact that Jay was too soft since he came from a very suburban neighborhood in Cheltenham, just outside of Philadelphia. He graduated from private school with flying colors. Jay never had much time to get into any real trouble with his church-going mother and captain of PA prison system father breathing constantly down his back. Jay did find Channey as a way out of the madness, so he jumped at the opportunity.

He loved the way Kelly made love to him. She always nibbled his ear in the midst of sexing, uttering she'll be forever his. Despite Kelly's slender frame, she was rather cute to be a dark skinned jawn, and her smile could chase sorrow away in the midst of misfortune. Most people compared her to Nia Long but with much longer hair. Riding Jay was very pleasurable, as she carved her signature into Jay's back with her fingernails. He didn't mind, as long as Kelly was pleased. Kissing her lips passionately, the two sailed into ecstasy. Jay was the type to do good by his woman. If he was with a chic, the world knew of it. Finding empty condom wrappers or uninvited females springing up causing problems was all un-heard of. Jay had shared only one love interest before Kelly. That ended with him being unable to maintain her lavish lifestyle. Those damn Gucci and Dior bags were just too expensive for Jay to provide, and they were too damn nice for her to fore-go. It took a long ass time for Jay to get over her. It's a story that Kelly knew all too well, which is why it was so hard for her to say what she had bottled in her heart. Dressing on the end of Jay's bed, she gathered her thoughts just as Jay was exiting the bathroom. She beckoned for him to have a seat beside her and she began to tear up as she sought control of her trembling hands.

"Jay, you know I love you and we've been together for a while. But, I don't see this going where I would like, and I just don't know what else to do," she said to Jay, who could not believe his ears.

"Well, what can I do? Why can't I fix it?" He wanted to solve it.

"Because Jay, the problem..." By the time Kelly finished, she managed to do all that she feared, hurting Jay! He couldn't believe Kelly was willing to walk away so easily, with little regards for what they built and shared over the last four years. He stood in the mirror after she left, trying to understand why it is that women dealt so unjustly with him.

Jay could see he was attractive, as his braided hair reached the shoulders of the caramel complexion frame that he regularly worked out.

"Kelly, da fuck buggin', Yo!" *I'm college educated, manly raised, and hood adaptable*, he thought to himself. He believed that's what most women wanted in a man. Why Kelly wanted out beat the hell out of him, but he knew he was going big places. Jay was fortunate enough to have spent a couple of summers with his cousin K-B in West Atco, New Jersey, before mom pulled the plug on that shit. Niggas was still a little soft in most parts of South Jersey, but you had a few who understood the code and respected it. His cousin shared jewels from the game with him early on, engaging him into fist fights to toughen him up. So, he wasn't a complete sucka on those issues. But, on anything concerning women, he wore his heart on his sleeve!

Days had passed since Kelly hit 'em with the Dear John story. Even though he strutted his shoulders with the 'whatever face' while Kelly broke off what was supposed to be forever, he was really hurting inside. He eyed his cell phone as if it were about to ring any minute with an apologetic Kelly, realizing she had made a mistake. Minutes turned into hours, hours turned into days, and well, you know the rest. It had finally dawned on him that it was official, which explained why he received no calls. But, what had been the reason for not seeing her around campus?

$ $ $ $ $

Kelly had thought about Jay over the weeks and wanted to check up on him, but had decided not to, as that would only complicate things. She admired the way the Gucci sleek dress hugged her slender frame, and it definitely created an image of a fat ass on her petite body. Kelly knew she would never possess nice things like that, had she stayed with Jay. Her thoughts were broken by a sales rep in the women's department of Nordstrom's.

"Will you be charging the $4800 to your Visa or paying with cash?" she asked.

"Cash. Can you please have it wrapped?" Kelly replied. The amount of bread Sideeq was breaking Kelly off made decisions like that thoughtless, whereas before, that would have been an entire year's worth of eating. Sideeq had shown Kelly what it's like to ball. Convincing her to take a few weeks off from school to explore the western parts of the states and the Caribbean, he turned her out on flawless diamonds and designer labels. How in the hell could Jay keep up with that? She hated rolling out, but damn, a bitch tryna get right. Even the sex was different. Jay made love and that was nice. But, Kelly wanted to get fucked, and Sideeq provided just that, filling her in ways Jay never attempted.

When Kelly returned to school everybody could see she had spent a few weeks bathing in money. Nothing from her attire spoke Kelly, from the one hundred and fifty dollar lip gloss, to the fifteen hundred dollar stilettos. She was that bitch. And, the college boys flocked to her whenever she paused like something off of T.V. Who said money can't buy you love, and some good dick don't bring you swagger?

American history was Kelly's last class for the day. Her Sidekick went off, just as the bell was ringing, with a message from Sideeq plastered on her screen, indicating he would be picking her up after class. Kelly attempted to type back while exiting and maintaining her books, two way, and Christian Dior saddle bag. Call it luck of the Irish; she crashed into out of all people, Jay! Dropping all within her carry, Jay helped collect the fallen items, icing Kelly's transformation with bewilderment in his expression. *Was this the same young lady I shared the past four years with?* He thought. Had she not said, "Oh Jay, you scared me," she could've gone on unnoticed. Jay had prepared what to say when he ran into Kelly again, all of which couldn't be remembered now if he was programmed to. They seemed to stare distantly, allowing the abruptness of their break-up to fuel the moment of awkwardness. Somebody had to say something.

"So, how have you been Jay?" Kelly caved in.

"I'm breathing, but that's about it.

"You not taking care of yourself, you look like shit, Jarrell."

"Yea well, this is the best I can do under the circumstances." Jay wanted to say something about Kelly's new appearance, but wasn't ready to face the bitter truth of her having somebody else already. I mean, the bitch looked like she was having the time of her life.

"Look, Jay I have to go. But, you can call me sometime when you're not busy," Kelly pushed out, ignoring Jay's last comment. Meanwhile, Jay's thoughts were *the nerve of this bitch*. Kelly said her goodbyes to a stale Jay and kept it pushing. He watched Kelly get smaller as she faded into the swarming students moving to and from classes. Jay decided to go after Kelly because he needed to clear his chest and add some real closure. If they weren't going to be together, he for sure was going to find out the real reason why. Kelly had reached the parking lot where Sideeq was to be meeting her. Sideeq slid his navy blue GS Lexus into the lot totin' a Newport he sparked moments before, his wrist chunky with Russian diamonds as his chiseled frame filled the wife beater perfectly. Knowing full well he had made eye contact with his chic through the passing students, it appeared to him a young bol just snatched her by the arm.

"What da fuck?" he chimed. Kelly, totally aware of Sideeq's presence and hood behavior, tried to inform Jay that now wasn't the time.

"Jay, I know you got a lot of things to say, but now isn't the time," she said calmly.

"Now is the time Kelly, actually when you left me was the time. You don't think you owed me an explanation, after all we've been through?"

"I didn't say that," she said firmly.

"Well let's hear it, because that bullshit you told me back at the dorm won't cut it." He became upset.

"Jay, what do you want me say? The shit wasn't working out," Kelly raised her voice a little.

"And, you're just now discovering that, after four god damn years?" Jay got excited.

"Don't fuckin' cuss at me, Jay! Now, I told ya fuckin' ass that I don't have time to talk about this shit right now," she barked.

"I really don't know what da hell I saw in you in the first place!"

"Kiss my ass, nigga," Kelly spat and turned to walk away from Jay, but he grabbed her arm to prevent her from leaving. Kelly reacted by snatching her arm back wildly as if Jay was hurting her. He couldn't figure out where the sudden personality change came from. He would, however, have his answer when Sideeq appeared.

"Kelly, go get in the car."

"Sideeq, please. It's not that serious."

"Go get da fuck in the car," he seconded, raising his voice. Jay could tell by the gesture that Sideeq was fucking with Kelly, and at the sight of his canary diamond chunks that wrapped his wrist, where Kelly had gotten her makeover from and reason for leaving. His evaluation was broken by Sideeq's baritone voice becoming aggressive.

"Naw, homie real loose with his hands. Nigga, dis my bitch. Da fuck wrong witchu?" Sideeq shot, pushing a protesting Kelly behind him.

Jay's eyes became intense, wanting to tear ass from limb. The passing students could feel the tension between the fellas so they began to linger. Jay wasn't a slouch, as he did quite well in his exhibition with his cousin. But, before he had a moment to gather another thought, Sideeq smacked the shit out of him, causing Jay to taste blood as it began flooding his mouth like a broken levy. Jay would attempt a sloppy left jab that had no chance of finding its target. By this time, Sideeq had begun dancing in a professional manner but without the bounce, rather flat footed and sturdy.

"Bitch ass nigga. Ya nut ass can't rumble, what?" Sideeq shot. Jay said nothing, as he concentrated on tapping Sideeq's chin and knocking his dick string loose for stealing Kelly. Sideeq faked left and threw right, which caught Jay flush on the chin, crack! Jay staggered into the picnic table, now being rushed by Sideeq like a thirsty hyena pack in smell of blood. As Jay crashed into the iron table, Sideeq doubled up on the hook, spinning blood from Jay's nostrils forcefully, all but knocking him out. A tired and beaten-to-the-punch Jay, shot two lead rights down the pike, shocking the shit out of Sideeq. It caused blood to stain his front teeth, as a distraught Kelly watched on. The two exchanged a few punches, nothing really landing flush. Intending the same overhand, the two entangled falling into a brief wrestling scuffle. Sideeq outweighed Jay by at least twenty pounds, a weight he knew how to use well being from the Tasker projects out of South Philly. Without realization, Jay was scooped onto his back, unable to defend himself. Sideeq drilled Jay relentlessly.

"I told you pussy. You. Can't. Fuck. Wit. Me." Sideeq shot, pounding on Jay's face until the campus security broke them up, allowing a beaten Jay to patch his wounds. Kelly felt awful about the ordeal, but Sideeq was her man. So, staying to help nurse Jay back to health was not possible. Jay watched the G.S. Lexus pull out of the lot with his winnings. The whole situation fucked Jay up. He had to go home to get his mind right. Shit was just that fucked up!

CHAPTER 4

Why U Frauding?

Chantel awoke the following morning with the covers half pulled over her body. The cheeks of her yellow ass split under her entangled panty line. She laid there gathering her thoughts concerning last night's actions. The police seemed to be everywhere trying to pick up the pieces of the unsolved murder. She guessed they got desperate for leads, as they went door to door asking if anyone had heard or seen anything. If you could depend on the hood for something, be sure to know talking to the police was an absolute no-no. They didn't even bother knocking on Ms. Pettiway's door. As they knew, talking to a sea lion was more informative than Shiz's mother. She hoped that none of Shiz's people had gotten locked up. Her cousin's whole team carried her like a little sister. The only altercation she had before with any of them was with Black. Whenever she came down, the boy would instantly start tripping, knocking on Ms. Pettiway's door for every reason under the sun: "Let me get some ice.", "Can I use the phone?", "Did the paper come today?" Of course, all of this was while Shiz was away. She hated being around him and would never leave her back turned towards him, as she could immediately feel his eyes planted on her ass, yearning to feel it slamming against his thighs. She mentioned nothing to Shiz about it because she knew he would flip. M was much cooler with Chantel. She believed he really rode hard for Shiz and she liked that. He was as loyal as it gets. She could tell M wasn't originally from North because despite his killer instinct, he was a gentleman. Once, he had been sent by Shiz to pick her up at her friend, Nettie's house. It had been raining considerably, so the sidewalk was flooded out. Chantel didn't want to get her suede Monolo wet, so M literally picked her up and carried her over the ankle deep body of water to place her into the warm car. She never forgot that and figured he must be from uptown. Regardless of such, the sight of M putting his murder game down in eye view of Chantel made her skin cringe. Call the bitch crazy, it kinda turned her on though. If she was to give the pussy away right now, M would be the number one candidate. If he could get past Shiz, that is. Speaking of Shiz, he had called her last night after her attempts to call him twenty times. She understood the power of booty, but damn, did he have to be out every night tricking, she protested.

She checked her cell phone for any messages from Shiz saying he was coming to Ms. Pettiway's house soon. She wanted to get her nails done before her cousin tricked any more money on them dumb ass brawds, and then have the nerve to tell her, he 'ain't got it right now'. She really didn't like going hard on her cousin's stash, but like he used to say, "I rather it be mines, than one of them niggas in the streets knowing full well how trifling niggas can get." She noticed she had no messages from Shiz, but a gang of missed calls from Markease. She gathered the strength to tear her sexy ass from the bed and go shower. On her way down the hall, she peeked in on a still sleeping Ms. Pettiway, surrounded by wrinkled chip bags and the ticking sound of the ceiling fan. Aunt Puddin is so pretty. After Darin died, she let herself slide though, spending all this time in the house watching soaps, eating snacks...*No matter what, I'm not gonna stop living as if I died too*, she promised herself.

While in the shower, allowing the warm suds to run over her lickable breasts and apple bottom ass, she began fantasizing about M's sexy ass rubbing his manly hands all over her. The thought was making her coochie throb, as her nipples hardened. She bit into her bottom lip, feeling the urge to touch herself. The steam that rose from the heated sprinkles made the mood so much more erotic. Circling her tiny finger on the clitoris of her shaven Georgia peach, she began envisioning M's massive dick running in and out of her soaking box, carrying her silky body on his chiseled physique while maintaining a steady pace. The pleasure Chantel was experiencing drove her back towards the wall of the shower. Her fingers soaked in her own moistness that the heavenly gate provided. With her back pressed firmly against the wall, and her cinnamon hair wet and wrapping alongside her neck, she was nearing her peak. The moaning intensified, and she hoped she wasn't within ear's reach of Ms. Pettiway because there was no way she had any intentions of stopping.

"Sssssss-Awwww, M." Chantel sucked in air through clenched teeth, as she chimed. "Shit. Yeah yeah, Sssssss-Shi...Omigod, yeah!" Feeling a break in her breathing and twitching in her coochie, Chantel massaged the pinkish nipples of her 36-C's. In a pornographic moan, she busted all over her fingers, as her heart beat uncontrollably. She finally finished what she started out to do, then washed thoroughly.

On her way out of the shower, she ran smack into Ms. Pettiway who she didn't expect to see up so early. Ms. Pettiway shot her a look indicating she had heard, but understood. Chantel was embarrassed to say the least, so she opted to say nothing, lowering her head as she squeezed past in a wrapped towel in tote of her belongings. After grooming herself with her favorite hygienic products, the small room encompassed the enchanted fragrances of cherry almond and cucumber melon, as Chantel lifted the blinds to allow sunlight to rip through. Wearing a bra and panty ensemble from Dolce and Gabbana, she decided to hit Markease. (Ring. Ring.)

"Yea?" a baritone voice shot, still bearing the morning cracks.

"Markease?" she inquired a little uncertain.

"Yea," he answered.

"This is..."

"Chantel," he finished wearing a smile.

"Is it too early? I can call you back?"

"Naw! I been thinking 'bout you all night, sis. After the phone cut off, I tried to hit you a couple times. I heard niggas out there bucking so I thought something happened to you. I was mad as shit...You good though?" Chantel blushed at the thought of his concern. She appreciated that he cared.

"I'm sorry for worrying you, but things did really get wild around here last night. I got a 'lil too into what occurred, but yea, I'm good though. I did, however, wake up thinking 'bout you." Markease wondered to what extent.

"Awww, that's what's up ma ... I'm tryna get at you today. What's up, how your agenda look?" Chantel thought he'd never ask. A day with Markease was definitely doable in her book, but she didn't want to sound 'pressed'. She was sure a nigga like him had plenty of hoes waiting around ready to ride his dick. So, she decided to downplay a bit.

"I don't knowwww," she whined.

"Whatchu got in mind, Markease?" sounding skeptical.

"We can go eat, hit the waterfront, or we can hit the mall." *Jackpot!* Chantel screamed to herself.

"Alright, sounds good. Let me get dressed and I'll hit you back with the address." Chantel ended the call, lowered her head, and thought of Markease's sweet voice. She then combed through the clothes she had down there with her, wishing she had brought her Gucci jumpsuit that seemed to stop traffic wherever she went. Just then, she remembered her cousin had taken her shopping the day before. Eyeing the Niemen Marcus bags in the corner beside the dresser, she decided to go with a white one piece Zayaani summer dress with a dropped back and open-toed Donna Karen six inches. Pulling her hair up with a few spaghetti strings to hang, Chantel could've stepped right off the runway. *He definitely gonna be feeling me in this joint here*, she thought to herself, admiring her reflection in the mirror. After notifying Markease of the address, it wasn't long before he was outside the door ringing her cell to indicate his presence. Markease couldn't help but adjust his sight when Chantel stepped out. If she didn't have the meanest set of legs and ripest body he had ever seen, he for sure wasn't black and dying. He helped his beautiful counterpart for the evening into the showroom BMW, closing the door behind her. The two were off, into the city that hosted the most murders that year and the one before.

M stared at Black, resting on the couch of the crew's Delaware apartment, wondering how Black could be so stupid. *You squeezed the known wife of another man's ass, then get caught sleeping on a pay phone. This is the typical shit Black got his ass whupped for and fucked up major dough because of. In the past fourteen hours, I know we could've at least flipped a half of bird. Niggas sitting on a gold mine! I know Shiz gotta be flipping over the bread we losing. Shit, I feel the same way, but I gotta keep looking at the dickhead that caused it...I gotta get at Shiz...What did he mean when he said leave that nigga down here? I swear, if he meant leave that nigga stinking, I'll flatten his shit right now. Look at this* *dude...sleeping! He don't even dig it, ready to lose his God damn life and all he want to do is sleep.*

"Black!" He screamed, startling Black half to death. The reaction squeezed a chuckle out of M.

"I'm about to grab some breakfast at the joint on Fourth Street. You good or do you want something?" M asked.

"Yea, grab me the same thing you getting," Black requested groggily.

"I'm out. I got the young bols D and Bam wit me. So, hold yaself down," M advised. Heading out the apartment he could hear Black shuffling on the couch. Black gathered himself up after M and the others left to freshen up and see the damage to his beaten body. Gazing at the wounds in the mirror caused an outrage in his heart. Black's eyes boiled, looking for someone to blame for the injuries so he could hold court. Motherfuckas didn't like Black for a reason, a good reason! Niggas knew how treacherous he could become in a heartbeat. There were just entirely too many slimy-ass stories circulating about him. And, his body count was ridiculous, mostly over bullshit. The value of life was cheap to Black, so letting that nigga sit behind you in the whip, or not giving him what he wanted, were costly mistakes that were proven to be fatal. Knowing that Dino's punk ass was behind his injuries and that nigga was dead, Black didn't get the opportunity to squeeze his chopper and satisfy his thirst. Naturally, it had occurred to him, If M nut ass was where he was supposed to be at, all of this could've been prevented. This wasn't the first time M failed Black on some sucker shit, he believed. But Black was dead set on making it his last. Over the years, this nigga M is becoming a real dick rider being Shiz's yes-man. *And, how this nigga Shiz gonna tell that nigga he ain't fucking with me no more? That's my money out there...My pull that got that strip doing the pussy. Fuck wrong with this nigga? Fuck, he forgot how I held him down. Watch, we gonna see what's good though.* Turning the pillow cushion in search of his twin 45's, Black tucked them into the front of his Dickies, then made a much needed phone call.

$ $ $ $ $

Markease glided the 750 into the city traffic, pondering where he should take Chantel considering that every time they crossed paths, she was wearing designer labels. First, it was Chanel and Jimmy Choo, now it's Zayaani and Donna Karen. He could tell someone had to be breaking the young brawd off some paper, because there was no mentioning of a job. Even if she had one, there's no way she could afford eleven and twelve hundred dollar items just to sashay around in. So, he had to be unique to impress Chantel, as all the usual high class stores that would normally make most heads spin were an average clothing store to Chantel. She wondered why Markease had been so quiet since they left the house. It kind of made her feel nervous. *Maybe he feels my dress is too short. I hope he don't got an attitude. I only wore this stupid thing cause of his ass.* Not sure if she should ask, she decided to let it go. The amount of jewelry on Markease's chocolate body made him look like a rap star. She found herself trying to guess what his hustle was. She hated to be stereotypical, but let's be honest...BM rimmed up, jewels twinkling, and his cell phone stayed on blast. *Dope boy*! She smiled to herself. Chantel switched the radio on Power 99. TI had a new jawn out with Monae, a soulful singer from the city that had the town on smash because even though she was R & B, she was gutter. They mostly compared her to Mary J or Keisha Cole, but to Chantel, she was better than both of them on any track. The mid day princess, Shamar, was ready to play the new jawn. She cranked the volume on the factory system, drawing Markease's attention.

"Oh, you like Mo?"

"Do I?" Chantel replied winding her hips with her hand stretched out the sunroof, totally in tune with the bass line. She sang along with it, after picking up on the chorus' catchy hook.

"She that bitch," Chantel shot, smiling like a heavenly angel, while the sunlight ripped through the roof causing her white summer dress to accentuate her fair complexion. Markease was digging it!

Shiz awoke that afternoon like, *Fuck, Tracy must've worn my ass out last night*, he thought to himself as he stretched out a yawn. Shiz didn't go for the sleeping in shit. Every day was a potential day of becoming a millionaire. So, when the sun came out, he was out on that paper. Last night's events had him stressing something crazy. Thanks to Tracy, she knocked the edge off with her timely 'don't worry's' and good ass pussy. Breaking his thoughts, the phone rang with M on the other end and faint voices in the background.

"You come up for air yet, nigga?"

"Naw, I was fucked up last night drinking that Henny and shit, plus Tracy had that shit poppin'. That bitch pussy good, dawg,' Shiz spat, brushing his waves down, as he sat on his bed corner.

"I know, I've been calling you all morning, babee," M returned, shoveling a slab of turkey bacon into his mouth, while the young bols beasted down there plates. Shiz apologized.

"Ay dawg, hold up for a minute. That shit last night, I should've been on top of it a lot better, and it's my bad for letting it go down like that. But, that Black ass motherfucka, mannn, he be on that nut shit, then think a nigga 'posed to clean up behind him, feel me?" M spat, putting forth his own apology.

"It's cool, dawg. You did what you do," Shiz chimed, as a brief silence joined the line.

"Oh shit, yea, dig it. The reason I'm calling is to find out whatchu meant last night when you said leave him down here? 'Cause I ain't got no problem dropping 'em off, but I wanna make sure that's what you meant. You know I don't fuck with the nigga like that!"

"Where you at now?"

"At the breakfast joint with Dee and Bam," M mentioned. Shiz reviewed if his statement was made in anger or if the nigga really fucked up the last of his paper. Knowing how vindictive Black is, he had to get dropped if Shiz wanted him out.

"M, my old heads used to tell me, niggas were like old shoes. You wear them as long as you can benefit from them, fair exchange no robbery. But, sometimes you outgrow them and you have to change them before they hurt you." M allowed Shiz's words to marinate in his brain before Shiz sang,

"Do what-chu do, M," in very chilling manner.

"No doubt. Cash Is King, nigga."

"Cash Is King!" The line went dead, leaving Shiz looking into the phone like he could see his words fading therein. The thought of Black's death bothered him none. In fact, it was best for everybody that he lost no more money and Black fucked no more up. The sound of cans rattling in the bathroom caught his attention. Shiz called out to Tracy. She responded by sticking her head out with the phone attached, indicating one minute with her index finger.

Tracy stood looking into the bathroom mirror naked and eyeing her reflection, as she waited on-hold, entertained by the Bank of America marketing ads until there was a break in the line.

"Umm yes, hi, this is Tracy Woods, client service rep. with the Jenkintown location. I'm calling because I was due in today under Mark's supervision, but I was informed of an emergency this morning with a family member. Can you notify Mark that I'm not able to make it in, but I will be there tomorrow? Yes, Um-hmm, thank you." Tracy closed the flip, not really knowing why she had done what she did. Shiz wasn't even her man yet and the nigga already had a bitch calling off of work. But, she couldn't control the circles her heart was doing when she thought of him. Tracy had never missed a single day of work in customer service at the bank in two years. Today marked her first. She just hoped it was worth it. She exited the bathroom, as Shiz closed the cell after unsuccessfully trying to reach out to Chantel. Shiz grabbed his pants nearby on a chair stationed by the table, unaware Tracy had surfaced from the bathroom. Shiz caught sight of Tracy's jiggling ass, as she stepped into the bubble filled hot tub that had been brewing before she entered the bathroom.

"Where you going?" Tracy cutely asked, tastefully nude with her hair pinned up. *I know he don't think he's leaving now*, she thought to herself. Figuring with the block shut down, there wasn't much to do anyway or more importantly than to fuck with Tracy all day in a room she was paying for, Shiz didn't check her questioning. Rather, he ditched his clothes and joined her in the hot tub, bringing a warm smile to Tracy's face.

Markease turned into the gated community off City Line Avenue. After two check points, they walked into a well kept building, appearing to be condos. He repeatedly told Chantel,

"It's a surprise, sweetheart." They parted the elevator on the top floor past the corridor, and greeted by two doormen, finally were led into a huge apartment laced with every amenity known to the lifestyle of the rich and famous. Without delay, a well dressed white female approached and offered, "Is it at all possible to interest the two of you in a drink?"

"No, I'm good," Chantel answered, amazed that their attendant wasn't off some place modeling.

"Yea, I'll have a Coke and Henny, please," Markease chimed. The attendant faded away with a mean ass switch. After Markease's drink was delivered, they were ushered to an adjoining room where there was a thin, frail guy patronizing Dolce and Gabbana, shuffling through tons of designer clothes. All of Chantel's favorites were there, except what she was seeing was not the items you'd find at the normal retailers. Markease then introduced her to Sway.

"Chantel, this is Mo's stylist and fashion consultant."

"Mo, Mo who?" Chantel asked confused. Markease, however, ignored it.

"Not bad missy. Not bad at all," Sway said in a feminine voice, overlooking Chantel's 'Lay', staring intensely over the top of his D & G frames. He grabbed her hand, soliciting a twirl for better observation.

"Girlfriend, ya ass is fierce in this Zayaani. And, them shoes! All of it," he sang, with his hands bearing a girlish rest. Chantel blushed, thinking, *oh Kayyy!* taken by Sway's assertiveness.

"Sway is here to assist you in picking out a few outfits," Markease clarified.

"Ay Sway, hook my girl up, all hot shit!"

"Definitely! Mommie got a mean shape, too. I can't wait to get her Beyonce hips in this Nicole Miller strapless," he said, holding the dress up. Chantel smiled the whole time. She enjoyed Sway's charisma, and the assistance made her feel like a star. She had to admit, Markease was truly that nigga, but she still didn't get the Mo's stylist part, until the French doors parted opposite where they were and Monae floated in wearing oversized Channel shades and a white terrycloth bathrobe with matching head towel. Chantel could identify Mo, if she was in the nosebleeds out of an entourage of thirty. Monae did have the most perfect mahogany skin complexion that Chantel had ever seen, and her teeth were so straight and white that her smile was truly a kiss of god. Feeling a bit inferior to her platinum selling idol, Chantel covered her face to hide her excitement. Monae ran into the arms of Markease, which also took her for a spin, until Markease introduced Monae as his sister on his pop's side, and told her that it was he who put out her first LP. Chantel just couldn't believe how small the world was that we lived in. Markease introduced Monae to Chantel, and right off the bat Mo liked her. She could see herself swinging with her. Mo just hoped that Markease didn't hurt her like the last one.

M wrapped up breakfast with the youngens, and informed them of the order that had come down. They showed no fear in what had to be done, which is why M and Shiz dug the youngens so much. When they first met them, the little niggas was on their way upstate for laying down a check cashing spot. Shiz was outside the store talking to M when the little niggas swiss-cheesed the joint, after gettin' the bread. If it wasn't for some plain clothes detectives investigating a murder which had occurred two weeks prior at the same establishment, they would've made off with the money. Shiz felt bad for the youngens and could definitely respect their drive to get that guap. He grabbed Brian McMonagle to handle their case and Janet Samarow to sit in as an advisor. The youngens eventually got off and had been under the team's wing ever since, putting that twirk in. M and Shiz kept the duo on paper and good game. As M handed out portions of the plan to blood thirsty youngens, they left with fire in their eyes and murder on their lips. Laced with forty calibers and Desert Eagles the murderous team entered the building, focused on their target. But, Black had quite a different plan for the returning crew. The sweat began beading down his temples and back, while he stood silent and still in the hot shuttered closet in view of the couch. His hands in firm grasp of the twin 45's with extra mags in his pocket, his teeth clenched so solid that a crow bar couldn't pry them open. With the look of lava in his eyes, Black was ready to lay murder down on the absent-minded hustlers. M entered, leading the trio as they filed in like infantry thirty nine. Dee and Bam cut through the kitchen hoping to surround a sleeping Black on the couch in the living room. M stepped into the spacious quarters with the iron behind him.

"Ay yo, Black! They didn't have no turkey bacon, so I got you this." MOCK. MOCK. MOCK. MOCK! Firing four shots into the sheeted couch causing cotton to fly through the bullet holes. M's blood began to rush. Black's eyes widened momentarily, and then returned to a murderous slit as the sparks of light streaked across his face. His mind raced, trying to figure his next move and fast, too. M uncovered the sofa, eyeing a disarray of pillow cushions arranged strangely. He gave the youngens the order, as the crew ran in search of the bedrooms. The findings of "Nothing!" ..."Nothing!" echoed throughout from Dee and Bam. As they stood at the end of the living room, the trio knew Black wasn't far because all of his shit was still there. Being one last place to check that could hide a motherfucka that size, M acted as if they had gave up and were set to leave, in order to fool him, if he was in fact in that closet. But, Black was nobody's fool. Five shots tore through the soft wooded door from Black's forty fives, striking Bam in the forearm, as the crew went diving for haven behind the kitchen wall.

"Oh shit...Shit, that nigga got me," Bam said, holding his arm while resting his back against the wall.

M instantly stuck his hand around the corner and returned five slugs of his own into the chipped closet door. MOCK. MOCK. MOCK. MOCK. MOCK! Caused pictures to fall from the wall, and a shattering sound. Black knew if he was to survive, he had to come out of that closet so he could better see their attack. With his back pressed against its deepest wall, he re-emerged, squeezing flaming lead from both cannons into the shielding wall the trio nested against, causing them to lower again. Chips of drywall and paint fell onto them, giving Black enough time to pull over the entertainment console he intended to use as his fort. Like a general in the thirteenth brigade, M ordered Dee to head towards the other end of the kitchen to get a better shot and position on fat boy, preventing him from leaving. Bam was to provide cover for M to make it into the bedroom down the hall.

"Ay, M!" Black bellowed out. "Ya bitch ass ain't got it in you to kill a nigga like me! Neither you, nor them nut ass toy soldiers you brought witchu."

"Yea! Keep talking that shit, playboy," M blurted back, while Dee reached his spot at the end of the kitchen just a few feet from Black.

"I hope you suck that faggot ass Shiz dick one last time this morning, dick riding ass nigga! Because, next time he see you it'll be without a face, pussy!" Black hissed with his cannons aimed at M's place of assault, over the heavy wooded console. For a split moment, he thought he saw something move on the floor by the entrance of the kitchen. *There it is again*, he thought to himself swiftly. It was Dee's untied shoestring wiggling about. Black quickly let the loud hammer off, sending three deadly shells through the wall into Dee's abdomen, and four towards M's location. The shells blew Dee to the deck in grasp of his stomach, allowing the forty cal. to slide across the kitchen floor. His agony could be heard throughout the complex. Black began laughing hysterically at the episode.

"Y'all better have somebody check on Dee, that nigga sound fucked up!" Black spat, on one knee picking off the self-named assassins. M gave the signal to Bam to send a barrage of deadly rain on Black's bunker, while M went in flight of the back room, bucking his 44. into the spacious living room behind him. Black had no choice but to keep low until the firing ceased. He used that time to reload his two grief causers. Sirens could be heard distantly, as well as muffled pleas of terror from the neighboring apartments. M was heated a thousand degrees that he allowed Black's bitch ass to take them to war. He believed Black couldn't fuck with them, and that little stand off in the living room was far from impressive. He wanted him, and bad at that. So, seeing him bleed and plea for his life before he changed his face made his dick hard as he thought of it, loading the chopper in the bedroom on the far end of the apartment.

"Ay Bam, that nigga 'bout to get you rocked. I'm telling you! You ain't got nothing coming fucking with me!...Matter fact, YOU-NIGGAAAS-ISSS-PUSSSY!"

He stood from the bunker with a face from hell, firing both cannons at the devastated drywall, causing a fire to blare from their snouts. The smoking shell casings flipped out their chambers like a winning slot machine. It was his last stand. He was determined to end the screaming of these bitches, but there was a monstrous click-clacking he heard under his fire...A sound he had heard before. Without warning the beast spoke. DA DA DA DA DA DA DA DA DA DA!!! Sounding like a gigantic typewriter printing out an essay. It lifted Black off his feet behind the shielding divider. M continued to ring off behind the firing torch that blew before him, while the sizzling shells that conversated with Black had ended his fight unbeknownst to M. When M's shooter's twitch relaxed, he eyed Black's bullet stricken bunker, as the gun fog descended slowly upon the damaged abode. Glass still jingled, as it dangled from the TV and coffee table. The dust settled from the sheet rock upon the plush carpeting, as M gave Bam the nod to check out Black's existence. When he got a few steps away, he could hear Black coughing and gagging on fluid, but before the wounded Black became fully visible, he knew he had one chance of escape from death the wolves were sure to put on him. He sprouted up in the last life-filled spirit he had left, and jumped his big ass out of the living room window, PUSHHHHHH! Shattering its glass. M and Bam rushed to view whether he had survived the two story fall. To their surprise, the nigga was maneuvering through the swerving traffic with a bad limp. The trail of blood that followed him was thick and consistent. Bam, aimed the .40 caliber at him, but M pushed it down, acknowledging the closing sirens, an injured Dee, and Black's heavy blood loss in the witnessing traffic. They needed to go, but M wouldn't rest until he received confirmation of Black's demise. On the way back, M hit Shiz's voicemail and put him on.

CHAPTER 5

That Was Dirty

Chantel was truly impressed. She had never met a man that could possibly outdo her cousin. This thought bounced around her mind, as Markease pushed the BM, eating 476 up. They were heading towards King of Prussia's Cheesecake Factory to have a bite to eat and some needed conversation. Markease, similar to Chantel, loved going out of the hood for all their services. Any reason became an excuse to avoid the unkempt products and poor customer service you often found in the ghetto. The ride was filled with laughs and fruitful conversation. Markease informed Chantel of his desire to be a full time producer, so he could open the talent doors of Philly up and put the city back on the map hip hop wise. Chantel was shocked to discover Markease had no children. A nigga like him was sure to have a few somewhere in the tuck, even if he didn't claim them. But, he assured her that he sincerely didn't and she believed him. She offered the same info, as she shuffled through his CD collection, admiring his choice selection. He had some bangers, but there was one in particular that caught her attention. She inserted the disc and Markease instantly recognized the intro. Tearing his eyes from the road, he placed them on Chantel momentarily, anticipating if she had in fact known what she was doing. Chantel noticed his stare, to which she responded by giving the 'You got something to say?' face.

"What the hell? You know about this youngen?"

"Boy please, this my shit, you don't know," Chantel retorted, rolling her lips. Even though she enjoyed the new school, she was definitely up on her throw backs and Rolls Royce's. *I'm Going Down* was for sure one of them.

"No, you down with that Mary J version," he teased. She sucked her teeth.

"Boy you buggin'. You gonna learn though," she said with confidence, as she began to belt the words and beautiful harmonious notes, resembling Rolls' version.

> *"Time on my hands, since you been away, boy. I ain't got no plans no,noo,nooo..."*

"Oh you can sing, ma," Markease asked surprisingly. Chantel just shot him the 'I told you I'm the shit' face, while she continued to wave her diva finger doing S's in the air, bearing her heart in the lyrics.

> *"Why'd you have to say good bye, look what you've done to me. I can't stop the tears from falling from my eyes ... Ooh baba."*

Markease couldn't restrain himself, so he joined in as the two floated down the Blue Route chanting the classic.

> *"I'm going dowwwn, 'cause you not around, baba!"*

Chantel was beginning to feel comfortable around Markease. He was so sweet and easy to get along with; she honestly wished she had met him sooner. When they arrived at the Cheesecake Factory, it was truly jam packed. The anticipated wait was two hours, and the faces seemed to reflect aggravation from the long delay. They say bosses are born and not raised, so after three crisp one hundred dollar bills and a few eye conversations later, they were seated and had their order delivered within minutes. The white folk who stood and waited were enraged at the seniority. Markease would say nothing except,

"I ain't begging, I'm buying," as they were led past the velvet ropes. The food was great and so was the atmosphere. The lighting in the restaurant had Markease iced out 'B' charm, encrusted with tropical-colored diamonds, twinkling and winking at Chantel. He caught her staring a few times but decided not to comment, figuring she had to be wondering what was the letter B all about.

"So tell me, why is it somebody hasn't snatched you up and locked you down yet? You supposed to be wifey," Markease mentioned, as he sipped away.

"Who said I'm looking to allow somebody to snatch me up and marry me?"

"Every woman has dreams of being somebody's wifey."

"Well, fortunately I'm not every woman. My goal is to get my bachelor's degree in Business Administration and Management, to make a proud mother out of my mom, and secure my family investment in my education by successfully running and owning my own company. Then, and only then, will my dreams resemble every woman like you was rapping about," she spilled, setting him straight. She wasn't your average girl. Markease hit her with the 'Excuse meee' face.

"No, that's what's up, sis. It's rare you hear that out here. You definitely a diamond in the rough," he flashed a devilish grin, thinking how nice it would be having such a threat on his team. She was truly amazing, eloquent, and intelligent. She had most women he met beat by miles. Blame it on the grace in her smile, the roundness of her ass, or articulation of her tongue, he had to know.

"Chantel, how old are you?" She thought to lie, but why? It was a solid number that she didn't feel the need to explain.

"I'll be eighteen next month," she replied with confidence. Markease shrugged it off, considering how she acted and looked. After tipping the waitress generously, he sat a Jacob & Co.box on the table, and then slid it across to an eyeing Chantel. She read it, as Markease nodded, indicating for her to open it.

"Nothing compliments a woman's beauty better than diamonds." Chantel's hazel eyes combed steadily over the six carat tennis bracelet, outlined in canary baguettes. Chantel was genuinely touched as her eyes watered, staring into Markease's killer smile. She leaned in to kiss him sweetly and affectionately on the cheek, pausing briefly before she removed her succulent lips from him. She was inspired, as no one had given her diamonds before.

The two decided to take a walk on Camden's waterfront to burn the food off, and take in the Philadelphia skyline. It seemed to illuminate the night as the city reflected off the river, dramatizing the crashing waves on the rocky banks. Markease had wrapped his jacket around Chantel to shield her from the breezy current air that the waves generated. It was an excellent way to top the evening off, placing Chantel back in the BMW.

$ $ $ $ $

M had checked Dee into the hospital in Chester on the way back to the city. He knew the police would have been all over them if he had taken him while they were still in Delaware. The amount of blood loss was life threatening, and it was unsure if he'd make it. Bam stayed with him because he also needed his arm looked at.

They were told to call the moment shit was stable, and a ride would be sent to scoop them up. M couldn't believe all that had happened, and found tightness in his chest about Black's survival. He knew Black took a few nasty wounds, he just didn't know if it was enough to rid the earth of his presence. He tried Shiz again from his cell phone, but still there was no answer. Shit truly felt fucked up. That feeling worsened when he saw detectives and homicide posted on their strip. With the troubling affairs tail spinning, he found nothing else he could do except lay the fuck down, rest up, and hope things found their way back to normal. Somehow, he knew things never found their way back; they had to be put back. They say 'when it rains, it pours'. Nothing was worse than that right now, except not having an umbrella.

Realizing it was getting a little late, Chantel checked her messages. She received three from her cousin and a few from a couple of scrubs. She knew she would get an ear full from her cousin for violating one of their major pillars...Don't go nowhere with anybody I don't know before letting me know. This just further added to the point that she should be getting home. Markease had asked her on the bank of the pier whether they could go back to his crib for a little night cap, as they were having the time of their lives. Chantel never answered him, but on the way back over the bridge, she informed him to take her home, so they could get up tomorrow. Plus, her cousin schooled her...Never accept the invitation of a man back to his crib if you're not ready to take it there. She wanted to be with Markease, but not at the expense of being a whore.

"Damn ma, I thought we was going to the crib to chill, you out?" he asked confusingly.

"I know, but my people are on my top when I don't show face all day," Chantel replied, thinking he would understand after the eleven hours they just spent together. Plus, she had every intention of calling him when she got into her crib and settled in. The long mute of Markease made Chantel a little nervous which she brushed off, considering how sweet and generous he had been all day, until he broke his silence.

"Ah, you wanna be on ya little girl jawn," he spat, thinking of all the pussy he missed by turning his cell off the whole day chasing Chantel.

"Excuse me?" Chantel said, with 'No he didn't' in her tone.

"Yea, you one of them little bitches tryna take a nigga for some dough, but don't understand the rules to this shit." Chantel remained quiet, knowing full well how her mouth could get, as she was no fool. Markease would, however, continue his rant.

"So, you just gonna play me like that? Take my money, eat my food...Wiggle ya little funky ass in my face all day?" Markease checked his cell and receipt of a call.

"You hear me talking to you, bitch?" he screamed in her ear. Chantel's eyes began to water. The hard words found a soft spot in her heart. It was definitely a new tone for her. She truly couldn't believe Markease had flipped like that. Where was the gentleman in the restaurant, the concerned tone he spoke in over the phone, or the warm smile that had its way with her? Where was he? Sure enough, not sitting beside her. This was some demon motherfucka that seemed to be bent over some coochie. Her thoughts broke by his hostility.

"That crying shit don't mean nothing over here," he spat, enraging Chantel.

"You know what Markease, I thought you was cool. But, I see you on some sucka shit. How you gonna act all sweet and stuff, tell me things about your personal life, then the first time I don't give you what you want, Oh, I'm a bitch now?! You got some shit with you, but it's cool though, you got that one." She was hot and could no longer hold her tongue, and that nigga needed to be checked.

"I got that one, huh? That's cute, you finished?" he sarcastically taunted.

"Yea Markease. Just take me home or let me out, one."

"Oh yes ma'am, sure thing boss," Markease said, to which Chantel shot him a sour look.

"Whatever Markease," Chantel sang.

"No bitch, it's not whatever." He reached over and punched the shit out of her. With blood in her mouth and a hysterical scream, Chantel went off! kicking, punching, and scratching a driving Markease, causing the BM to swerve into the other lanes. The trailing vehicle's could see the war that Chantel was putting up against the one armed Markease through the rear window, but were more concerned with the fool causing an accident as he ignored the blaring horns.

"Bitch, you the fuck crazy?!" he spat to a flaming Chantel, before pulling over on a barren block to choke the shit out of her. She tried to free his hands from around her neck, but his grasp was to strong. She couldn't believe no one was out to see her attacker and come to some assistance. Any other time you couldn't keep a motherfucka out of your business. She attempted the exit latch, but it was locked. Markease punched Chantel in the stomach draining life from her soul.

"Stupid ass bitch, now get the fuck back here," he growled, winded from the struggle. But, that didn't stop him from pulling a weakened Chantel into the back to have his way with her. Ripping her panties off, instantly he could smell the scent of pussy, not because it stank, but because he had done this so many times he was a pro when finding it and was accustomed to the mildest scent. Chantel tried to resist him and screamed, but with the weakness she found in her body and covering hand of Markease, it was no use. She did manage to squeeze out a few pleas.

"Markease, please don't. Please. Not like this," she begged in faint tones, but he wouldn't hear of it, as his massive penis tore through Chantel's pussy and she gasped. In and out he pumped, fondling the hair, thighs, and ass of Chantel, ripping the one piece down the middle, exposing her succulent firm titties which he groped. Seemingly ripping her insides to shreds, she could only hope he'd cum soon to end the ordeal, as her tears soaked her angelic face. As Markease fucked her, she could feel he was touching things that weren't meant to be touched. Her pussy started bleeding profusely, and he could feel the difference, but had no plans of stopping. Chantel fell unconscious a few times, but another death stroke had woke her up to witness his grunting and moaning until he finally busted all over her, deflowering her more so. Markease wiped his dick on Chantel's summer dress, and then pushed her forcefully out the door onto the asphalt, bruising her shoulder.

"It didn't have to go down like that, bitch. Next time, I'll let you eat my dick though, a'ight?" He pulled off, leaving Chantel raped, battered, naked, and distraught. She laid there unnoticed for a while before she found the strength to get to her feet. She staggered down the chilly Philadelphia street, holding her stomach and ripped Zayaani dress, covering her nude body.

M pulled on the weed, while he steered Black's BM up the heartless city street, pumping Big's *Life After Death* CD. He was on his way down west to get some pussy when he noticed a run down light skinned sister in bad shape, attempting to cross the trash encrusted block. The halogen lights beamed into her cinnamon hair as M drew near.

"Damn sis. You alright?" Still dazed from the ordeal, Chantel faced the voice and collapsed on the door, just inches away from M. His heart sank into his stomach, containing an ocean of extreme sorrow seeing that this helpless, shredded cloth wearing female was Chantel.

"What the fuck's going on?" he growled, immediately helping a battered Chantel into the wagon. Confused as to what could've happened and upset at what did happen, M couldn't believe the day he was having. It was like his entire world was like, fuck that old shit it's a new day! En route to the hospital, M repeatedly checked on Chantel who was slumped over in the passenger seat, as he accelerated the BM.

"Chantel, who did this?" he asked, but she said nothing.

"Chantel, who the fuck did this? Let me know so I can go at 'em. Where you coming from and what da fuck happened to your dress?" But, Chantel remained silent, unable to relive the events. She threw her head in her hands, and started sobbing intensely. She could see blood dripping down her inner thigh, which saddened her more. She felt like shit, and could only imagine what kind of damage was done. The only thing she could bring herself to say was,

"Don't tell Noodles, M. Please, don't tell 'em," repeatedly, she chimed.

"Come on Cee, I can't do that, ma. Niggas would die behind this one. I don't know what happened, Cee, but somebody da fuck gonna die! Yea, you can believe that shit." M. wouldn't lie to her. Shiz was his man and some shit like this, he needed to know.

CHAPTER 6

My Turn

Ms. Pettiway opened the refrigerator door, combing through seeking her unfinished Pepsi. She loved the way Pepsi tasted, chasing the poisonous Newport smoke she lit moments before. It was these lone moments she enjoyed best, after Shiz's father Darin died. Realizing she was spending an excessive amount of time in the house putting on unwanted pounds, she desired to be free again. The moaning of Chantel in the bathroom earlier made her reflect on what it felt like to be young, ready, and willing to explore sexuality. It had been a long time since she opened that door. Sure, she had allowed her firm ass to become a bit chunky and gravity had taken its course on her once perky breasts, but she was no slouch. She could easily be mistaken for Angela Basset. Chantel reminded her a lot of herself when she was younger, priding herself on upkeeping her wonderful figure and not trusting people. *She's just a baby,* Ms. Pettiway thought to herself, which is why it kind of worried her not hearing from her all day. She noticed Chantel leaving in a white car this morning. It was sort of funny to her how Chantel did her when her son wasn't around, but was sure to jump on her ass for not telling her where she was going before leaving.

$ $ $ $ $

The bar in Wilmington, Delaware was jumping with the hoodrats that normally lingered the block. Repeated shots of Patron rose to the mouth of a dark figure sitting under dim lighting in the corner, before a small table. The shadow watched local dealers flirt with the chicken heads, pressed to be bought a drink. The screw face stare that plastered the image face made everyone keep their distance...It was Black and he was still alive. Overly preoccupied with the thoughts of what had unfolded hours ago had him piping hot. Despite feeling like shit, the drive to avenge his assault completely fueled his bullet stricken body, and caused him to abandon mandated hospital treatment. Three slugs tore through his rotator cuff, causing a substantial blood loss. However, the stubbornness he fostered led him to rip the IV out adding to the loss, and flee the hospital. He could think of nothing or no one except getting at them niggas. It was then that his life binding vendetta was born. The one thing he planned to use to his advantage was his survival. The fact that the crew didn't know for sure if he was dead or not meant he could exploit it. It was on, in his mind, so staying low was the best thing he could do, especially when he was in the city. Shiz's ear was so extensive; being sloppy could prove to be fatal.

Just then, a short stocky brown skinned individual walked in, wearing fatigue bottoms and a white tee. Hoovering a Black and Mild, his eyes canvassed the bar until he spotted Black. He joined him at the seated table, unceremoniously kicking his feet upon it.

He viewed Black's beaten face, slinged arm, and gauze wrapped shoulder in a tedious manner.

"So now what, my nig?" Trig shot disappointedly, blowing a stream of smoke out. Trig had one of those Young Jeezy type voices, his swag was similar to Jim Jones, but he looked a lot like Camron. He was definitely the wildest of his family, considering juvy hall served as his second home during his adolescence, until finally he was sat down for a bump...Seven and a half to fifteen upstate PA for aggravated assault charges and weapons' violations. He'd been home for two years now, and was just starting to eat a 'lil something, but his gun game wasn't to be fucked with at all!

"Fuck you mean, NOW WHAT!? These niggas tried to lay me down and I'm getting at 'em," Black spat.

"So, why we sitting here? Let's jump on these niggas heads."

"Trig! Look at me. How the fuck I'm rocking out like this?!" Black fired back, pouring himself another shot of Patron as Trig shook his head, aggravated and on edge. Black continued.

"Man, fuck that shit anyway. What's up with what I asked you over the phone? Is it on or what? Let me handle them nut ass niggas. You just worry about what you promised... (Silence) What's up, dawg?" Trig blew out a dense cloud, removing his feet from the table.

"Yea nigga! You know I'm already on that shit. Who gonna tell me you can't come out here and get this money with me, but I'ma tell you, you nuttin' yourself letting that shit ride." Trig put out the Mild on the bottom of his Tims feeling like--HIM.

"I need a whip, cuz. Don't you know these niggas had the nerve to leave in my shit!?" Black returned, ignoring Trig's last statement. He knew vengeance was his and didn't need to be hyped up to put that twirk in. He would strike, but when the moment was right.

"Awww, fuck outta here, cuz! Them niggas got your shit, too!" an appalled Trig retaliated. Black shot him a 'Don't make me fuck you up' type look.

Weaving the BM through traffic, M rushed Chantel to get some assistance. He could see blood that leaked down her leg consistently, staining the carpet under her feet. Although he didn't know the details, it didn't take much to figure out she was raped, and bad at that. An unconscious Chantel's breast freely jiggled from the turbulence of the ride, to which M covered her nudity. Wheeling the wagon on the outside lane and occasionally hopping sidewalks, M was serious about getting Chantel the help she desperately needed.

"Come on Cee, don't do this right now, a nigga needs you. Shiz needs you! Hold on, ma," M spoke to Chantel, who appeared not to be breathing. Holding her soft cheek between his fingers, he felt a slight chill in her temperature. Fearing the worst, M accelerated the BM engine, causing the V8 to purr into the entrance of Temple medical emergency unit. The MTU's assisted M in getting Chantel out of the car and onto the stretcher, circling it as it moved speedily towards the O.R. where M was refused entrance. Watching the stretcher fade down the tunneling hallway, M thought about how much he admired Chantel. She was truly a sister that reserved a soft spot in his heart. Shiz had done a wonderful job with grooming her to be the wife of a hustler who would respect and cherish the gem he was in possession of. In fact, Shiz's words still lingered in his head the night M first met Chantel. M thought he was trippin' when she stood in the doorway wearing a Baby Phat bodysuit, flashin' her pearly whites, as Shiz handed her a couple hundreds before returning to the car. Her hips were the epitome of femininity, her ass, a cushion of bliss, and her lips, softer than pillows. Whereas, her breasts sat up so perfect and firm, to wear a bra was a pinch away from disrespect. The only thing absent from the waving eye candy as they pulled off was a pair of wings that could match her angelic face.

"Who the fuck was that, dawg?" M questioned with an arched voice, giving away his excitement and position to a detecting Shiz.

"That's my LITTLE cousin, dawg! And, I don't want nobody fucking with her, ya heard me?" M said nothing, as Shiz explained his desires for her.

"See my nigga, she gonna be a boss ass bitch. None of that fucking for 'get high' and Reeboks shit. I give her the game, M. These motherfuckin' streets will chew a bitch up, and most girls don't know better but to chase the shit that offers. Not Channy! She gonna get this game right the first time around. Trust what I'm saying, her little ass is gonna do it big. So, I don't need nobody getting in her head, feeding her the bullshit until she clear on her part. If a nigga can't trust nothing, she'll definitely be a bred that will ride hard for a nigga to the bitter end, feel me?" M reflected on Shiz's words. From the color of her chinky eyes to the adorable laugh she chuckled, M enjoyed every moment of Chantel's presence. If she didn't make it, half of him would die, but all of his man Shiz. Not sure how to inform him, he tried Shiz from the lobby's pay phone since his cell received no signal. Still no answer, M hated Shiz turning his phone off so frequently as shit was always unfolding that he needed to be aware of. With no other option, M jogged for the BM to head for the hotel Shiz had last mentioned.

In the home that nested his early childhood memories, Jay laid on the suede sofa of his people's Cheltenham crib, watching New Jack City on the big screen that his peoples managed to upkeep since the early 90's. It had arrived at the part where G Money's girl wanted to fuck with Nino because of the wealth and status he held over the city. Instantly, the cruddy ass move reminded him of Kelly's departure from him, chasing that very same life. The coffee table before him bore a few bills he had emptied out of his pockets, along with some other items before taking the couch. He reached for the unfolded twenty, dimming his eyes as to scrutinize the soul of the bill. *What the hell is it about this piece of paper that people murder, steal, respect, and throw away love because of it?* He asked himself. He was no dummy, as he understood the purpose of money and the use of it in the world. But, at the end of the day, he believed people shouldn't be so shallow as to allow a piece of crumbled paper to be the motivating factor in matters that involved the internal.

"Fuck this shit. I'm not ever letting anybody play me again over some money. If money make the world go 'round and my girl go down, then I gotta get my hands on some ASAP." Jay found what he was looking for on his computer, a little nervous with going forward as he pondered the consequences. He didn't want to be in jail behind some bullshit, but he knew if he wanted to be the man now, then he needed money. He figured Rome wasn't built in a day, why should he have to make a decision about something so important in one? Jay didn't spend four years in college for nothing. Even though he wanted to make a move, it was his better judgment to think it through before it really popped off.

M phoned Ms. Pettiway in the car on his way to get Shiz. His spine grew chilly when the screams of Shiz's mom pierced through the line. He did manage to give her some details and the hospital's name. M parked the BM leaving the car running directly in front of the entrance of the Days Inn. Approaching the reception desk, M found the same bronze foreigner Shiz had, watching the black and white. He hit the bell a few times to which the man looked him off.

"Yo, what the fuck, I'm invisible or something?" M growled at the clerk. Reluctantly turning down the volume, he returned fire.

"What you want guy, fuck?!" He returned in a rich Indian accent.

"Fuck you mean, what I want," M responded, shooting a look that threw a thousand daggers. The deadliness of his glance told it all, he would kill in a heartbeat. Too bad the clerk didn't pick up on it. He walked slowly towards the desk.

"I'm looking for Sean Pettiway's room. Where he staying at?" The clerk combed through the log, licking his fingers excessively with every turn of the page on some nasty shit. That sight alone made M want to smack the shit out of him.

"No Pettiway. Now, you go or I call the police," he said before mumbling, "Fucking roach monkey." M's face wrinkled like a pit in command of sick 'em. Fed up with the antics of this dickhead, he snatched the foreign clerk by the collar, pulling him completely over the desk and landing him on the stinging floor. M stood over him, still in grasp of his shirt and .44 caliber which he whipped out right before he barked.

"Dawg, you don't know what to say out your mothafucking mouth...Now get da fuck up!" M ordered, after nudging him in the chest with the nose of the gun, causing a dog like whimper the clerk used for bitching. M stood the weeping clerk up and forced him to check the log for Tracy.

"2-0-6, 2-0-6," he shot speedily. M choked the phone cord around his neck and smacked the shit out of the back of his head with his metal.

"You even think about calling the police, I'll buck the shit outta your monkey ass!" M spat, before searching for Shiz's room. M arrived at suite 206 and knocked on the door, to which Tracy answered rather quickly wearing the bed sheet neck high.

"Where Shiz at?" M spat. Before giving Tracy a chance to respond, M entered causing Tracy to step to the side.

"SHIZZZ!!!" he screamed to a sleeping soldier, making him awake and grab his iron beneath the pillow.

"Who the fuck is screaming? What's up, fuck you doing here?" Shiz returned a little discombobulated. M threw Shiz his jeans from the table, as a confused Tracy watched on.

"We got problems, homie," M clarified. Without rap, Shiz got up and met his man, waiting in the running BM. As soon as Shiz stepped foot in the whip, M pulled off speedily.

"Yo! What da fuck happened to the clerk?" Shiz shot, but M ignored him as he ripped down the boulevard. Shiz tried to put together what could be the emergency.

"What the hell is this all about, dawg?" he asked, as M searched for the words to put to his man concerning Chantel. The hesitation in M's response made Shiz think of the worst with matching scenarios, but nothing could prepare him for what M blurted next.

"Somebody did some nut shit to Chantel, man!" M said with disgust in his tone. "She's in the hospital, Shiz." Shiz's heart froze over as M had to fill his man in on what he knew, being the bearer of yet another bad episode. Shiz was 1000 degrees, with his hand clenching his .40 cal tightly; thirsty to lay murder on whomever came in sight of Chantel this day. Niggas knew Shiz's murder game was for real, and he could turn it up at an instant making the city bleed. M could say nothing except,

"Whatever, you know how we get down," fully supportive of any wildin' he wanted to lay down.

Shiz and M hit the entrance of the E.R. at Temple hospital. Ms. Pettiway, Chantel's mother Aunt Patricia, and her two cousins, along with her old man Greg were all stationed in the waiting area in support of one another. Ms. Pettiway fell into Shiz's arms as soon as he approached her.

"What's happening?"

"All they keep saying is she lost a lot of blood," Ms. Pettiway replied over her consistent weeps.

"I don't know what to do Noodles, sh ... sh ... was beaten badly." Just then, the doctor emerged from the O.R. calling 'Pettiway'. Everybody began gathering around and bombarding him with multiple questions, until Greg seized control.

"HOOOLDDD UUUP! Let 'em talk! If we be quiet, we might learn something," he hammered. The doctor took it from there, clarifying,

"Chantel suffered from a vaginal puncture, afflicting a rupture in her abdomen. We were able to stop the bleeding, but it doesn't look like she'll be able to have children. I'm sorry...I'm very sorry." Aunt Patricia burst out in tears over her daughter's sad condition, drawing weakness in her legs. Her head became woozy and before anybody noticed, she crashed to the floor. The doctor rushed to her aid, flashing light into her pupils and performing normal procedures to verify her stability. After the doctor finished instructing the aiding nurses, Shiz managed to squeeze in over all the commotion and hysterical screaming from the women and family.

"Doc, where is all this coming from?"

"Well, it appears Chantel was brutally raped. Now, you guys will be allowed to see her soon. But, from the amount of blood loss, she will more than likely be unconscious for a while." The doctor gave his apologies and moved on to the next family. The entire world moved around Shiz, as he stood silent in the very same spot the doctor explained Chantel's condition and assault. M was the only one that could see the murderous tint coating his man Shiz's body, like the closing drapery at a Vegas show. His face was like chiseled stone as a single tear rolled down the left side of his cheek, while he stared into the 6 x 9 window viewing the empty hallway. M led Shiz outside, passing by a few detectives on their way. Off to the side, M rolled up, sparked, and then passed Shiz the blunt. The conversation was silent but deadly, quiet but informative, mute but very clear; as the two men stared at each other with the smell of bud lingering the air.

Greg had come out to inform Shiz they were being let in to see Chantel. As he entered the lobby, he could hear his mom's voice.

"All I know is she left in a white car this morning," she told the detectives, who were making notation in their flip pads. Ms. Pettiway walked clean off when she noticed the family moving towards the double doors. Before being led in, the nurses reminded the family that they couldn't stay long, as Chantel needed her rest. The muffled cries and sorrow were well on their way when the family saw Chantel unconscious, with tubes affixed up her nostrils and in her arms. The sound of the heart monitor made the viewing that much more dramatic. The visible bruising clearly indicated Chantel was beaten by a man, as her once flawless skin hosted blackened blemishes with scrapes covering her elbows and forearm. There were even bite marks along Chantel's neck and cheek. M asked a passing nurse,

"Excuse me, nurse. Did the young lady say anything at all that might be useful in figuring out why this happened to her?"

"I told the police everything I know, sir," she answered and then continued to descend down the hall. As if a bag of nickels had fallen on her head, she stopped her pace, sucked her teeth, then hollered back,

"Young man, Young man! There was one thing she mentioned..."Why Mark?", but that could've been just the effects of the anesthesia, as she was heavily sedated," she provided and then continued her rounds.

"Thank you, ma'am," M rewarded. *Why Mark, huh?!* He thought to himself before entering the suite again. Chantel's bed was encircled with loved ones towering over her beaten body, trying their best to relate to what she had endured. Chantel's mom, Aunt Patricia, sat rocking and weeping in a chair, cornering the room with Greg massaging her back to ease her tension. She was clearly thrown by the situation and TICKING TO BOOM.

"This ain't right...Umm-ummm, this ain't right," she mumbled incoherently. "She don't belong like this, Lord! Why my baby in that bed? Didn't I give generously to your cause and feed your people at the orphanage picnic? This is wrong, THIS IS FUCKIN WRONG," she fumbled on in ear's reach of the occupants witnessing the sudden change in her tone. "And I know DAMN WELL they don't care nothing about my baby like that! Up here crying and shit, pleeeaasseee," she continued, receiving crooked looks after ruffling the family feathers. Greg tried to calm her down, as Shiz looked on. "No Greg, THESE MUTHERFUCKAS DON'T CARE ABOUT NOTHIN' EXCEPT MONEY! They wouldn't let my baby come down there until I started giving them some of my money. They don't give a shit about Chantel, THATS WHY NOBODY KNOWS SHIT!!!" she screamed, with tears pouring down her face.

"You know I had just about enough of your shit. Who in da hell do you think you talking to!?" Ms. Pettiway checked in.

"You and your crooked ass son. Don't think I don't know how fast Chantel had become hanging around his ass, filling her head with that hood bullshit," she revealed relentlessly.

"Bitch, please! As I recall, it was you begging ME to allow Chantel down here, while you carried your self righteous ass to Atlantic City to gamble. My son has done nothing except steer that young girl in the right direction. If you would talk to the poor girl more, you might know that. And, as far as that money goes, bitch, you can shove that shit up your ass. Fuck you and that money!" Shiz attempted to calm his mom down, as the escalating noise had the nurses and security staff run down. The family was being asked to leave, while Aunt Patricia and Ms. Pettiway continued exchanging blurts of 'Fuck You's & Bitches'. Chantel's left arm had been under the covers, but Shiz could see something protruding from it. As the family walked out, he lingered behind to expose her wrist. Shimmering under the room's lighting was the diamond tennis bracelet she was given by Markease. He unattached it before exiting with the rest of the family, at the beckoning nurse's request.

M drove Shiz back to his truck before heading towards M's crib to sort out the recent events. With everything moving so fast, Shiz had forgotten to ask M about the C.H.E.M.E. (Cash Have Everything Murked Easily) on Black. M sighed, rolling his hand over his wavy hair.

"Damn, dawg. You got to start answering your phone or checking your messages, one."

"Why? What's good?" Shiz asked, frowning his brows.

"Nigga, I don't even know where to start from, feel me!?"

"How about with what I asked you? And, where the fuck is Dee and Bam at?" M's eyes met Shiz's, as his face revealed the same look it had hours earlier, right before he told Shiz about Chantel.

"What the fuck's up, nigga?" Shiz pressed on.

"We ain't get 'em," M gave up reluctantly.

"You ain't get 'em. You ain't get who? I know you ain't talking about Black, 'cause that muthafucka dead, right?"

"Shiz, on everything, I wish that be what it is, but the nigga got away. He was bleeding bad, but I can't be sure if he died or not, 'cause 5-0 was right around the corner."

"And, what about the youngens?" M briefly lowered his head, fearing the worst since he hadn't received a call yet.

"Dee took some nasty shots to the stomach, and Bam got an arm wound. I left them at a hospital in Chester so they wouldn't get picked up on some bullshit. I told them to call when shit was stable and a ride would be sent. That was earlier Shiz, BEFORE I found Chantel. The niggas still didn't get at me. I think the boyz got 'em." Shiz couldn't believe what his ears were serving him all day. Bullshit after bullshit. As if the heat that arose on the block wasn't bad enough, now you got Black, Dee, Bam, and Chantel in the mix to bring the current from bad to worse. It was situations like this that made clear who was a 'bred' from them 'lames', and a 'gangsta' from 'goons'. Being that Shiz was a bred, tough situations never made him give up, but only go harder!

"M, dig this. Call the bitch Mona up and tell her I said to call that hospital, and see what's good with my youngens. If any problems occurred, let her know to take care of it ASAP. I don't give a fuck if their bail is a hundred G's. If they still breathing, I want them back in the city by tomorrow. As far as that Black thing, I'm not feeling you, letting that greasy ass nigga cause these kinds of problems for us. You gotta see to it that nigga ain't breathing. Shit like that can have bad effects for all of us, dawg." M made a mental note to handle it all.

"Shiz, I know how you feel and you know I'm wit you one hunnet. But, what's up with this shit with Chantel? We gotta settle family business first before shit gets any crazier," M said urgently, hoping Shiz was still focused despite Chantel's mom's bullshit back at the hospital. What M was in hope of is that Shiz had already moved beyond that point, reserving an ocean of rage for Chantel's attacker, which would fuel his search even if it took him to the end of the globe. There was nothing more important to him than shooting that mutherfucka's face off. He pulled the diamond tennis bracelet out of his pocket, holding it up to admire, wondering where she had gotten such an expensive item.

"M, this shit with Chantel is fucking me up, dawg," Shiz admitted.

"Listen, my hand is STILL twitching, seeing Chantel on the dirty ass street, dawg. I wanted to murder somebody..." M said, unable to bear the thought of a raped Chantel flashing in his mind.

"Ay, M. This bracelet, this piece ran a nigga some money, dawg. And, I didn't grab this for her. So, this faggot ass nigga got some paper, yahn-meen."

"That's some nut ass shit. Niggas ballin' AND STILL tryna take some pussy! Dawg, you know who used to be good for some shit like that?" M waited a few seconds before continuing. "Mutherfuckin' Butter from West. You don't remember how that nigga used to be throwing shit in young bitches' drinks and shit, so he can take pussy?"

"Yea, didn't the bol have a case in the paper a few years back on some rape shit?" Shiz chimed.

"Exactly, he be doing that shit, too. On the real, when you showed me that bracelet that's who came to mind."

"But, the nurse said Cee mentioned somebody named Mark, and Butter bitch ass handle is Keas-se," M said to a daydreaming Shiz, when something did catch his attention.

"Whatchu say, M??" Shiz asked quickly.

"What part?"

"The part 'bout Cee saying a name."

"Oh, she said, why Mark?" Once again, Shiz couldn't believe what he was hearing. Despite the fact that M didn't know Butter like that, Shiz did because he went to school with the bol. And, he knew that Markease didn't like people calling him by that when they were younger. So, he would tell people his name was Keas-se or pronounced as Key-say. Shiz hopped off of the couch, drawing his forty and pacing. Similar to Shiz, M also heard Shiz's mom saying Chantel left in a white car. So, M placed a call to his jump-off down West and she verified that Butter does have a white BMW with Giovanna's on it. Shiz stopped his repeated chants of "Dis nigga da fuck crazy," when M informed him of the results. Like it had driven up and knocked on the door, Shiz remembered that car the day of he and Chantel's outing.

"I'ma ROCK DIS NIGGA, M!!!"

CHAPTER 7

They say Pussy run Da game

A few weeks had past, and Black was feeling Wilmington, Delaware like a masseuse. He wasn't 100% yet, but he was moving well, and that was in every sense of the word. With Trig being a native down there, Black grabbed a half of bird and had Trig collect a little crew to put out there to nick-dime it. The way these niggas set up, Black could instantly see why Trig wasn't making no money like that. Right up the block, New York dudes were under cutting the whole game with better coke, at a cheaper price. In fact, the only reason crackheads copped off of Trig was because they were scared of him. Black needed his little bit of money to work, if he was to ever get back at Shiz and them. He knew full well the money Shiz was seeing off of the corner was close to fifty thousand dollars every week and a half. That money would continue to translate into power. He had to make his shit work. His thoughts were broken by Trig's ringtone, as the duo sat in Trig's smoked out Buick Lesabre, across from the townhouse the New York niggas were hustling out of. There was a Spanish looking guy talking to some brawds, overly concerned with making their presence known. Most of the hustlers seemed to be referring to him as well. Trig passed Black the weed as they watched on.

"You know what, playboy? Niggas really fucked up letting these niggas eat down here. These niggas are really gettin' a lot of paper out this mutherfucka." Black pulled on the weed, as Trig cleared his mind.

"I been watching these Ricans move. And, that nigga right there with the "fronts" be bossin' these cats. I think he was like the first one out here."

"Papi da boss?" Black asked, as the 'gaink' filled his lungs.

"Fuck that nigga, yo," Trig replied. Black ejected the whip with his signature .45 out behind his back. He walked towards the unnoticing hustlers, grooving to D-Block and circulating spliffs of haze. Before Trig had time to react to Black's swift actions, he had already cocked the iron back as he screamed,

"Ay yo, Papi! Who got that Yayo out here?" Directly in front of the crews leader. Before he could even blink, Black blew his face in. POP, POP, POP, POP! Sending his hollow head crushing into the gate in front of the townhouse. His man reached for his joint, but was refused access by three flaming slugs from Trig's .9 Milli. Awakening his thirst for blood, he began dumping on everything that moved. No one was safe from Trig's deadly rain, as a barrage of shells flew down the block, shattering windows and triggering alarms. Like scattering pigeons at Central Park, the entire clique ran in fear of the gunfire. Black reentered the darkened whip, leaving Trig to empty his clip in the middle of the street, before taking his place within the car, burning hot and winded. Black grabbed the burning blunt in the ashtray and pulled on the weed calmly as if nothing happened.

"So, now we eat," nonchalantly, Black chimed.

Over the last few weeks, Shiz and M were covering much ground on how Markease moved in the city. Shiz decided that after he calmed down, murdering Markease alone wouldn't quench his thirst. He needed him to hurt from all angles, before sending him to his bloody death. The duo knew Markease was getting it, but this shit was retarded. They discovered his number house in Frankford, a barbershop in Germantown, a recording studio up in Mt. Airy, and an off-the-hook coke strip on 47th Street down West. Markease played his girl games in the city, but true blue to the hustler's manual, he had something nice in the tuck...A bad ass Chinese bitch that he regarded as wifey, he kept on the low and far away from the hood bullshit. She was living out in Coatesville, in a $700,000 townhouse Markease provided for her comfort. The chick played Russian Minks in the winter and Hungarian silks in the summer. Some reports came back that she could be seen in a Bentley GT flossing diamonds the size of golf balls in and out of high end retailers. Markease had proposed to the Asian mommy and was set to marry her in the winter. He trusted nobody except her. She was his go-to guy when shit was rough and he depended on her to be his outlet and safe haven from the streets. He kept her out of ear's reach so no one could spoil her image of him. Shiz intended on using every inch of the new info to make Markease's life as miserable and worthless as possible, before the grand finale of murder for shittin' on his cousin the way he did.

M, in heavy thought, decided to go see Chantel. He found himself thinking about her a lot, and he needed to make sure she was turning out alright. What he didn't know is that since the incident, she was requesting Percocet to deal with the depression she underwent. Needless to say, the pills had her sleeping harder than Alice, and she really didn't say much when she woke momentarily. Be it as it may, M in tote of a circus worth of balloons with different pictures of Chantel's past living happier days featured on them, went to visit her. Entering the suite that was flooded with dozens of white orchids and red roses he had sent before his arrival, he sat a Hallmark card along with a large box of chocolates. M grabbed the hand of a sleeping Chantel, wishing he had found her sooner. Maybe he could've caught that joker in the act and settled all scores then and there. M was only a short distance away while Chantel was being raped. He couldn't understand why someone would want to hurt something as soft and beautiful as Chantel. Overlooking her silky hair that wrapped to her shoulder, M had a little thing for Chantel and somehow her current crisis made him desire her more. He knew he could hold her down the way someone as bossy as she deserved. Unable to expose the tenderness he felt inside at the time, he kissed Chantel's forehead, exiting to avenge her pain and agony.

Shiz had been running meetings all over the city to finalize his plot against Markease. Assembling his team of young Hyenas, he promised they would be set up nicely, if they followed his orders precisely. Mona was Shiz's lawyer he had used since he was a juvenile. Over the years, the two had become quite close, but he never hit it before...close, but not quite. M's suspicion had turned out correct; Dee and Bam were detained for questioning for a few days. But, Mona had gotten them off by as much as a simple phone call. She was truly that bitch. Having Dee and Bam back made Shiz feel like shit was starting to look up. He had called his man Rob in from D.C. to handle the most important part of the plan, while he had Tracy plugged into Markease's under boss. Shiz knew Tracy could fuck well enough to make most succumb to her wishes. It took some coaxing, but she reluctantly agreed, hoping she would bring Shiz closer to her. Pussy run da game, so he made it do what it do...Run Game!

$ $ $ $ $

Steering the black Range Rover up the long cobblestone driveway leading to the contemporary townhouse in Coatesville, Markease ejected the vehicle wearing a Zayaani linen set with black Prada soft walks, in tote of a gym bag. The home was truly a work of art. It was a stately stucco faced two story home, with manicured lawns and French doors. Sensored path lights led up the entrance walk, that activated as you proceeded. Oval Anderson windows complimented a centered full width sun view, overlooking Coatesville's landscaping. Closing the door behind him, Markease found a full blooded Rottweiler with an emerald encrusted collar greeting him zealously.

"Hey Rocky, how my girl?" He said, in a pet owner voice, ruffling her fur. The interior of the house was immaculate, with marble tile throughout in pearly white cubits, a gourmet island style kitchen with granite countertops, medallion cabinets, and a stainless steel stove and refrigerator set. A 52" high-def. flat screen hosted the living room's ivory colored walls, coordinating well with the coffee brown carpeting. The master bedroom carried his and her toilets, sinks, and shower heads englassed in crystal. Markease ascended the spiral staircase leading to what he loved most about his crib, 'KASHI.' Lounging on a mink coated stretch chair, her 5 ½ pedicured toes dipped relaxingly in the warm bubbles the foot massager generated. Her eyes under cucumbers, her skin looked softer than satin. Her shape was beyond worth pulling over for.

"Keas-se, is that you?" She asked, as Markease stared at the diamond he found vacationing in Europe five years ago.

"Yea, it's me Kay."

"Well, it's 'bout time, Keas-se," she said, removing the eye covering to jump lovingly into the arms she believed could do no wrong.

"Kashi was worried about you. Why didn't you call me?" She questioned cutely pouting her lips, staring through slanted eyes that resembled green oceans, as Markease's arms went wrapping lovingly around her slender waist. "Did you call the florist for our wedding like you promised?" She shot, releasing her pinned up hair and allowing it to fall over her princess face. He studied her full lip shape that was becoming more enticing with every formulating word.

"Answer ME," she chimed, beating playfully on her lover's chest.

"Did I ever tell you how in love I am with you? You are truly amazing and beautiful, and I just want to say that I appreciate everything we have together...I love you, Kay." Kashi blushed, as Markease untied her silk robe with dragons printed on the left side, exposing her perky breasts and shaven pussy. He slid his two fingers into her wet slit, and then made love to her passionately on the plush carpeting.

Markease exited the shower after his intense love making session. Kashi laid on the bed naked, zooming from the dick her fiancé laid on her. She turned to observe what Markease was doing. After finding the black gym bag, he carried it to the flat screen on the wall. He encoded a few digits, miraculously sending the screen up, revealing a gold plated safe door. Markease input the combination and instantly the door swung open, revealing three filled shelves of neatly stacked big faces. He began shoveling rubber-banded rolls of currency onto the very bottom shelf.

"Are you going to play with your money all day, or with me?" Kashi said, drawing his attention with her legs wide open.

Tracy stood with a confused look by the hood of her Honda Accord, watching it smoke on the corner of 47th Street. Shiz had paid for her hair to be styled to perfection on some real live Hollywood shit, while her outfit was to match her bossiness. The corner trappers couldn't keep their eyes off of Tracy's bootilicious body, and the way the Dolce & Gabbana jeans were huggin' her ass was bananas. Rocking Dior strapless four inches to match her halter top was the right look to make any hustler drool. Jab asserted his seniority over the workers, making them stay put while he assisted Tracy with her automotive problems.

"Damn sis, you good?" he asked, eyeing a troubled Tracy.

"No, I don't know what's up with it," Tracy returned, fanning its fuming smoke. Jab leaned in, acting as if he knew a thing about fixing cars.

"Sis, dis is fucked up. Let me call my mechanic to look at it."

"No, I don't have time. I gotta go and get home before the mail comes," she shot. Jab saw the perfect timing to introduce himself. The two exchanged names.

"Look, I know you don't know me like that, sis. But, I can take you to the crib, while my boy takes care of your whip. No bullshit."

"Now why would you want to do all that for me, whom you just met?" Tracy sang, resting her hand on her thick hip smiling seductively.

"'Cause I'ma nice guy, sweetheart...Stop trippin' and let a nigga help you out," Jab replied slyly with a devilish grin.

"Umm-hmmm, I'm sure," Tracy shot, rolling her lips, eyeing the young hustler head to toe, feeling his swag. In particular, she was feeling his name tattoo, J.A.B., which was on his forearm bringing out the diamonds that wrapped around his wrist.

"I don't know, Jab," she whined.

"C'mon sis, I got you," he returned, disarming the black Dodge Charger sitting on twenty-two's.

"You better not try nothing slick, boy," she said suspiciously, before entering the car.

"I ain't into that, ma. I got you!" He convinced before pulling off. The duo could hear the corner hustlers talking shit as they exited. Namely Ra, saying Jab wasn't getting any pussy, and Tracy was way too much for him. The ride to Tracy's crib was very intriguing as they learned a lot about each other. She could feel that Jab was attracted to her and without much flirting, he was already telling her things he normally would've sat on, all in the name of pussy. The duo arrived laughing, Jab occasionally patting Tracy's thigh as they exchanged giggles. Feeling the awkward moment nearing departure, Tracy asked Jab if he wanted to come up for a bit. Without thought, Jab jumped at the opportunity. Jab found himself a seat, while Tracy checked her messages. She fixed Jab a drink after turning on the shower, throwing him a sandwich Ziploc filled with an ounce of weed.

"Roll-up!" She said, as she wiggled out of her D&G jeans before Jab. Tracy glided toward the shower, totally comfortable with her curvy figure. *With a cold drink, an ounce of killa, and a sexy ass bitch he just met, Jab's luck had never been this good had he worn a horseshoe shirt, ate rabbits' feet for dinner, and rolled with a grant-wishing leprechaun*, he thought to himself. Jab stared at Tracy's humongous ass wiggling, as she walked into the bathroom laced in her sheer black panties and halter top. *That shit is crazy,* he thought. Jab turned the TV on, eyeing how clean she kept the apartment. No matter what he did out there on the couch, roll up the blunt, channel surf, text, he could not ignore the tingling feeling in his stomach that he was about to get some. Tracy re-surfaced wearing boy shorts and a wife beater, taking a seat beside Jab on the couch. He sparked up while Tracy inquired about her whip.

"Ma, I got you, babee. It'll be fixed and in front of your door within the next hour. I do what I do, sweetheart." Tracy smiled her pearly whites, indicating she believed him.

"You alright? Do you need anything, 'cause once I get comfortable, I'm not getting up, boy," Tracy shot, as Jab passed her the blunt.

"Nah, I'm good," but he replied too fast, hating the fact that Tracy arrived at the couch quicker than he expected, and he didn't get a chance to lust over her ass in those boy shorts. The two chit-chatted about the hood life and money. The whole time, Jab wondered if he would be feeling how Tracy's ass cheeks felt slamming against his thighs. After the crash course on who's-who, the weed smoke had Tracy feeling it so she decided to get shit poppin' by changing the DVD. She wiggled her ass at Jab as she bent over injecting the disc into the player. Jab's dick instantly got rock hard, pulling Tracy onto his lap wearing lust in his face. The softness of her ass plastered on him was sheer bliss to Jab. Nothing else in the world was of any significance at that moment. Tracy decided to top him off since she could tell he wasn't ready for her bomb ass pussy, as he was twitching off her head game alone. She didn't want him to bust so she stopped to fully undress him, fingering her pussy while a cum-chasing Jab beckoned her on. She planted wet kisses from his neck to his chest, ending with rolling the condom over Jab's average sized penis with her mouth. She boarded, sending Jab's ass straight to an explosion! After the first round, Jab found the strength to put up a more fulfilling performance. Tracy lay across Jab's chest, while Jab relaxed comfortably on her fluffy pillows with his hands tucked behind his head like King Dingling.

"Your wheel outside, Trase," he shot, rubbing her luscious ass.

"How you know, boy?" she returned, sucking her teeth.

" 'Cause I just heard John's raggedy-ass pick up truck pulling off." They both laughed heartily, as Tracy began drawing circles on Jab's chest.

"Jab, you don't think I'm a freak, do ya?" She asked sincerely. He paused before answering.

"Naw, I mean...Well... no. Why? 'Cause we fucked?" He fumbled.

"Nigga, please! You can't even answer me without stuttering 'n shit." Jab displayed a confused look, wondering where she was going with it.

"Let me explain something to you, sweetheart. I pay my own way; always have and always will. So, if I want to give a nigga some pussy, then that's my grown ass adult decision, even though I don't be out here fucking like that, 'causc I do respect myself. But, I'm responsible enough to do me and I fuck with them condoms H-E-A-V-Y. My point is...I fucked you 'cause I'm feeling you, not 'cause I'm some freaky bitch turned on some dick. But, don't be confused, roll when your done," Tracy spilled flat out. Jab could do nothing except respect what she said. The bitch was real in his eyes, and definitely somebody to keep around.

"That's what's up, Tracy, that's some real shit. I'm glad you put that on blast like that because I HATE an extra-bitch drawing and shit." Jab wanted to show he related.

"Well, let me tell you what I hate. When my mom be singing on the toilet," Tracy revealed, breaking into a hard laugh, lightening the moment.

"Naw, I hate when dope heads be bringing all this change to the corner, counting nickels and shit for like twenty minutes."

"Uh-huh, I really hate when a bitch be stunting 'cause they got a little car note, knowing damn well that bill whuppin' that ass," she giggled, snapping her fingers.

"Right, right," he said smiling.

"Aww shit, hold up, I got something crazier than that," he began laughing. "My man, Butter, go get his car washed every week down West, but not to clean his car. He just wanna watch the bubbles through the sun roof," Jab's laughter intensified. "That nigga ... that ... that nigga be on some nut shit sometimes." Tracy laughed right along with him.

"Ill, that is weird. Why he do that?" she asked, recovering from the humor.

"He said it helps him think better," he shared, wiping the tears from his eyes. She instantly knew what he spilled had to be worth something. Inwardly, Tracy smiled, patting herself on the back for how bomb her pussy was. Acknowledging the fact of her back shot when she threw it back was irresistible, and pillow talk is a motherfucka!

CHAPTER

8

You fuck with me, now it's a must that I fuck with you

Chantel awoke in the hospital suite buried in colorful flowers and floating balloons, with pictures of her on them living happier days. Candy and fruit baskets seemed to cover the white tile on the floor, bearing Hallmark cards attached to the necks. She had faint memories of M carrying her into the car and hospital, being very gentle with her fragile body. She also imagined M coming to visit her, where he caressed her hair and kissed her forehead lovingly. Unsure if the thought was actually a reality, she pondered how sweet that would be if M really felt something deep for her. She smiled at the thought of M taking her away from all of her problems and incredible men drama. Just then, she felt the soreness in her neck and stomach, reminding her of the ordeal she had with Markease. Bringing tears to her eyes and a throbbing in her heart, Chantel's mood switched dramatically. She felt dirty and disgusting, somehow blaming herself for the sexual assault and wishing things could be different. *M will never want me now, nobody will,* she thought to herself, snorting fluid back into her nostrils. Chantel had no choice but to cry herself to sleep, believing that everybody would think she was a whore.

Shiz informed Tracy to play Jab super close. His wish was her command, and she was not to fall short in fulfilling it. Tracy understood well and accepted her task like it was her own idea. Sitting at her desk in the Cheltenham branch of Bank of America, straightening the out of place items on the surface in preparation to leave, she dialed Jab from her desk phone.

"What's up, Trase?" He answered, peeping her job number on his display screen.

"Nothing really, I was just wondering if you could pick me up and take me to my hair appointment downtown?"

"Where ya car at and how you get to work?" Jab replied.

"I rode in with my girlfriend. Why? If you can't do it, don't worry 'bout it."

"Damn, did I say that? Shit a little busy out here right now, that's all." He got excited.

"It's cool. I'll catch the bus...And, you didn't have to get smart, Jab."

"You never said what time the appointment was."

"In an hour and a half."

"Shit!...Yea, I can fuck with it, but you gotta be on point, Trase. I'll be there in twenty minutes. Be out front, none of that I'm coming out now bullshit, BE OUT FRONT!" He spilled, wheeling the Charger through traffic.

"Alright."

"Nah, I'm serious, BE OUT FRONT!" he emphasized.

"A-L-R-I-G-H-T!" she countered his aggression, knowing he liked that shit. Tracy thought to herself about how intense Jab sounded. Maybe this was the one where she could finally be done with the young thug. Catering to Jab was a handful, for it had only been a few weeks and he was already trying to pull condoms off in a futile attempt to lock Tracy down with an unwanted baby. Jab had fucked many chics before, and the bread he was seeing off of 47th Street definitely had a couple of dimes thrown his way, but Tracy was cooking, cleaning, and fucking him good. She even gave him a set of keys to the spot which Jab utilized in particular at night, when he snuck in to bust her ass. He found a good hustler wife in Tracy. She was cute in the face, thin in the waist, with a gigantic ass. Tracy never sweated Jab about his comings or goings, nor asked about any of his personal business outside of what they shared. In fact, Tracy would remind Jab to keep that part to himself, citing the rules to the game...the less your bitch knows the better. And, to top it off, she had a professional streak to her, working in the client services department at the Bank of America. Jab didn't want anybody clowning him about how he fell for Tracy in a short period of time, so he kept it on the low from Markease, who would more than likely say he was pussy-whipped. While in fact, he just finally found a bitch that truly knew her role and didn't need to be coached. Jab pulled up to the awaiting Tracy, standing in front of the bank wearing a white skirt set by Nicole Miller with her hair pulled into a sideways ponytail that bellowed out at the end. Her curvaceous figure filled the suit perfectly. She smiled her pearly whites and Jab melted into a complete puddle. Tracy hopped in, tossing her Dooney & Bourke bag into the back after she kissed Jab's cheek. No sooner than when they pulled off, he received a call from Markease.

"Little buddy, where you at?" Markease wanted to know.

"Uptown, on my way down."

"What da fuck are you doing up there when my people be at the spot in twenty minutes!" Markease barked through the line. Tracy could hear the enraged man screaming through but pretended to be preoccupied, shuffling through her pocketbook she grasped from the back.

"Dawg, I was gonna send Ra and them to grab."

"No the fuck you wasn't! Matter of fact, what da fuck on ya mind? Nigga you trippin'! You been acting real funny lately, Jab, like you got something clouding your muthafucking judgment. We ain't starting nothing new. Go get my shit!" Tracy knew what was in question was what Shiz was after, so she texted Shiz to alert him, 'It's going down', and let him know where she was to be dropped off.

"A'ight B. I'm on my way, dawg," Jab spat to a disconnecting Markease. He noticed Tracy texting on her cell phone.

"Who da fuck you texting?" angrily he fired.

"Baby, why you cursing at me, what did I do?" Tracy asked calmly. After marinating the thought and coasting the Hemi towards the freeway, Jab apologized for the moody behavior, acknowledging that she had nothing to do with how Markease jumped on his ass. To clarify the acceptance, she leaned over and kissed him on the mouth intimately, while fondling his dick through his jeans. Jab was feeling it, and if he didn't have to be somewhere, between her legs he would've stayed.

"Now, if you must know, jealous man, that was my stylist. I let her know I'm on my way," Tracy dropped, making Jab feel even more foolish.

Shiz notified M, Dee, and Bam that shit was about to pop off and be in place, NO MISTAKES! Everything had to be perfect in order for the plan to send a crushing blow to Markease, as their hearts felt he deserved. Shiz was smiling inwardly, when he received the call from Rob that Kashi had been home all day by herself. Everyone was in place, even Markease who had been followed for three days now.

Jab dropped Tracy off as promised at the salon. Unbeknownst to him, M and the crew awaited him at the shop in a black Dodge Caravan. Following him at a safe unsuspecting distance, Jab led them to the parking complex of Dave and Buster's on Delaware Ave. Parking at the other end, the clique eyed Jab as he entered into a white Bentley Flying Spur. After about fifteen minutes, he ejected the Bentley with a shopping bag, heading towards the Charger as the Bentley pulled out of the complex. M gave Bam the signal behind the wheel to move in. Just as Jab was nearing his whip, the trio pulled up swiftly, skkkeeeeerrrrrrrtttttttt! Sliding the cargo door open simultaneously, Dee bailed out with the S-K, while M leaned out the window with his .44 marked at Jab's head.

"What the fuck?" A startled Jab blurted. Before Jab had a chance to reach for his heat, Dee slammed the butt of the gun into his skull sending him unconscious. Jab was then scooped up into the van along with the shopping bag, disappearing with little to follow.

$ $ $ $ $

Markease coasted his 750 back into the city. His temperature was a thousand plus, not receiving confirmation that the coke touched down. His first thought was to check how the strip was poppin'. When he arrived on 47th Street, Markease could see his team out there shooting dice, with the normal hoodrats hanging not far away.

"Yo, where the fuck Jab at?" He questioned, after leaving the whip. A pudgy looking kid took the initiative of responding.

"We ain't seen that nigga since earlier." Markease pondered that response briefly before moving on.

"Where Ra at? You ain't seen him either?"

"Yea, he around the corner screaming at Naesha."

"Tell that nigga to get at me ASAP. And, what's up with that money? How that money running out here?" Markease asked quickly.

"The money right, it's the work we fucked up on, Butter. We was waiting on Jab to get back, but that nigga probably out fucking something while this dough keep sliding through."

"Jab didn't drop nothing off since this morning?" Markease inquired, trying to place an explanation on Jab's mysterious actions.

"Na, we got our OWN work out here right now," a dark skinned young man draped in a Mezaan hoodie interrupted in an arrogant manner.

"And who told ya little ass to do that?" The regulars, sensing Markease's anger, knew better to stand down while the general addressed the recent recruit.

"What, we supposed to just sit back and let money walk because niggas ain't on point? Shit, I'm tryna get rich, too!" The brave heart spat. Markease's jaw tightened and fire displayed through his eyes, while his heart became coated with the predatory instincts.

"Yea...You little niggas got the game fucked up!" Markease swiftly drew the Smith & Wesson and shot him in the leg, tearing through his Roc jeans as the onlooking hustlers gasped. Now, standing over the bitching soldier,

"See, if I murk ya little ass, the first thing niggas'll be saying is Butter be trippin'. Don't never get it fucked up 'cause you don't see me out here, DIS MY SHIT! And, if I ever find out you selling something else out here without asking me, I don't care if it's socks and boxers, nigga. I'ma kill ya muthafucking ass!" Markease looked into the faces of the rest of them, making sure they understood it applied to them as well, sealing his statement with an exclamation mark that slammed into the brave heart's hip. BLUCK!

"Now, get this bitch off my block," he spat to the watching hustlers.

Ra descended down Naesha's front steps after sucking on her neck for like twenty minutes in her doorway. Reaching the second landing, he received a chirp from Pudge on 47th Street, informing him Markease was looking for him and he was around there trippin', 'Shooting mutherfuckas.' He also told him, Markease was looking for Jab. Ra knew that Jab was spending a lot of time with Tracy, although he didn't know her by name. He hoped that shit wasn't fucking money up because it would fall on his neck as well, since he was Jab's right hand man out there. As he reached his pine green and gold Acura RL, he dialed Markease's hitter to see what's really good, as he entered the whip.

"Butter, what's up? It's Ra."

"Where you at?" Markease growled, coasting the BM.

"I'm around the corner at the bitch Naesha's crib; about to pull off, what's up?"

"Where the fuck is ya man at?"

"Last time I talked to him was this morning. He told me we had to go grab, but he never got back at me."

"Yea, ya 'lil man running 'round here with ten large, and I'm about to start dropping muthafuckas if that 'Yo' don't turn up soon," he threatened, in which Ra was absolutely clear who was on his shit list.

"Butter, all I know is he been spending a lot of time with a bitch from North with a gold Accord," he explained. As Ra further elaborated on this brawd Jab had been running around with, he failed to notice the black Caravan that pulled up directly on the side of him, boxing him in with the parked cars before and behind him. Feeling a presence smiling down on him, he turned to see the annoying figure with his eyes. At that moment, Bam squeezed the chopper, sending an uncountable amount of deadly shots into Ra's car and body, just as Markease made his closing statement. Markease had thought that he heard gunshots before disconnecting but waved the idea off as foolishness. He floated on, thinking about a missing Jab and the ten keys, hoping he'd pop back on the radar soon.

Whoppp!!! Shiz back handed the shit out of Jab, sending blood splashing onto the wall, as Jab sat strapped naked to a chair in the basement at an abandoned North Philly row home, surrounded by M and Dee.

"So, ya man like taking pussy from young bitches, and you think that's cool?" Shiz mentioned with a chill in his voice. Jab spat a wad of blood onto the floor.

"I don't know what the fuck you talking 'bout. I don't know no Butter, no bitch named Chantel, and you can suck my dick." Dee smacked him with the .9 milli, causing blood to trickle down his bearded cheek. Jab moaned in agony, screaming,

"Fuck you's and pussies!" Jab knew he was a dead man. It was more than likely they were going to kill him because, if they didn't, Jab was dead set on returning the visit. Plus, Markease was his cousin, not just his man. So, betraying him would be betraying the whole family, and giving up any information was non-negotiable.

"I'm done fucking with you, dawg. You gonna tell me what I wanna know or you gonna be the perfect height to suck my dick, you gay ass nigga!" Shiz gave M the signal, to which he ascended the stairwell. Jab's mind raced the whole time strapped to that chair. He wondered who would find the $300,000 he had stashed in his mother's pantry. Would Markease make the city pay for his murder? Who would attend his funeral? Would his baby mom finally miss him and regret playing him out while he was locked up? But of all, he thought about Tracy; wishing he could taste her love juices, feel her sweet touch, or hear her laugh one last time. She had become quite dear to him over the last month and he would give a lot just to have one more day with her. Had he known this would happen, he would've definitely fucked her in the car before he let her out to enter the salon. His thoughts were broken by more of Shiz's threats and the nudging finger on his temple.

"Dig dis, dawg, what the fuck I look like a sucker?" Jab responded, ready to be laid to rest like a terrorist embracing his destiny on a suicide mission.

"Nah, no, not at all. You ain't no sucker, you a bred. But, you gotta be wondering if you gonna fuck my 'lil bitch Tracy again...That pussy good right?" Shiz struck a nerve, receiving a confused look from Jab that mostly displayed through his upward gazing eyes. Nodding his head, a detecting Shiz continued.

"Yea nigga, you ain't in this situation by chance," Shiz laid on, destroying Jab internally as he questioned himself, *was it all a game?*

"You feel like a sucka, huh? It's nothing! Your problem is she only fuck with niggas my height and down," Shiz spat, gaining a retarded ass look from Jab. M appeared out of nowhere with a chainsaw. He began hacking into Jab's kneecap; the pain sent him rushing in and out of consciousness. The hysterical screaming and flickering of blood and bone gristle brought goosebumps to Dee's skin. M managed to saw through the entire legs, sounding like a thawed-out steak slab smacking against the concrete.

"Aww, you bitch ass niggas, cut my fucking leg off!" He bellowed with spit particles flying from his deeply pronounced words. The tears flooded his face, eyeing his wigging nub in excruciating pain and not believing this was actually happening to him.

"Now look at you, all fucked up. You wasn't like this when you came, main-man. Tell me what the fuck I want to know! Where Butter goes to get his wheel detailed at and what time, dawg? My patience is getting real thin fuckin' with you," Shiz spat, watching intensely as the blood streamed like a river from Jab's leg, having no effect on him. Jab began to stutter, to which Shiz gave the order to M. Moving the chainsaw closer, Jab gave up.

"Hold up, dawg. I think this nigga ready to rap," Shiz said arrogantly.

It had been a full 24 hours since Markease had heard from Jab. Nobody in the street knew anything, except he had been spending a lot of time with some big butt girl from the North. The whole thing puzzled him, along with the fact that ten keys were missing with him, which made matters go from worst to murderous! He often questioned himself if Jab was on some sucka shit, as Markease had been a little hard on him the past few weeks. After some more thought, he brushed that notion off, knowing Jab was a bred. In fact, he handmade him himself. Jab made Markease a lot of money, and it didn't take much for Jab to determine street life was his most promising ticket out of the hood. Since Markease put him on, he promised death before dishonor, loyalty before betrayal. All of that was fly, and Markease believed he would hold to that if he got booked. But, the one thing he'd rather figure out first was,

"Where da fuck is my dope at?" Markease blurted, pulling up in front of the Coatesville townhouse.

Entering the nest this evening was awfully different from the norm. Usually, Rocky could hear his wheel pull up and would be waiting at the French doors, eager to play with her raiser. This was often known by the barking when he inserted the key. Markease smelled a strange aroma encompassing the household. Kashi, every now and then, would try to hit off with one of her back home meals, even though he never liked them. A smile came to his face when he thought about the leg work he had to put in to prove to her parents he was worthy of marriage. The Chinese are very protective over their children. They are raised to honor their culture and keep to the bloodline. So, when she informed her father she wanted to marry Markease who was American, and black at that, it sent him into an outrage. Markease many times considered letting the idea go, and her as well, because without the blessing of her father she wasn't willing to go forward. But, every time he looked at the Asian mommy, he had a change of heart forcing him to go harder. During one of their seasonal getaways, he offered to go visit her family in Hong Kong. For years, her father begged and pleaded for her to come home and visit. He even used her siblings to persuade her, but Kashi was dead set on never returning to the land where her mother was murdered. It was the one thing that would cause her to disobey her loving father. Markease understood her plight, but reassured her safety with his life and love. After a few love making sessions, a Bentley GT, and a ruby anklet, she was standing before her father in the land she vowed never to step foot in again. Markease was in; her father regarded such an act as priceless, and he had proven he had the morals and integrity for a man befitting to be marrying his Kashi.

Markease couldn't wait to feel Kashi's lips pressed against his face, for he hadn't seen her since the day before. He thought to surprise her in the kitchen while she cooked. He always enjoyed how her ass felt pressed against his dick, when he held her from behind. As he glided towards the kitchen, he noticed Kashi's silk robe on the staircase. His thoughts were on relieving his street frustration on his fiancé's wet box, because talking about what went on in the street was an absolute no-no. The last thing he wanted in the life he'd shared with Kashi was some hood bullshit. Markease was confused to find, Kashi wasn't in the kitchen supervising the over-sized pot with boiling suds dripping onto the sizzling burner. Tip-toeing over the puddling water in front of the burner, curiosity obliged him to open the lid. Scaring Markease half to death, he dropped the lid in shock of Rocky's head floating at the top of the boiling pot. His eyes raced frantically around the kitchen trying to understand what was going on. He grabbed the .357 from the cabinet, instantly beginning to notice every out of place item. He saw some of the crystals knocked over on the dinner set and wood chips on the paw printed floor, which caused him to look down the hall to notice a sizable hole at the bottom portion of the door. He could hear the TV on in the bedroom. Markease's mind spun in disbelief that somebody had obviously came to his home and brought hell right along with him. With the .357 in hand, he ascended the spiral staircase, stopping to pick up Kashi's robe. He smelled it, inhaling her scent deeply; his heart sorrowed and fearing the worst. Passing the bathroom, he could see blood splattered on the floor and door. His stomach knotted at what he might see. His vision served him an image of a headless Rocky swimming in a shallow red pool beneath her. Murder was in his heart. Feeling the rage pulsate through his veins, he belted her name.

"KAAASSHHIII!" Several more times he screamed it out, as he searched the luxury townhouse, but got no response. Entering the bedroom, he found a bunch of weird shit; giant dildos, rope, and butt beads. Furniture was overturned and wrecked, but absolutely no Kashi. Then, he realized he kept all his dough in the crib, so he speedily punched the code in that raised the screen and opened the safe door. Shocking the shit out him, it all seemed to be there.

"WHAT DA FUCK IS GOING ON?!" He barked, figuring that someone had to have gotten in and apparently had Kashi, but didn't make her cough up the bread. Kashi knew the code and was far from a ride-or-die chic, but yet the money was still there. He began searching for a ransom note or anything to explain what the hell happened. His head sent him in a thousand directions, but none made sense to him. All of Kashi's clothes were still there, as well as her jewelry that Markease bought over the years. Descending the steps like a lion hungry for blood, he noticed Kashi's six carat engagement ring lying just beyond the French doors. He held it in his hand, reflecting on the very moment he gave it to her and remembering the same words she uttered.

"I wear this ring as a symbol of my devotion and a sign of my safety." Markease didn't know if it was a sign, or something overlooked by her abductors.

"FUCK MANNN, DIS, NUT ASS SHIT!!!!" He screamed, sitting on the bottom steps, voice echoing, squeezing his hammer tightly.

CHAPTER

9

Who you loving, who you wanna be huggin'?

Jay's cousin K-B came down to see how his cousin was making out. His mom didn't really like Jay hanging out with him much. She believed Kyle was living to die in the street, and wanted Jay far away from that nonsense. Jay emerged from the house, wearing a polo sweatsuit with matching Bathing Apes; his color scheme was crazy. He hopped in his '08 Maxima on dubs to join his cousin within.

"That was your mom at the door?"

"Yea, that was her," Jay responded, flipping the visor down to brush down the edges of his braided hair.

"She still be grinding me up?" K-B asked, already knowing the answer.

"Yup!…Why else you not allowed in the crib?" Jay returned jokingly. K-B laughed knowing full well his aunt didn't fuck with him like that. The assault weapon she found in Jay's closet that he was holding for K-B didn't help either. If she'd had her way, she would lock K-B up herself to keep his absent minded ass away from her Jay. The two had a nice 'lil agenda for the day that involved getting money and relaxing, but first they planned to hit South Street to get tatted. After they arrived and overcame the incredible task of finding a parking spot, they walked into the shop, doing obviously well in the business. Bitches were in there something crazy, staring at Jay and K-B as they looked over the demo book placed on the counter. K-B checked his darkened complexion repeatedly in the mirror, making sure his lay was right. He loved some Philly brawds, citing the fact they kept it gutter. Instantly, K-B began flirting with the birds. The ladies were entertained by his crazy sense of humor which kept them laughing hysterically, watching K-B crack jokes on the occupants and passing shoppers.

Hearing the jingling bell affixed to the top of the door go off, everybody focused their attention on the entering customer, mainly to see if they were wearing anything K-B would crack on them for. But, this one was beyond jokes. This bitch was SERIOUS! Identical to the video vixen, 'Angel', but just a tad bit lighter, she had a walk that could shut Naomi down. She breezed past the eye hustling occupants to place an image on the counter which she planned to have done on her lower back. It was obvious she had work done before. The name tattoo on her neck read, *Da bomb.* Most sat in awe, jealousy, and admiration, listening to her instructions to the artist. Many wanted to say something, but dared not to. Before she spun to leave, there was only one person that she could see at all worth any of her time. With her quote in hand, she raised her perfectly manicured nails accentuating the gold bangles that dangled from her arm and said, "Hi!" to Jay before leaving. K-B wanted to say loudly so bad, GO IN!!, but he didn't. He would, however, keep a watchful eye on him the rest of the day. Still boiling for letting that bad ass dime slide out on him, K-B noticed the whole time in the shop, Jay didn't holla at nothing. Even the tattoo artist that worked on his arm was nice looking, throwing Jay all the right signs, still nothing! He was acting like these bad ass chicks were invisible. So, on the ride to the barbershop, K-B decided to confront him.

"What the hell is your whole thing, squad?"

"What you talking about Kay?" Jay replied.

"That bitch fucked you up like that, son?" K-B asked. Jay stared out into the scenery, reflecting how Kelly played him chasing after some minute paper.

"Fuck that bitch, yo!" A bitter Jay barked back.

"I'm good right now. I don't need no freak bitch looking to fuck for dollars right now slowing me down, feel me?" K-B shrugged his shoulder with the 'whatever! face' inscribed in his brows.

"Well, if you ask ME, some good 'ol fashion pussy is exactly what you need. So, what, you ain't gettin' no head if we go down the China shit? Stop tryna fall in love with every bitch you meet, son." Jay pondered K-B's last words thoroughly, wondering if that was the real problem and reason that had set him back in life. Every female he dealt with made him instantly imagine them in wedding dresses. He hated to treat women like a pack of wild whores because he saw all women like his sister, mother, and any other female family associate. But, it was coming to the point where he had to accept shit for what it is!

CHAPTER

10

Twenty-four Hours Before (Luxury Townhouse)

Kashi stood in the mirror putting her hair into a ponytail, eyeing her reflection as she carefully checked for out of place strands. She could hear Rocky barking downstairs, as the echoing 'ruffs' were beginning to make Kashi nuts.

"Oooh, I'ma kill her if she don't shut up," she grumbled to herself. The thought that she might be hungry crossed her mind. Kashi grabbed her satin housecoat with dragons printed down the side and proceeded down the staircase to feed Rocky. She hated that Markease left Rocky to her care, even though she understood the dog was for her protection. But, Kashi felt she had better things to do than opening cans of Purina for an oversized K-9 all day. After reaching the first floor, Kashi noticed Rocky was propped against the window seal, apparently barking at somebody and intensively staring at nothing in particular. Kashi looked out the window but saw nothing.

"What is it, Rocky? Why are you acting up?" Petting the neck of the black Rottweiler, she then led her to the kitchen where she filled her bowl with steak chunks and her fluid container with mineral water. She proceeded back up the staircase as Rocky began barking again. Kashi yelled, "SHUUUTT UUUUUP! Her voice echoing down the hallway. Rocky, within ear's distance of the command, obeyed. Kashi began relaxing in the tub, not thoroughly wet yet, Rocky commenced her growling 'ruffs'. Fed up with the noise, Kashi robed up and descended the stairs to a nervous Rocky, sensing Kashi's anger. A frustrated Kashi led the dog by her jewel encrusted collar into the basement and locked the door, entrapping Rocky to the muffling lower compartment. Climbing the staircase, she uttered,

"You so hard headed, Rocky." Just then, the doorbell rang. (Ding-Dong) Kashi stopped mid stairs and headed back down, wondering who the unexpected guest was. And, had she known, she would've boarded, bolted, nailed, and chained that motherfucker out. Rob was the kindest and most soft spoken person you'd ever run into these days, but underneath it all, he truly didn't give a fuck and was crazier than a mutherfucka. Washington D.C. nurtured his madness, as he grew up in the murder cap. era, learning by eyewitnessing D.C. vets like: Wayne Perry and Lil Dame and them. You call a nigga like Rob in when you want some dirty shit done! She opened the French door to a dark skinned gentleman wearing a Dickies set with a noticeable scar under his right eye, holding a meter reader.

"How ya doing, ma'am? I'm Robert Hall from Coatesville Electric Company, here to do an accuracy test on the electric meter."

"Nice to meet you, Mr. Hall. But, we weren't scheduled for another reading until next month," she replied, with her hands folded over her housecoat.

"We're so backed up that we had to dispatch earlier. It's only a few seconds, do you mind?" Grabbing the suitcase by his feet before receiving a response, he stepped well within the main foyer of the townhouse. Kashi, shocked at his boldness replied,

"Excuse me," sharing his attention with the loud barking of Rocky who had been ruffing since Kashi opened the door.

"Nah, you should've said that shit when that nigga asked you to marry him," Rob countered, punching her in the mouth and landing her inches before the steps. Rob slowly turned around and closed the door, as if he owned the beautiful townhouse. Rocky seemed to detect the incident as she was snapping from behind the locked chamber. Kashi rose to her feet swiftly, in an attempt to escape Rob's assault. Stumbling up the stairs, he caught hold of her robe which she slipped out of, allowing the garment to fall on the steps. Nearly tripping over the top landing, a naked Kashi fled toward the bedroom with Rob on her heels closing in fast. Her nose bled fluently, soaking a portion of her face in blood. Rocky began slamming her head against the door, causing a trembling of the dinette set. Clearly detecting Kashi's fear, her thrust became harder.

"Oh my god, what did I do? Why are you doing this? Please leave me alone, PLEASE!" Kashi screamed, tearing drops from both ends. She was hoping Markease returned to save and protect her, like he promised when he moved her way out there. But, the more she prayed, the faster she realized she was on her own. Rob tackled a naked Kashi, just as she entered the bedroom. She began fighting off her attacker by kicking, screaming, and scratching anything she was in reach of. Tasting blood on his bottom lip, Rob grabbed her hair and began banging Kashi's head into the door. Rocky's barks were becoming ferocious, as she continued pounding the door, causing blood to drip off of her fur. Kashi grabbed her Gucci shoe and began defending herself with it. Back on her feet, she attempted to cross over their king sized bed to get to the nightstand where Markease kept his 9mm. But, Rob met that attempt with a swipe at her feet, causing her to tumble off of the end, nearly snapping her neck. He began reaching for her, as the struggle to get loose was well on its way. Overturning several items, she did manage to make it to the nightstand. Rocky's pounding the fragile door began to pay off, as the wood paneling began cracking at the bottom. Rob had Kashi pinned to the floor, as she struggled to pull the nightstand drawer out.

"Calm da fuck down, bitch!" He blurted, licking her face while his hands fondled her ass and titties. Finally her hand latched on, pulling the drawer completely out as she fumbled for the inching 9-milli. Unbeknownst to a molesting Rob, she grabbed it, putting it hairs away from Rob's temple. Closing her eyes as the tears poured profusely, she squeezed what she anticipated to be the ending of Rob existence...CLICK! Rob instantly recognized the sound under the loud crashing of wood, growling, and four-legged footsteps. He knocked the pistol out of her hand, sending it sliding under the bed. Realizing the bitch could've just taken his life, he delivered a blow, knocking her unconscious. He could still hear the rumbling footsteps drawing closer. Appearing like a ghost in the darkness, Rocky finally locked on Rob's ankle. The wrinkle faced Rocky could taste blood, as she shook deeper into Rob's leg, tearing through ligaments with each twitch of her massive neck. A panicking Rob searched for the 9mm under the bed, while the beast shook his leg like an old rag doll. With the 9mm in hand, he could only hope it was loaded. He cocked back the iron, firing hot lead into the blood hungry beast and knocking him down. But, Rocky returned to her feet and charged Rob again, to which he put three more in her. Boc, Boc, Boc! Sending Rocky away, curled up and whimpering. Rob went into the bathroom to patch his wounds before executing the next part of the plan. He didn't consider this job would nearly claim his life. Eyeing his reflection in the mirror, he could've sworn he heard a growl. Before his instincts served his conscience, a bloody Rocky burst through the door landing on top of Rob, where the two scuffled on the bathroom floor.

"ARRRRRRRRRRRRRR, RUFF, RUFF, RUFF!!!"

"Aww shit! Get the fuck off me, you fuckin' mutt!" Rob blasted in a futile attempt to end the ordeal.

Why the fuck did I leave the gun on the god damn bed? crossed his mind as Cujo bit through his arms and hands, delivering devastation. He managed to grab the folded knife from his worker pocket as a last resort to win life from the vicious Rottweiler, painting the house with his splattering blood. He unfolded the blade with a swift jerk of one hand, while Rocky feasted on his remaining one. Rob jammed the seven inch blade into the savaging beast's neck, causing loud cries from the attacking Rocky. A winded Rob pushed the limp K-9 onto her side.

"Get da fuck off of me, crazy ass mutt!" Rob spent the next two hours beheading the lifeless Rocky, and cleaning his wounds.

Kashi awoke in the bedroom with a sore head and blurred vision. She had remembered dreaming about something awful, but from where she lay on the bed everything looked normal. The sheets had a softness to them that made her want to return to snooze world, but her headache was killing her and there was still laundry that needed to be done. That's when she realized that her feet had been shackled to the bed and hands bound. She began to cry, recalling the awful event. Out of nowhere, Rob's ten and a half inch dick plummeted deeply into her ass in one quick motion. She gasped, believing she would never find air in her lungs again. With the camera in his left, and Kashi's hair being tugged on in his right, he was loving the sweetness of her brown walls. He flashed a flick, highlighting the jiggle in her firm ass, while he pumped mercilessly into her rectum, causing a mind blown Kashi to scream for dear life. He pulled it out, then shoved it into her pussy, wrapping his hand around her neck while he applied a little pressure from the pleasure he was experiencing.

"Stop! Please! Ahh, no, noooo please don't. I have, ahhh!" Another death stroke ended her plea. Rob turned her onto her back so he could cum on her chest and face, making sure to smear it on her titties. Kashi was depleted from the long dicking Rob had put on her, and began to slip into unconsciousness. Meanwhile, Rob went to retrieve his suitcase from the lower level, preparing for shit to get messy as that was only part one of his assault. And, since that bitch got him all bit-da-fuck-up, he planned something special for her in particular. With Kashi asleep, Rob untied her from the bed, keeping her feet and hands bound.

"Yo ... Yo! Wake up ma," he said, smacking her face. As Kashi came to, she screamed after seeing Rob's face towering over her.

"What do you want? Why are you here?" She questioned, noticeably frightened.

"Calm down ma, calm down. You want me to leave?" She nodded her head, unsure if he was telling the truth and would respond to her request.

"Then, I'm going to ask you a few questions. If you answer what I ask honestly, I'll leave. Just like that, ya hear me?" She nodded.

"Do Markease got money in the house?" He asked and she nodded once again.

"Is there a safe or stash spot?"

"Yes, a safe," she spoke, just over a whisper.

"Do you know the combination?"

"Yes" she cried. He unfastened her bondage for her to show him. Kashi walked towards the TV and encoded the numeric secret. Rob's eyes opened wide when he saw the screen slide up, revealing the gold-plated safe door. She got the door to swing open, showcasing more money than Rob had ever seen in his life. As Kashi stood naked in front of the safe, Rob's dick got rock hard again. Kashi could feel it poking her in the lower back as he stood behind her, breathing on her hair. She began to weep uncontrollably.

"Why, no. You promised, you promised," she uttered, as he began feeling on her titties and inserting his fingers into her pussy. He threw her to the floor and she gasped heavily, right before he back handed her hair to another direction. Rob pulled out the .9mm, as he stripped from his clothes.

"Bitch, I swear if you move, I'ma blast ya muthafuckin' head off!" Rob began to insert giant butt beads into Kashi's rectum. She tensed up every time he inserted a ball. The way her camel toe smiled at him from doggy style, he had to put it back in. Kashi's insides felt like fire, as Rob laid another pipe beating on her abused kitty cat. Every four or five strokes, he'd rip a ball out, sending Kashi screaming in agony. Once they were out, he stuck his dick in replacement of the beads to thunder fuck her some more. By this time, Kashi's insides were mush and her tear ducts had dried out. As she weakened in her legs, her bowels released stool and urine all over Rob's dick, catching his abdomen, thighs, and hands as well.

"Aww fuck!" He said, with his hands raised above his head. "You just gon' SHIT on a nigga like that," he spat to a distraught Kashi.

"Bitch, clean this shit off before I shoot your ass." Kashi slowly moved to grab a rag by the TV.

"No bitch, witcha mouth. Lick all this shit off!" Kashi looked up with a trembling lip, in disbelief at the request. Rob smacked her with the .9mm, sensing hesitation. A recovering Kashi began cleaning him like a whistle. Halfway through the ordeal, she fainted. Rob began to stage the money, realizing he traumatized Kashi for a life time. Carrying her out the door, he could smell 'Brewing Rock'. In a dramatic daze, she slipped off her engagement ring, seeing it jingle on the floor as they exited. Talk about rough days!

CHAPTER 11

Revenge is the Sweetest Joy Next to Getting Pussy

"Ay, Pudge! Why da FUCK is this nigga not answering his phone? Ya better tell that mutherfucka, I ain't working with a lot of patience right now!" Markease growled through his cell, on his way back to the grimy city. He knew all of this was connected, and he was damned if he wouldn't turn the game on its head to figure out what was up with his bitch.

"Butter, I thought you knew," Pudge replied.

"You thought I knew WHAT, nigga?" Markease was beyond the edge.

"Ra, somebody killed Ra yesterday. Over the bitch Naesha's crib sitting in the car, a nigga hit him like twenty times." Markease was still flaming over Kashi, his coke, Jab, and now Ra got dropped, all within twenty-four hours. He knew somebody put him on their shit list, but he honestly couldn't pinpoint who because he'd been shitting on everybody in preparation to exit the game when he married Kashi. So, everybody gotta die! If you had a C.H.E.M.E. on you that wasn't carried out, or took a corner that a nigga was holding wrong, or a bitch that you played out, or so much as a little argument, you had to go. That was the best thing that he knew, to lay murder down. Niggas will beg to bring Kashi back, to make him ease up.

"Butter, you there, Butter?"

"Yea, I'm here Pudge, Damn...Ay listen, where you at now?"

"On Woodland Ave. on my way to Ra janazah," Pudge gave back.

"That's where they praying at?" Markease asked.

"Yea, down Daarul hadith, the masjid on 67th and Woodland. Everybody out at this joint right now."

"A'ight, I'll be there. Tell everybody not to leave. I got some real rap." Pudge confirmed the command, and then hung up.

"As-Salaamu Alaykum Wa Rahmatul-lah...As-Salaamu Alaykum Wa Rahmatul-lah," Abu Muhammed Al Jamakee chanted, ending the funeral prayer over Ra's body that laid out before the congregation shrouded in white, in wait of the masjid's Wakils to take hold of the body for its burial. Markease's eyes met with Pudge, who was wearing all white. They continued to exchange glances with other members of Markease's deadly 47th Street hyenas, acknowledging Markease's presence and need to speak with them. As the brothers began to pour out of the masjid from the front, the sisters did the same thing from the back. Markease found his way to the hood of his BM where he waited on his team. He thought about Ra and the way they killed him, and about how long it had been since he was in the masjid. Too bad it took something like this to get him there.

After the prayer, the brothers began to pair off in cars to follow the funeral procession. As the Muslims scattered about, Pudge, Zakee, Sajad, and Hasan found their way over to Markease, in response to his order. He really didn't have anything fly to say or any fancy way to put it, so it just came out.

"DEATH! I want mutherfuckas to start droppin'. If we can't get to them, then whoever is close to them; mom, dad, sister, whoever...DEATH! Any nigga that even breathes wrong, looks wrong, hates, DEATH!" His voice boomed, careless of who was in ear's reach. He was clearly emotional and enraged, from the redness of his eyes to the trembling lip, he was hot. Markease ordered murder for Ra, a missing Jab, and most of all, Kashi. If niggas wanted war, then so be it. Everybody that wanted a piece of his empire was all a target. He had never been hit this hard before, so he promised a million dollars to any of them that could make sense out of what was going on, and bring it to an end. He had **CASH** for whoever could **ELIMINATE** his **OPPOSITION**. The crew traded vicious looks of murder to resolve the current, fueled by the death of their man and Muslim. And, now the million Markease promised would push their ambition to high-max. From amongst the names he dropped was Chantel, including the address where he'd picked her up. When he said everybody, he meant EVERYBODY!

Markease coasted the heartless city wide open, with no intentions of cutting anybody breaks. And, it really didn't matter what anybody did today, any excuse was a good excuse to open somebody up. The situation laid so heavy on him, he thought to call his cousin, J.R., which was so unlike him as he was the type to handle his own affairs. But, this shit had him spread thin. Junior, or J.R. as they called him, was the bol out of Baltimore. He'd been out there since fourteen, originally from Philly, but stepped off with his mom who received a nice job offer out there. He was another wild ass gun slinger that got the game from E-A and then, from uptown. Mostly everyone that was a bred, pretty much was because they got the game from niggas that held it down before them. So, Markease respected his outlook, and maybe he could see something in the occurrences that Markease missed. After informing him of the whole spiel, J.R. offered his apologies, sympathizing with his cousin's misfortune. He knew how dear Kashi was to him, and the shit about Jab had him ready to throw the city on smash.

"Dig, let me send a few niggas down there while I tie some shit up here?" J.R. spat, wanting to help out.

"Nah cuz, I got too many running around right now tryna sort this shit out."

"I feel you, damn. Let me think on this shit. Something ain't right...hmm, listen Butter, I'ma wrap up and I'm on my way down." Markease felt better knowing that his cousin was coming down, acknowledging that the two together could squeeze juice from a rock. They were a natural ingredient for disaster that would far surpass the efforts of any team of wolves.

Zakee and Sajad sat in the parking lot of Cheltenham Square Mall in Sajad's black Dodge Durango. Zakee chain smoked Newports, while he watched the entrance of the movie theater hawkingly. Sajad flipped through the radio stations. Their target led them to the last featured film of the night, 'Nasty'; A loud mouth Pulaski project bol that was getting some paper down there since A-vex and them got locked up. Markease told Nasty to surrender the projects before he took it. Without thought, Nasty told him to suck his dick. That was three months ago. Markease had put a C.H.E.M.E. on his head, but that contract got lost when Markease heard that he was grabbing off of Dollface. Incidentally, that wouldn't be enough now to keep Markease off his head. The duo had followed Nasty and his lady friend to the theater from the projects. The movie ended, and Zakee's eyes locked on Nasty as he pushed through the exit with his out-of nowhere entourage. Nudging the arm of Sajad,

"Nigga, wake da fuck up, ock. You supposed to be on point and you fuckin' searching for club music," he said, cocking back the assault weapon he dusted off for the occasion.

"Bra, I'M ON POINT. Just don't miss this motherfucka," Sajad replied, pulling out of the parking lot into the customer pick-up lane.

"Turn da music down dawg, you trippin' man!" Zakee fussed to an ignoring Sajad, as they reached the curb in front of the entrance where Nasty and his party had emerged. With the window down, the M-16 went crackling, sending deadly fire into the entire crowd; watching them fall like life-sized dominos into the cemented graveyards. Nasty and his party didn't have a snowball's chance in hell of surviving the murderous rain from such a close distance.

While Zakee and Sajad were dropping everything on Markease's list, Pudge was staking out the crib where Markease picked Chantel up. Despite the consistent movement on the block, he saw no one enter or exit the brick row home. He heard that a bol named Noodles' mom stayed there. Regardless of how he felt, he had strict orders to kill whoever was connected to the girl, Chantel, no matter how long it took. So, on that block he'd nest until somebody came through.

$ $ $ $ $

Since rocking Papi from New York, Black was making the kind of dough he used to see during the Fat's era. Niggas out in Delaware were paying homage to him like he invented the game. Trig couldn't have been happier with Black's actions. He reclined deeply on Trig's leather sofa not far from the strip, smashing a wing & fries combo from the Chinese store.

"What's da count, Trig?" Black eagerly wanted to know.

"Hold up."

"Nigga, what's da fuckin' count?!" Black asserted on Trig, feeding the money counter from trash bags filled with old currency.

"Bol, you gonna make me fuck you up, dawg! It's $97,000, not including the ones." Black finished the tray, then brushed the crumbs off of his Evisu jeans.

"How much coke left?"

"Like a half of joint, but I swear these niggas robbing us, straight up! You ain't notice how weak that shit gettin'. I can smell some bullshit." Trig cleared his chest.

"Yea, them niggas think somebody stupid. We gonna get right though. You try to put a few dollars in a nigga pocket and they try to play you on some nut shit. That's why I don't be giving niggas shit, mutherfuckas is greedy," Black said, greedier than the niggas he was talking about.

"Ay listen, I want you to meet my old head from down here. Money thorough. I fucks wit him like dhat, a nigga good peoples."

"What's his name, dawg?" Black questioned, picking chicken meat from his teeth.

"Reese-Cheese. Squad that nigga. Not on some dick-riding shit, the nigga serious, he serious Black." The two sat back, eyeing the bread on the top of the table. Shit was different now, the momentum was stronger. Niggas was getting RICH!

After considering the whole situation, Markease realized the master piece to the puzzle was the chic Jab was fucking with. If she wasn't somehow involved, then at least she would know what was on his mind before he turned up missing. Each passing day was worse than the one before it. Kashi didn't deserve what she was going through, and he knew he was responsible. Markease refused to believe she was dead, so he had to crank up the search. If the chic liked fucking with ballers, then she was bound to frequent the same circles he knew. And, there was no doubt the bitch, Star, from North would for sure know her. *How many bitches with Accords and asses her size?* Floated through his mind. He had to see what's good with Star. Markease arrived on Diamond Street, where he found Star's sexy ass with the music on blast, her girlfriends nearby, and plenty of cold Coronas.

"Oh shit, look what the fuckin' wind blew in!" She screamed, seeing Markease's BMW pull up in front of her door. "I know it's gonna snow now," she continued.

"Cut that shit out," Markease shot back, ejecting the 750. Star was a bonified North bitch that had some sexy ass dimples and killa good pussy. Most times, it was her high yellow complexion that covered the fact that she wasn't that pretty, and kept her on the arm or speed dial of some baller.

"Give me a hug, sexy," he spat to a sitting Star.

"You want something to drink?" she sang while studying his eyes, trying to guess what the real reason was she had the honor of the legend paying her an unsuspecting visit. "What you want, Butter?" she asked suspiciously, enjoying the twinkle from his diamond 'B' charm.

"Why, I gotta want something to come through?"

"Nigga, you cut that shit out…I've known you for too long, a bitch ain't crazy." Star stared unblinkingly into Markease's eyes.

"Let's go in the crib, I do need to scream at you." Star knew this had to be serious, if he wanted to talk to her in private. The two found themselves a seat and Markease went in.

"I need some info on a chic out this way." Star's eyes read, *Why? What happened?* loud enough for Markease to pick up on it.

"Don't hit me with that look Star; you know how I am, SERIOUSLY. Somebody very dear to me is in harm's way, and I need to find this chic before shit really gets crazy, feel me?"

"A'ight, why you coming to me, Butter?"

"C'mon Star, everybody knows all the bitches that fuck with get-money-niggas hop from one dick to the next. So, you bound to know who just got off your man's dick," he spieled, to which Star didn't find it at all humorous.

"Fuck you nigga, I ain't fucking with you!" She spat.

"My bad, Star. I didn't mean it like that...But, you know what I'm saying though," he apologized. She eyed him intensely maintaining her silence. She chuckled.

"I don't know why I fucks with you. What's her name?"

"I don't know."

"How you don't..." Markease cut her off.

"Look! All I know is she's from North, got a gold Accord, with a super fat ass, and was just fucking with Jab." Star rolled her eyes and lips at the typical-male info...Her ass was like this and her car was that color.

Pudge was surrounded by wrinkled chip bags in his all black on black Chevy Caprice, knocked da fuck out. It'd been almost a week since he started staking out Shiz's mom's crib. The tint on the windows shielded him from the setting sun rays that still beamed down. As of yet, still nobody had shown up. But, Markease was sure that was in fact the right address. Pudge didn't know what the girl Chantel did that could've warranted murder. But, it really didn't matter to Pudge since Markease had $50,000 on everybody that lived in the house. With his Philly Fitter smashed against the window and drool sliding from his mouth, the goon was officially sleeping on the job. Both of the rear doors slammed swiftly. BLOOM! Causing Pudge to jump from his sleep with eyes bloodshot red, fumbling for his .40 caliber. Relieved by Zakee and Sajad belting laughs from the backseat, Pudge wiped the drool from his mouth, clearly upset that the duo was playing like that.

"Man, what the fuck is wrong with y'all niggas?! Y'all on some nut shit!" Pudge growled not amused, while the duo laughed harder at his saltiness.

"Fuck is wrong with us…Nah! Fuck wrong with you? Lying out in front of some nigga crib knocked the fuck out with the doors open. Call yaself tryna murk somebody…Get da fuck outta here." Pudge could say nothing momentarily, while Sajad laughed on. Zakee was all the way right, and he knew it. The joke got old so the laughter ceased, while Pudge brushed his hair looking in the rear view. Sajad sparked up the blunt he had nesting in his ear.

"Ay, Pudge. How long you been out this jawn?" Sajad asked.

"For like a week, dawg. Fuck!" he replied, heated that he might be chasing his own tail. Sajad passed him the blunt.

"Ain't nobody come through?" Pudge shook his head, inhaling the weed smoke.

"NOBODY!?" Sajad asked again, in disbelief, as Pudge shook on.

"There go somebody right there!" Zakee spat, eyeing an average looking woman entering the row home, just as night coated the sky.

"WHERE?" Pudge excitedly wanted to know, searching for his .40 that he had forgotten was tucked under the armrest.

"You gon' do that old bitch, dawg?" Sajad asked teasingly.

"Nigga, I've been out here for a week. I'm killing somebody out this motherfucka," he replied, while Zakee snickered. Pudge slid to the door, while his boys watched on from the car across the street, blowing the remaining weed. He thought to knock, but instinct made him reach for the knob. It was open! This crazy bitch done left the door open. *'Bout time shit start falling my way*, he thought to himself, looking over his shoulder at the team before entering.

Pudge could hear water running upstairs, as he stood in the living room shutting the door behind him. The home was in average North Philly condition; worn out sofa set, scraped hardwood floors, and a reeking smell of roaches nesting. He ascended the stairwell, tiptoeing to the second landing. The entire floor was dark, except the bathroom, which gave off a heavenly glow illuminating its passage. Hot water splashed into the deep sink's body of water, causing a steam fog that seeped through the cracks of the door. The whole thing reminded Pudge of some movie shit, but it would take more than that shit to keep him from offing her ass and collecting that fifty from Markease. He pushed open the door with the .40 pointed just before his chest. But, the steam had become so dense that he couldn't tell if she was in there or not. So, he began BUCKING everything within, until he heard a voice.

"That's fucked up, you gon' do my man's mom like that?" Rob said standing behind him still wearing the blouse and dress he had entered with. Before Pudge could react, Rob shoved a needle filled with Clorox, injecting it into his neck. Instantly gagging for air as the substance ate through his flesh, he dropped his weapon in reach of his neck. But, Rob refused him by pushing Pudge forcefully into the bathtub, which had been filled with acid. The deadly fluid splashed over Pudge's body, melting his fleshy mahogany tissue off his pudgy frame. Agonizing screams of excruciation pierced the hallway and stairwell, as Pudge melted away like the Abominable snowman. The multiple shots Pudge let off could be heard on the slender block. It made Zakee wonder why he would use such force on an old brawd. The shit sounded like he was going to war in there. He told Sajad to stay put while he went to see what Pudge was up to. He left instructions to leave the car running. With Sajad behind the wheel fucking with the radio, Zakee went in.

"Pudge! What da fuck is you doing, ock? You got niggas hearing shit outside," he said as he ascended the steps to the second floor. Zakee pulled his .40 from beneath his tee, as he drew closer toward the bathroom door.

"Pudge. What's up? You hear me, Ock?" He inched open the door with his weapon by his back leg, frightened when his sight served him a dissolving Pudge sitting in the tub with flesh oozing off his face into blood red water.

"FUCK niggas done did to Pudge?" He spat with crackling in his voice, right before Rob bolted down the hallway knocking Zakee crashing out the second floor window. Sajad was blowing weed, tapping to Beanie-Sigel's *I Can Feel it in the Air*, and beating on the steering wheel. Sajad's tune was broken when shattering glass, along with Zakee, hit the car top in front of the house and then fell to the pavement, cracking his neck. It sent fear through Sajad's heart that he would be next. So, with the gear in drive, and the gas pressed firmly…he was out.

Shiz knew it wouldn't be long before Markease delivered himself right into his hands. The way he loved his bitch, he knew he had to be causing havoc trying to resolve it. So, before he got at him, he moved his mom out of that crib down North, acknowledging Markease might come after Chantel where he had picked her up. Regardless of how much blood his team caused, he didn't feel better, as his mind continually returned to an unconscious Chantel on that hospital bed. He wanted Markease! Shiz stayed away from the hospital while Chantel made her recovery, so the image of her assault could remain fresh in his mind from the night he saw her. With all the scheming and plotting, he thought very little about the block that provided for his family. If all went well, he'd be able to move at a larger level and really run shit. His thoughts were broken by M's entrance into the locker room with two jumpsuits, bearing high-tech logos on the sleeves. The duo got dressed without conversation.

$ $ $ $ $

Markease depended heavily on Star, tracking down the faceless booty queen. She said she would email it to his cell phone when she came up on something. He knew in his heart Star would come through, it was just a matter of time. Her ear game was extensive when it came to who's fucking who in the city. Markease intended on blessing her something crazy. He eyed the hundred thousand on the floor of the BM, sitting in Kashi's Louis Vuitton messenger bag that he'd taken from the safe a few days ago. Shit was so serious with him; he carried bread on hand to utilize in finding his peoples' whereabouts. The cell sitting on his passenger seat rang with a call from Hasan.

"Hasan, what's good homie?" Markease asked.

"Dig. You ain't heard from Pudge and them?"

"Nah, not since yesterday," he said, turning his diamond encrusted 'B' charm back right as he steered the BM through the city.

"Well, listen. I got this strange ass call from Sajad. This nigga all stuttering, shaking, and shit; talking 'bout Zock got dropped. I'm talking about on some real noit shit."

"Did you call Zock and see if he was good?" Markease asked concerned.

"YEA, I tried, but he didn't answer. Then, I tried Pudge...Nobody's picking up. Man, something ain't right," Hasan added.

"This nigga Sajad gonna make me fuck 'em up. Keep trying that nigga!"

"A'ight, ONE!"

"ONE!" What Markease didn't know was Sajad was already on 95 out of town, with no intention on returning or looking back. Sajad knew that Markease would've killed him for leaving Pudge and Zakee out there alone. So, he kept it pushing, with at least plans on saving somebody's life ... HIS! Markease considered the possibility of another death on his team and what that might mean to him, safety wise. He hated the congested city atmosphere. He could never think clearly with so much going on, and it was what he needed most at this time. Realizing his greatest thoughts came in the car wash, he noticed coincidently, it was Friday, when the wash offered their extended service where he usually went to think. When he pulled into the complex of HI-Tec, he endured the usual wait for cars that had beaten him there to traverse the bubbly tunnel. He decided to try to catch the weekend forecast on 1060AM News radio. While he crept to his turn, he reflected on the life he was leading, and boy how shit does come back around. He carelessly observed workers passing out rolled sheets of white paper, promoting upcoming specials the complex was offering.

"Twenty five dolla, get your supa soak, twenty five dolla!" A short Mexican man blurted out over the running engines. Markease pulled to the entrance where a hatted man handed him a tightly rolled paper. After sending the window up, he relaxed with hand in tote of the rolled paper. Markease rested his head, totally in tune with the drill, as the automated voice directed:

"PLACE CAR IN NEUTRAL. NO BRAKES, NO STEERING. THE WASH WILL GUIDE YOU THROUGH."

Markease began to ponder the ten kilos that would've pushed his bread over the three million mark, leaving the 47th Street strip to Jab when he stepped off with Kashi. He began to think about her full lip shape and how those lips pressed against his. He thought about her father handing Kashi's hand to him, trusting him with her life, before they boarded the plane to leave Hong Kong. He thought about their wedding that was set to be off-the-hook in St. Tropez, with a honeymoon to follow in Greece. *Damn Kay, it wasn't supposed to end like this, baby. Damn. Stay strong, Kay, stay strong, baby.* His thoughts intensified, as the wash threw thicker suds on the BM, and its soft brushes shined the car back to showroom. He thought about Chantel. Maybe she was behind this, but he brushed that thought aside, seeing that he had done that to so many chics before her. What would make her any different from the others? While considering how different her pussy was, his thoughts were broken by a special news bulletin by KYW.

"Police are seeking a rape and murder suspect of what they call an execution. A naked Oriental lady appearing to be in her twenties was found in a Crown Victoria with Coatesville Electric company logos. She was brutally raped, sodomized, and beaten by an unknown black male who allegedly posed as an inspector. Neighbors called authorities on a thumping sound coming from the trunk all night. When the police arrived, they found something truly startling...The young lady was smeared in blood, but it wasn't her own. After further investigation, officials say they discovered human body limbs that seem to have been dumped on her. There are no leads on the identity of the corpse, other than a forearm name tattoo that reads J.A.B. The woman has been admitted to the I.C.U. of Jefferson hospital. If you have any information on this..." Markease whole body tensed up after what his ear just captured. His hand in tote of the rolled paper relaxed, causing the diamond tennis bracelet to slide into his lap. He picked it up, confused as to how it had gotten there. Then, he recalled giving that jewelry to Chantel the night of their outing. He frantically opened the paper, revealing a photo of a naked Kashi getting fucked in the ass by a dude with a dick that was as long as train smoke with his hands wrapped around her neck. There was also a photo of his gold plated safe, empty! Under the picture, the caption read: THIS HOW YOU RAPE A BITCH! His breathing picked up as he looked at the bag of money on the floor. He grabbed it to ruffle through his 'Safe money'. To his surprise, all of the stacks had blank green paper underneath a shell twenty that surfaced it. His heart beat uncontrollably, trying to process all the occurrences. His hearing faded, and pretty soon all he heard was his own thumping heartbeat, while his mind raced. There was a knock at the window, as faint Mexican voices could be heard at the ending tunnel. The wash was coming to an end, as the suds dripped off the BM's windows. He could see figures moving about as his paranoia picked up. With his hammer in grasp, he emptied the clip on everything moving. The shots echoed the wash tunnel, but it was impossible to cover every angle. There were entirely too many ways to attack, if he was under fire. It was too weak a position to fight from. It was too LATE!!! Shiz's pistol grip pump and M's twin forties fired endlessly into Markease's BMW from the driver's side. CRACK, CRACK, CRACK. BOOM, BOOM, BOOM, CRACK, BOOM, BOOM. BOOM, BOOM, BOOM, BOOM!!! They went off, leaving Markease like a used dart target with holes through him, some as big as tennis balls. Knocking the shattered window out completely with the shotgun, Shiz reached in and snatched Markease's 'B' diamond charm off his neck. He uttered coldly,

"CHANTEL, PUSSY!!!" before loading his face with three more pellet shells. BOOM, BOOM, BOOM!!! Shiz stood there overlooking his body in the bloody tunnel, while the sprinklers sprayed on him. He finally found an ease, a comfort, a satisfaction. The man who raped, gamed, and assaulted his baby cousin was no more. He had completed his task flawlessly, and now it was time to rock the fuck out!

CHAPTER

12

Two Weeks Later

Chantel had made a full recovery and was set to be released from the hospital. It was too soon to determine if she might be able to have kids later. The doctors gave her several prescriptions for discomfort and depression. Aunt Patricia had decided, in light of the recent events, to move Chantel to Atlanta. The change up was well needed. Philadelphia was far from the city she grew up in, as the city hosted the highest murder rate three years in a row. Chantel deserved better and her mother wanted to give her every opportunity to obtain it, even if it meant losing thousands on a quick sale of her home to provide a better environment in Atlanta. Most of the family seconded the move, but couldn't understand the rush because they were set to board the plane immediately upon Chantel's release. The entire family waited in the lobby so they could say their goodbyes to a departing Chantel. The time she spent in recovery served her well, as her skin was back to normal, providing that usual glow. She was sad to be leaving Philly, but also needed something new. Chantel gathered her things from around the spacious suite. Opening the closet door, she stared at her appearance in the full length mirror, curve checking the fit of her Pound Cake jeans that she played with a white wife beater and open toe four inches. She began pinning her hair up, holding the clip in her mouth as she gathered the right look to pin together. Suddenly, she noticed M's reflection in the mirror standing behind her, causing her to jump.

"Oh boy, you scared me," she said, bracing her chest.

"My bad, sis. You a'ight?" Chantel nodded, breaking into that diamond smile that always had its way with M. She loved the way he played his facial hair. He rocked it like Nelly, complimenting his deep sea 360's over his pineapple complexion. She wanted to say a thousand things to M regarding her feelings, but feared rejection as the incident knocked a lot of her confidence.

"So, you leaving us, huh?" M said, hating the thought.

"Yes, I need a little time away. It's hard, M," she admitted, hoping he would know what she was referring to.

"Cee, you a soldier. Tough times always pass. It's the people that remain. You don't owe the world an explanation. Fuck that! It owes you one. But, until you find it, brush that shit off ya shoulder and troop this thing out, sweetheart." She nodded her lowered head while he finished his last statement. M always said the right things when it came to her. He was so much like Shiz. She smiled, flashing her whites and thinking, that's probably why we were so close.

"M, I know I don't really have to say this, but...I really appreciate what you did for me. You always looked out for me and I remember it all. So, when and if ever you need me, I'ma hold you down," she said, just as the nurse entered the suite's doorway.

"Ms. Pettiway," she announced.

"Yes," Chantel replied.

"They're ready for you," she said before spinning off. Chantel moved towards the bed where she grabbed her baggage-on-wheels, returning before M, who spieled,

"Damn, Cee, I can't believe you rollin' out on me. I watched you grow into this amazing sista, and it's kinda fuckin' with me you won't be around no more. A nigga really ain't feeling this."

"Well what do you want me to do?" she protested.

"I don't know right now, but not leaving!"

"My mom invested a lot of money in this move already. She sold her house, M! Plus, the city really shit on me. I just need to get away and clear my head," she said, fastening the pin in her hair. "AND, why are you so headstrong on me not leaving? It's not like I see you everyday anyway."

"That's not the point," he spat.

"It is the point!"

"Cee."

"I've been though a lot of shit, and everybody's still thinking about them. I haven't even seen Noodles in God kno..."

"Cee!" M tried to interrupt.

"I was the one that nigga RAPED in the back of that car!" She started crying.

"CEE!!"

"What?!"

"I NEED YOU, MA," M cut in.

"Huh?" Chantel was dumbfounded. She had never heard M say he needed anything before, and here he was telling her it was she that he needed. Still somewhat confused to his words' meaning, Chantel searched his eyes for the answer.

"I shoulda been wifed you, but you was a 'lil young then. You of age now and a bol like me needs a chic like you. I can hold you down, baby." Chantel fought to hold back the tear that streamed down her face, as shock filled her brow hearing of M's hidden feelings.

"But, M..." He kissed her lips hungrily, meeting his tongue with hers as she gave back the same intensity. Her body melted into his, while his hands grasped the back of her neck. The two went at it like a returning war hero exiting his flight. M kissed her pain away. Her sorrow, agony, and regrets fell from her heart, as he sucked on her lips. She loved being wrapped in his arms and valued his sincerity. She knew from that very moment on, she would always be his, and nothing or nobody could replace what she felt for him. But, with every bone in her body that screamed and yearned for his companionship on any other day, today was the one day she would refuse him.

"Wait a minute, M..." She said, breaking away from the lip lock.

"What, Cee, what's wrong?" he asked. But, before she had a chance to respond, her mother's voice chimed,

"Chantel, we don't have all day. You got people and planes waiting for you!" Aunt Patricia said from the doorway. It was the moment of truth, as they stood there before one another, still winded from the kissing. They exchanged stares of 'Don't leave me' and 'Don't hate me' until finally it was settled.

"Chantel, if I sayyy..." Her mother interrupted, biting her lip for emphasis.

"Mom. Al-RIGHT!" She said firmly. Chantel darted to the nightstand, where she penned her number quickly. She returned before M to take hold of his hand.

"Call me," she pronounced deeply, meaning every letter of it. She hugged him tightly, inhaling his scent before exiting to an awaiting Aunt Patricia.

All of the family rushed Chantel when they saw her emerge from the double doors into the lobby. She could see wrapped gift boxes with bows stacked on the chair. Saks Fifth Avenue and Tiffany & Co. logos plastered the bags that sat along the floor. Chantel's release wasn't the only thing being celebrated; her birthday had been just a few days ago. Faces she hadn't seen in ages all made an appearance to big up Chantel. She appreciated everybody's support, but hoped her business wasn't thrown around in the street. Kissing and hugging her way through the swarming family members, she looked for one face in particular...One that she hadn't seen since her tragedy began. Her eyes combed the room thoroughly, expecting to see the one she loved most-----NOODLES! But, the more she searched, the faster she realized he wasn't there. She felt abandoned and crushed. It saddened her that he wasn't there to see her off. It was bad enough that he didn't find time to come visit, and now she was leaving but he still was M.I.A! Shiz was like a father to Chantel and she'd do anything he commanded. Acknowledging the fact she had violated set principles made her think that Shiz was upset with her. She figured he felt like he wasted his time dropping game, when at the end of the day, she was no different than her other female cousins. Ms. Pettiway could see the displeasure on Chantel's face.

"Chantel, what's wrong with you?" She wanted to know.

"Where's Noodles at, Aunt Puddin?"

"Is that what you worryin' about? You know how your cousin is, that boy stay in the streets," she replied, thinking he had at least been to see her. But, Chantel just shook her head seeing the real reason was that she'd been cut off. She wrapped up the goodbyes and had the car packed for her departure. Chantel sat in the back by the window with a throbbing heart that displayed through her eyes. Her mother and Greg entered the car, set to pull off when a black CLS 500 with limo tint pulled up. The door cracked and young money hopped out, wearing this colorful ensemble by Zayaani; line up chiseled, heavy on the wrist, and pinky. Chantel's heart popped in excitement.

"NOODLES!" She screamed, jumping out of the car into Shiz's arms, weeping like a toddler.

"Baby girl, stop crying. Everything gonna be alright," he spat, wiping the tears from her gorgeous face.

"I thought you hated me, I,I,I was..." She offered.

"Channy stop, that's not necessary," Shiz cut in.

"Well, why didn't you come visit me in the hospital or answer none of my phone calls?" She asked, wanting an explanation.

"Because I had to tend to something, momma, but best believe you'll always be in my heart on some real shit." She gave Shiz her diamond smile, feeling foolish for ever thinking he would abandon her.

"Look, I want you to take care of yourself down there. And, I want you to call me every week to keep me posted on everything, ya hear me?" Shiz shot, to a yessing Chantel. He handed Chantel a vanilla envelope.

"That's for you. Remember what I taught you." The two embraced, and Shiz kissed her forehead, placing her back into the running car.

"Aunt Pat, take care of my baby down there." She nodded, acknowledging the request. The car began to pull off while Chantel stared into his face with a smirk.

"HOLD ON!" Reaching into his pocket, he pulled Markease's platinum chain with the tropical diamond encrusted 'B' charm, placing it in Chantel's hand. He stared intensely into her eyes, as she searched her memory for where she had seen that chain. As the car descended down the low traffic street, Chantel's heart stopped, realizing where she had seen that chain before and whom it belonged to. With her cheeks soaked in tears for her heavenly protector, she ripped open the envelope to place the chain within, finding an unspeakable amount of money inside, seeming to be all Benjis, she gasped. There was a note attached that read:

> *As long as I'm breathing, no one will ever cross you, then live to talk about it. Never value yourself less than a diamond. With you so far away Channy, I need you to use what you learned to stay sharp. Being a lady comes from within. Never compromise that beauty, as it will keep you the queen that you are. Pussy run the game. Use it when needed, and don't allow it to use you. Enclosed is a hunnit grand for you to do you. Be responsible! Happy Birthday and I love you always; you know the number ... Get at me! -----Noodles*

CHAPTER 13

We in this bitch

The night of Chantel's departure, Shiz decided to hit Fusion nightclub with the clique in celebration of the new start. He had hit the whole squad off nicely, so he anticipated everybody doing it big. He had become a self made millionaire the hood way, by taking money. Shiz thought to call Tracy and let her partake in the night since she also played her position well, but he opted not to. Even though he appreciated how she held it down, the last thing he wanted was the bitch breathing down his back while he popped bottles. So Shiz decided to get with her on the solo. The mirror didn't lie at all when it reflected, he was that bol. White Armani linen over the v-neck Cavalli Tee played richly with the black Louie

Vuitton loafers. The ice chunks on the charm & bracelet were damn right insulting, keeping the forecast cloudless. Shiz viewed his appearance in the mirror while spraying a hit of Unforgiven cologne on his neck. The image was right. The beeping of M caused him to exit the row home, but the sound of the horn wasn't the usual airy sound his STS Cadillac made. That's because M had copped up. The S550 Benz fully loaded on twenty-two's, cleaner and meaner than a motherfucka, shitting on everything on the tiny block. Shiz could see the jewels shining on M's neck and wrist through the window. Shiz entered the wheel, finding M also in all white, except it was Versace.

"Nigga, you copp heavy, huh?" Shiz asked grinning.

"Yo! Let me hitcha back," M said, ending the call.

"What da fuck you talking 'bout, dawg?"

"You KNOW D-A-M-N WELL what I'm talking 'bout, when you grab this bol?"

"This afternoon, you feeling this piece, Shiz?" M asked with a chuckle, enjoying Shiz's excitement. Shiz overlooked the lit gauges of the gadgets on the dash and console, the soft leather upholstery that felt like butter, and the marble wood grain, but the panoramic glass top; that was a mighty fine touch. Shiz had to big-up Benz for the latest model, as he gave his man a nod of approval.

"Yeah, dis shit hot, I'm feelin' it." They inched off into the erotic city night life.

When M and Shiz arrived at the club, they could see the city had that bitch poppin'! The birds had no problem letting it hang out. Flocks of dime pieces entered the club on 6 inches, fresh from the hair & nail salon. Niggas balled out with diamond jewelry were playing everything from Gucci to Ferragamo, stunting on GXR's,

R1's, and Kawasaki's. You would have thought the city just won the chip. After ejecting the whip, which also received its fair share of attention, Shiz and M proceeded to the entrance. Eyeing the overwhelming amount of pussy in the parking lot, the two knew they were leaving with something tonight, as the brawds exchanged looks of 'He's already mine, back off!' Niggas knew their bossiness as well, as the crowd before the door parted, allowing them to reach checkpoint. They were waved off by the security overseer, who just happened to be Black's uncle. Some of the enviers in the line couldn't restrain themselves from the hate of the star-like treatment, plus the 'Wet' had the thugging crowd already on edge.

"Dem niggas ain't no fucking celebrities!!" rang out.

"Don't get mad, GET MONEY BABEEE!!" Shiz hollered back, as the duo disappeared into the darkened club. The two were escorted by security to the V.I.P., where they were to meet the clique and discuss the business, post Markease era. Dee and Bam both had the club on smash, rocking black Gucci over the cocoa brown Louis Vuitton sneaker shoes, killing them Diamond Troy reptile frames. Rob wore eggshell white Cavalli that coordinated well with his arm cast. Bottles of Champ were in heavy rotation as they sat under dim lighting. Shiz and M joined them right when Dee sparked up, while Lil Wayne's voice filled the club.

> *"Started off hustling, ended up ballin', nigga I'ma shit, get da fuck off my toilet."*

"My niggas look good wearing that designer shit," Shiz spat, admiring the crew's prestigious look, just as Dee was handing him the blunt.

"Y'all niggas, see when we go hard, we make it do what it do!" He said, taking a pull from the weed.

"So, where we go from here? I mean, I got a couple dollars and all, but a nigga tryna get right, feel me?" Dee shot.

"Exactly, that's what da fuck I'm talking about. I was hoping y'all niggas didn't let that dough go to ya head, and y'all be on that 'I'm rich shit', 'cause you got a couple hundred thousand and now shit all good. That bread ain't nothing. And, if we can learn something from that nigga, it'll be how easy that shit can go, and not just 'cause he didn't put that shit in the bank. A dude gotta learn how to secure their investment, dawg. This street life is just a means to get right. I'm tryna have that kind of money where I can park my Lamb in front of the Federal building and know my shit straight! Fuck around and see me on B.E.T., dancing with Puff and spilling Champ in the air." The clique smiled and laughed at Shiz's last statement, as they watched him unfold a bigger picture. Shiz pulled on the weed, then continued in a smoke filled voice.

"And, I want that for all of us," he said, exhaling trees.

"So, we gotta go harder and smarter, ya dig?"

"All that sound good dawg, real good. But, how you suppose we get to that point where we secured and not fucking wit the street no more?" M asked, readjusting his diamond face Breitling as Shiz popped the cork of the Champ, filling their glasses with the bubbly suds.

"That's a good question M. We obviously ain't there yet, so in the streets we be until we get there. However, what I'm suggesting is we go hard like never before, for like two years, NO BULLSHIT. And, then we go all in together on something legal and profitable, where we ain't gotta ever look back, only forward to better investments," he clarified.

"So, basically whatchu saying is, don't carry this drug or street thing or whatever like we gonna be here robbing, trapping, and gang warring twenty years from now. Still tryna be hood with it, go hard and get right," Rob shot, bringing Bam's mental a clarifying moment, while the rest let Shiz's words linger in their minds.

"I don't know 'bout the rest of these lames out here, but we tryna get this money and be out here to spend it. Fuck a block, when we can have the state. Our vision has to far surpass what's in the hood. When we move, we move intelligently with our long term goals in mind..." Shiz took a moment to knock the ashes from the blunt.

"If you really think about it, most cats that used to have a little name, a little money...Aaron, Fat Cat, Preem, all doing wheels in the box chasing them short goals. Yea, they was them niggas, them dudes, them bols, and all that, but they didn't get out when they had their shot. So, we gonna learn from that and be them niggas for real. R-E-A-L-L-Y, H-O-L-D,
S-H-I-T DOWN!!!" Banging his fist on the table, he continued. "C.E.O., dawg," Shiz held his drink in his right, spliff in his left, and raising his drink to solicit a toast, while his 'WE GET IT' charm swung from side to side in glistening diamonds. The rest of the clique rose, eyeing one another bringing their glasses to crash as Shiz sang,

"Cash IS King, NIGGA!!!"

On the opposite side of the club, Sideeq chain-smoked Newports, watching his men down shots of Patron, cracking jokes on one another. The consistent flow of ballers that the club hosted brought the squad out, trying to catch a nigga slipping in a sloppy attempt to floss un-reported currency.

"Nigga, look at your fuckin' TEETH. Da fuck you been doing...chewing rocks or something?" Pig said laughing hard.

"Fuck outta here, nut! Look at your bitch, nigga, nappy ass weave and shit." Spank got back.

"Pussy, I know we ain't talking 'bout pussy, are you serious?! When the last time ya funny looking ass even smelled some pussy? And, I ain't talking 'bout that crack head shit," Pig struck hard, gaining deep laughter from the whole table, while Spank stared on with the 'you got that one' face.

"This nigga be fucking all night dope heads. I'm talking 'bout the ones that be scratching and looking like they be on some shit. Ay Spank, keep it real, don't make me call Diz." The crew rolled on in laughter, while Spank flagged them off. See, Sideeq wasn't any average stick up kid. In fact, he did quite well off his stings alone. If you weren't a sectional boss of the city, he wouldn't even consider your candidacy. Anybody working with a hundred thou or less was a strong arm case for Sideeq, which opposed his 'run up with ya gun up' policy. So, you were safe from him and his wolves, or at least until you stepped your game up. It was funny to Sideeq how as soon as a nigga started touching some money, the first thing that came to his mind was the floss. He knew if he laid in the cut, it wouldn't be before long when his mark would expose himself.

Shiz and the crew dispersed from their seating to blow off some steam by flirting with the bitches that came out to shake there asses. When M bought out the bar, the club went crazy! The women swarmed the dance floor when Hov's *Brush Ya Shoulders Off* started quaking the club. Everybody's eyes stayed glued to Shiz's team, as they threw stacks of big faces in the air. The club rushed the rainfall like the Spaniard's bull rush. Dee and Rob sprayed gold bottles of champagne into the dancing hood girls. Niggas were hype seeing the bitches dive to the floor chasing that bread, allowing their breasts and asses to jiggle freely. After this, most of the clique spread out leaving the V.I.P. to make there personalized presence known. Shiz stood by the railing with Dee, smoking haze he had rolled moments before, eyeing the dance floor partiers who spared no expense in enjoyment.

"It's some bitches up in this jawn tonight," Dee mentioned.

"Why you ain't out fucking with nothing then?" Shiz said, inhaling the blunt and keeping his eyes on Dee.

"These bitches ain't going nowhere, Shiz...Look at these niggas though, mutherfuckas is going in," Shiz smirked at the sight of M, sweating wet and pounding on the ass of mommie like he was hitting that. Bam was buying the bar out, while Rob had his hand up some chic's dress.

"What's ya whole thang, Shiz? You don't see nothing out here, with all these bitches in here running around? You ain't hollerin' at nothing??" *He probably got that bitch on his wig*, Dee thought, eyeing Shiz and waiting on his response.

"Nigga, you trippin'! As soon as my speed walk in this jawn, I'm poppin' off," he replied. Dee passed his drink to Shiz urgently.

"Hold this, I gotta use the bathroom bad as shit," he mentioned before walking off, grabbing his genitals, and squeezing through the cluttered club.

"Drunk ass nigga! Stop drinking so fucking much!" Shiz screamed after him smiling. As Dee faded, he was raising his middle finger above his head so Shiz could see his response. Diamond Cutz had the club jumping. Even if someone wanted to sit down and rest up, another banger was pounding the wall, sending the club into a frenzy. She then faded into Pop Champagne by Jim Jones, screaming over the jam.

"All my go-getters and bosses, pop them corks if you a baaallllleeerrr!!" Surfacing in the middle of the floor was the Angel Lola look alike with her hair pinned to the side. Wearing a white one piece short set that stopped above her thighs, her plush pink Jimmy Choo's matched her cotton candy finger nail polish perfectly. She began winding her hips and poppin' her ass as the bass crashed, making everybody stare at her erotic ass shake without moving as much as a blink. Grabbing their genitals and biting their tight lips, the guys lusted, drooling over the 5'6" brick house with green eyes and an ass that was a miracle of physics to fit into that Pound Cake one piece. And without saying, they did exactly all that they could do...WATCH!

Dee hurried into the bathroom to relieve himself. He found an additional club therein higher than helicopters engrossed in conversation. The two men took turns rattling on about some meat head nigga that slid in the club talking reckless like it can't go down. They didn't mind Dee in ear's reach of their topic while he relieved himself.

"I keep telling niggas, watch ya fucking mouth, 'cause when it pop off, I ain't tryna hear shit," the young man spat slurring, as Dee flushed the urinal and proceeded to wash.

"Dawg, you ain't doing shit. In fact, da fuck up wit all that nut shit, you blowing my high," his man challenged, exhaling the wet.

"Oh, I ain't doing shit?! Nigga, you da fuck trippin'," he said pulling the .40 caliber from his waist and cocking one in the chamber.

"See, that's that bullshit right there. Nigga can't even come out and chill without you fake ass niggas drawing."

"Say no more, you must got me fucked up," he said threatening and pushing open the door with blood in his appetite. Dee left right behind him, hearing his man's laugh echo the bathroom.

Shiz had appeared out of nowhere, grinding on the behind of the young lady everybody stared at in amazement. She turned to see who was brave enough to grind on her ass. Noticing the shining jewels on his chain and bracelet prevented her from doing what she intended to do, leave! His swag captivated her, as her feet became nailed to the floor. She had many before play that big willy shit with her, but Shiz truly had a look of confidence in his green eyes that displayed clearly, even in this dark club. But most of all, the smirk of a smile Shiz showcased was enough to make most women climb into bed with him in a moment's notice. He reached for her hand to raise high with his, as the bottle of vintage wine poured carelessly onto the floor. Shiz sang along with the chorus.

> *"We pop champagne...Oh, Ooohhh!!! ...Shorty, we can be friend, Shorty, we can be friends. But right now, I wanna see you dance, see you dance..."*

Gaining a reluctant smile from the brick house, she resumed her flirtatious booty dance as Shiz captured the sweet scent of her long hair and better sight of her neck tat that read *Da Bomb*.

Dee made his way back to the V.I.P. where he found M, storing the Puerto Rican chic in his I-phone.

"M, where Shiz at? Shit 'bout to get wild."

"Why you say that, what's up?" M replied.

"Nah, some young bol in the bathroom with a .40 calli talkin' 'bout airing some nigga out screaming, 'Don't get mad, get money' or some shit like that at the let-in," M recalled that statement well.

"Yeeeaaahhh, here take this and go find Shiz, Dawg," M ordered over the thumping music, passing him the forty. The two split up to round up the team and hip them to the potential threat, even if it was nothing.

Shiz was serving up his second set with shorty, while Drake had the club on fire. The hatin' assassin finally spotted Shiz on the dance floor, as he crept through the mass of dancers seeking to put that twirk in. Carrying the.40 behind his back, he swerved around to get a better position on Shiz, namely a clearer headshot. Shiz began fondling the ass of the brick house dancing before him.

"Don't cha think you should tell me your name first, before you start feeling all on my butt?" She said sassy, gazing carelessly over his shoulder at the screw-faced grin. The youngen smiled, pointing the .40 cal in their direction.

"Shiz, love. My name, Shiz," he said, oblivious to the hit. Her eyes resembled golf balls, tapping his shoulder but unable to find the words of warning over her panic.

"What sis, you alright?" Shiz asked, shifting his weight backward. Regaining her sense, she screamed, "SHHIZZZZ!" milliseconds before a multiple shot of gunfire rang off. MOCK, MOCK, MOCK, CRACK, CRACK, MOCK, MOCK, CRACK, CRACK, CRACK, CRACK, CRACK!!!

The music came to a screeching stop, as a brief silence combed through the club before the storm. Gun smoke lingered in the air, creating a light fog as the screams and stampede erupted suddenly. Pandemonium was well on its way. Shiz lay bleeding on top of the hysterical brick house, who felt his blood soaking her outfit. He was injured, but still breathing. He gasped for air as he noticed Dee lying not far from him, moaning with steady leg movement to cope with the pain. Through the treading partiers, Shiz noticed M approaching.

"Shiz, Shiz! Get up, dawg! Dawg, get da fuck up!" M said, fearing the worst as blood covered his sports coat.

"GET 'EM OFF OF ME, GET 'EM OFF OF ME!" the brick house screamed.

"M," Shiz whispered, which was all M needed to hear, as he and Bam helped him up.

"Rob! See what's up with Dee, dawg. He over here, he over here, dawg!" When Shiz made it to his feet, he noticed what really had occurred in a matter of moments ...WAR! Tons of people were still down, bleeding from God knows where, as friends and family rushed to their side calling for help. Piercing screams of "OMIGOD" rang out as sirens could be heard drawing closer. The bar was demolished, as was the club; broken bottles, vomit, and blood could be seen on the floor, walls, and steps. Partiers were still being rushed over, as the masses attempted to exit by any means, crossing over the legs, backs, and necks of others. The brick house sat on the floor, staring intensely at her blood-soaked hands, experiencing shock. Shiz thought to grab her, but M's voice broke his trance.

"We out, Shiz. We out, dawg, come on!" M belted. As they walked passed the young assassin plugged with multiple slugs, Rob stomped the motionless body.

"Mutherfucka," he growled, as the crew staggered out of the disrupted club, blending in with the stampede.

CHAPTER

14

Sideeq : "Let me find out"

Is these bols sweet or what? All that flossin' in the club, throwin' money, spraying Champ, and all that. But, you let some faggot ass young bols get close enough to get at your Boss. These niggas is soft. Shit could've really got wild if my squad didn't rock out. I was gonna let that little nigga ride, but he would've fucked up my paper and I can't have that. Shiz, as they call him, fit the bill of my mark; loud, flamboyant, with plenty of money. Although I never met Shiz before, the word travels fast in the city. He be gettin' that guap down North. The only reason I didn't go check for that nigga before was that he was still nick-diming it, which was an indication you ain't really poppin' yet. In fact, that type of movement is nut shit. Irregardless as such, homie must have run into some serious money, judging from the way the whole little squad balled out last night on some boss shit. The wheels all crazy, diamonds glistening, and the bar being bought out two-three times. Yeah! This nigga definitely gettin' it, and I'm certainly finding out how much. Bam gave me his number after we all got outside, before they took Shiz and Dee to the hospital to check out their flesh injuries. When youngen started bucking, a couple of shells hit Shiz in his vest he was wearing, and lucky him on some real shit... (Keys rattling in the door)

"Da fuck!" The door flew open and Kelly came waltzing in, mule kicking the door closed behind her, carrying plenty of Saks Fifth Avenue bags. I can't believe this bitch spendin' like this.

"Where da fuck was you at?"

"Please don't start with me Sideeq...Where do you think I've been at?" She said, raising her bags above her head as she marched into the bedroom.

"Who you gettin' smart with, Kelly? Your fly ass gonna make me fuck your 'lil ass up."

"Whatever, Sideeq!" She belted from the bedroom. Kelly way out pocket, running up in here with bags and talkin' shit. Now, I don't have a problem with a bitch doing her school thang, but god damn, a nigga can't get no head? All this shit is coming to an end, real fuckin' soon.

"Sideeq, where my love and basketball DVD at?" She asked standing before me.

"WHAT?!"

"Ain't no what. Ya heard what I said."

"Don't you see me chillin', yo?"

"Damn that! Where my god damn disc at?" She pressed on.

"I-DON'T-KNOW!! So, leave me da fuck alone before I wig out on your ass," I said, with my eyes fastened to the flat screen.

"Won'tcha lying ass stop playing! I know you let one of your 'lil stupid ass friends hold my shit without asking me, didn't you?"

"HERE, HERE!! Take this shit," I said throwin' twenties at her. "Go buy a hundred love and basketballs, JUST leave me da fuck alone."

"Since you throwin' money out, nigga, give me some. A bitch needs her toes done," she said, irking the shit out me.

"You know what? Instead of washing vegetables and thawing out steak slabs to cook for a nigga, you been out spendin' his money up all day. Or, instead of running the jacuzzi, so we can go fuck, you up in here fuckin' with a nigga while the game on?" Kelly didn't even blink. In fact, she looked at me like I was stupid or something.

"Whatchu want, some dough? Here, I got you, come get it." I acted like I was searching for some bread, while in fact, I used the opportunity to get a 'lil closer to Kelly.

"Where is it, Sideeq? You play too much, boy," she said, shifting her weight to one side with her hand out. But, what she received was a whole 'nother thing. I grabbed her by the waist and bent her over the couch swiftly, unbuttoning her jeans.

"Un-unh, boy! We ain't doing nothing, STOP," she protested.

"Nah, dis what da fuck you wanted. Keep fuckin' wit a nigga. All you had to say was bust my ass, but you want to be on ya bullshit."

"Sideeq, I'm serious. You ain't getting' no pussy until my DVD turn up!"

"Shut up," I growled.

"So, you gonna just fuck me like this when I said n… Ahhh!" She pushed out when I slammed it in.

"I said, shut da fuck up!" Instantly, her pussy got wet, as I lead myself in and out of her warmth.

"You still want your DVD?" I said, over the clappin' sound that Kelly's ass cheeks made.

"You-play-too-much-booyyy!!" She moaned in ecstasy. While I fucked her, I noticed the price tag on the new bag she just bought: $6,300.00. *Oh, HELL NO!!* I thought to myself.

"So you out spending my shit up, huh, huh, huh, BITCH!"

"Awww, Sideeq, damn baby, ooh shit, it feel soo good."

"When I tell you to drop these drawers, drop that shit!" I moaned, punishing her.

"Fuck! I can't take it baby. Please slow down, shit, I'ma explode. I dug deeper into Kelly's pussy until I hit that spot where she jumped three melodies. Her body began to convulse just as I was nuttin'. Then, she did what I have only heard about but never seen...BLACKED OUT!!! At first, I thought I killed the bitch, but then I realized she was sleeping. Only two things could possibly come from that; an eased conscience and a swollen ego.

The weather was nice, so I decided to pull my all candyapple 929cc Ducati out. I had to go check Spank and Pig anyway, so there ain't nothing wrong with lettin' that thing rumble. When I pulled up at Tasker projects, I found them niggas blowin' trees sittin' on Pig's F-150 on twenty four. The project was at a normal: fiends, hoodrats, and petty hustlers in consistent flow...All of which made me feel right at home. Spank and Pig came off the steps late, but when they did, mutherfuckas was wishing they went right back on. And, that's some real shit! Plus, them niggas 'bout money...So, I knew if I put them on some major paper, they would stay loyal. Over the years, we been puttin' one another on money, but my shit always left us satisfied. Soon after, they realized fuckin' with me keep them niggas filthy. As I got off the bike, you could see that big ass hammer bulging from my Y3 t-shirt, while Spank blew weed O's from the blunt smoke.

"Yiz-zo."

"Yiz-zo, what's hood, 'Deeq?" Pig asked me, jumping off the F-150 to pound me.

"Same shit, different day. What's up with this nigga?" Referring to Spank.

"Who knows what kind of period this nigga on today," Pig shot.

"Ay Pig, you gonna keep playing me out until I wind up fuckin' you up all crit-nazy?" Spank spat, receiving a flag from Pig.

"I'm good 'Deeq, what's poppin'?"

"I just want to put y'all niggas on game."

"What's up?" Spank jumped down, sensing this could be important.

"Dig this…I'ma 'bout to go all the way in on these niggas sumthin' crazy. So, shit might be different for a 'lil while, ya heard. Remember how we did Rus?" They both nodded with this wicked ass grin.

"Well, the same thang, but instead of using the bitch, I'm going in. Peep game, I need niggas to get his whole MO, everything, dawg. The bitches this nigga fucks wit, addresses, his team, supplier, who grabbin' off him, everything cannon. It's sumthin' 'bout this nigga, man, straight up. I don't know, I can't put my finger on it yet. But, on everything, I feel like this nigga gonna be the one that have us sitting on an island, sippin' from coconut drinks through umbrella straws."

"Yeaahh, you think that nigga holdin' like that, babee?"

"On some real shit. I ain't one-hunnit, but you know I can smell some money."

"A'ight, say no more. We on this nigga top!" Spank chimed.

"A'ight, that's what it is. Get that game for me and we on our way. The young bol, Bam, should be hittin' me soon. We want to be right when he does, feel me?" I left knowing my youngens would handle their handle and the nigga Shiz was over…Damn, I can't wait!

CHAPTER 15

Da Game Plan 1 Of 3

Jay was home finishing his political science report, scrolling the mouse through the data that plastered his laptop. He realized his mind was distant. He was thinking about Kelly, which urged him to pursue what he was researching earlier. That shit with Kelly still fucked with him. He viewed what he turned up earlier; Asian engineers had determined U.S. currency was the easiest to duplicate. In fact, several people had been known to manufacture the greenish dead presidents, belonging to the most envied country in the world. They explained the process in the simplest terms possible, including needed ingredients. They gave him the game that allowed his bills to go undetected when he went forth with his plan. Jay began ordering the needed supplies. Regardless of how long it would take, Jay was hype at the thought of becoming rich, so Kelly and the rest could regret fucking him over. Jay closed his bedroom door, and then went to the armoire to shuffle through some clothes, in order to unravel the .50 caliber his cousin gave him to hold. He loaded the chamber by cocking the iron in the mirror, putting his best gorilla face on, rehearsing killa remarks, and wondering if this was the lifestyle for him. Jay definitely had a mean streak, and with the right buttons pushed…who knows? His thoughts were put on hold at the sound of the ringing phone.

"Hello?"

"Hello…Is Jay there?"

"Yes, who is this?"

"It's Michelle, babee! Jay, what's up with you?" She said excitedly, noticing his voice.

" 'Chelle! Damn, what's up? Long time no hear," Jay said with shock in his tone.

"I knowww. I just came back from Cali. And, I was in the Gallery when I saw your crazy cousin K-B there, tryna floss with his stuntin' ass." Jay and she laughed briefly.

"An-y-way, he told me to get atchu. So, here I am."

"Damn 'Chelle, it's good to hear your voice. So, what are you doing today, stranger?"

"Nothin', I was hoping to see you, to be honest."

"Word!? Yea whatever, you wasn't thinking about me."

"Yes, I was. I'm calling you, ain…"

"Well, come through then!" Jay cut her off.

"A'ight, give me the address and I'm on my way…And, Jay…I heard what happened with Kelly. Don't worry, I got somethin' for ya ass," she purred seductively. Jay used to talk to Michelle a while back and she wanted to fuck him then, but Kelly was in the way. Chic or not, the new Jay was dead set on busting her ass today. He was beginning to like the idea of doing him--No strings, no commitment, just whatever the fuck he wanted. A nigga was coming into his own.

CHAPTER 16

Da Game Plan 2 of 3

In the back of the restaurant, Black and Trig sat in the booth of their favorite breakfast spot, waiting for Reese Cheese. The smell of pancakes, turkey bacon, hash browns, and scrambled eggs with cheese made Black's mouth water, as the waitress brushed by their table.

"Damn, that shit smell good as shit," Black said to Trig who was sitting before him.

"Yo! What's up with this grub? Let's get this grub right!" He roared to the passing waitress. The last time he was supposed to get some of their famous breakfast platters was the day of his half ass assassination.

"Will you calm da fuck down? Ya fat ass gonna eat."

"Nigga, fuck all that...LET'S GET THAT GRUB OVER HERE!" He blurted again. Ignoring Black's unruly behavior that she was previously informed about, his waitress appeared before them with a large tray carrying their food.

"You know, you need to stop acting like you gonna die out here…Here!" She said passing them their plates, as Black eyed her, noticeably amazed at her beauty.

"Damn, sis."

"Is something wrong?" She asked, arching one of her eyebrows.

"If it is, then not on you."

"Yea, yea, whatever. Ain't nobody drunk with those bar pick up lines," she sang, as Trig busted out laughing.

"And you LOUD as ever."

"What! That wasn't me," Black said lying through his teeth.

"It was you! Don't even front. LET'S GET IT…LET'S GET IT," she imitated.

"A'ight, you got me. My bad, sexy," he bowed out gracefully.

"So, y'all straight?"

"I'm good," Trig chimed.

"You already know what I want."

"You don't stop, do you?" She asked, as he began eating his meal.

"Nope! Not 'til I get what I want."

"AND WHAT'S THAT?" she spat, shifting her weight to one side with her hand pinned to her hip, in true hood girl fashion awaiting a response. He laughed.

"Just ya number, sis. Ya number, that'll do for now." She grabbed the menus from the table, allowing her breast to jiggle just inches from Black's mouth, overlooking his dark complexion and good hair grain.

"We'll see," she uttered to a smirking Black. Heading to the back, he kept his eyes glued to her bouncing ass rumbling in her waitress one piece.

Umm! I wanna fuck that, straight up, he thought.

"Sis, whatcha name?" He hollered after her into the aisle.

"MOET!" She replied, walking past a late thirties gentleman with honey brown complexion, medium well maintained build, and darkened shades that completely hid his eyes. His Bossalini bore a slight tilt, which matched the linen suit perfectly. But, the Salvatore Ferragamo shoe boots, those joints were mean! Old head paused when he reached Trig and Black's table, in grasp of a black handbag. He looked over Trig's wrist and neck glimmering, as the duo beast down their plates. The man smiled to himself, thinking how far Trig was willing to go when it came to money. He had the right ambition, wrong attitude.

"If you displayed that kind of hunger on the block, you'd be a millionaire," he said to Trig who was tearing through his pancakes.

"Yiz-zo, what's up, my nig? Da fuck good with you?" He stood to embrace him.

"Living babee, just living."

"Cheese, dis my peoples. He from Philly, and niggas trying to get right."

"Black," he said, extending his hand to introduce himself.

"Reese, babee..." taking hold of his hands, while he searched his eyes for weakness.

"From where in Philly you from?"

"North, right off of Lehigh. Have a seat, dawg. Can I have the waitress bring you somethin'?" They scooted in.

"Nah, I'm good, babee...but ah, I knew quite a few good soldiers that were from North. Niggas made a lot of money down there, too."

"Ay Reese, a nigga really been hearing some good things about you, dawg," Black mentioned, ignoring Reese's last statement.

"That ain't shit. The streets not only listen and see, but they talk as well."

"My peoples tell me you are nice with that heat, and we can really use somebody that ain't scared to put that twirk in. These bitch ass niggas out here ain't tryna rock out. And, once the flames start flying, you know the rest. We hittin' our number out here, but shit could be better, a lot better, smell me?" Black shot to a nodding Reese.

"The problem is, niggas overcharging, while they keep steppin' on the shit."

"Black, I'm sure you understand the game well, so you know it's not just one candy man. You can buy at a better price and product."

"Yea that's true, but I feel as though if a nigga selling me some bullshit or some garbage, then he's stealing from me. And, if he steals from me, then he took something from me, and nobody takes something from me without me gettin' at that ass!"

"Dis your show, but this game been around for a long time and will be long after. You see youngen, there's rules to this thing. When the streets get hungry, the streets gonna eat, and mutherfuckas got to realize that. Blood is never the first reaction for men of power; da shit is bad for business, babee. And, there's something else..." Reese smiled to himself.

"The game is sold not told, so do whatcha heart tell you, naw-talkin'-'bout?" He asked to a blank staring Black who ate on. Reese had been in the game for awhile, and he got it from niggas that used to move out with the 'M' in Philly. He always learned to test everybody that he intended to do business with, citing the ancient hood anthem, 'First we learn, then we trust'. He figured if he was able to change his mind about some work he needed done, then maybe the police could get him to change and roll on him. So, he wouldn't fuck with you if he succeeded.

"Try to understand what I'm saying, ol' head. Either way, these niggas go down! I got thirty thousand and I want all the coke you take off those lames at eight a bird. Everything else is yours. $25,000 I hold for bail, lawyer's fees, or whatever the fuck you want taken care of if shit get fucked up. You wanna fuck wit it, there's a bed and breakfast bag waiting up front for you with everything you need in it, including 15k from the rip," Black spat, finishing his meal.

"So, what's good, dawg?"

"Black, I myself don't fuck with people who can have their mind swayed. Niggas fuck around and roll on me. I don't pick and choose who lives or dies. If the money right, anybody can get it, babee. I don't give a fuck if he was scheduled to meet Harriet Tubman and 'em at the Underground Railroad. I'm on your ass, naw-talkin'-'bout?" Reese revealed his true position, and Black could see that he was a thoroughbred. Being as such, after they reached an understanding, Reese excused himself, got up, and departed, keeping business and pleasure separate.

"Whatchu think, my nig?" Trig asked Black, wanting to know his view, as Black sparked up the Newport to chase his meal.

"Like he said, when the streets get hungry, then the streets gonna eat. Mutherfuckas got to realize that," he said, exhaling the twirling smoke.

CHAPTER 17

Da Game Plan 3 Of 3

M woke up with the young Spanish chic who he'd met in the club beside him. He looked over to her, noticing the hump she caused in the sheet from her heart-shaped ass while lying on her stomach. He sat on the edge of the bed, checking his messages on the I-phone. Shiz had hit him with: GET AT ME. The e-pills still had him slow motion, as he gathered his thought from what happened in the club. Awakened from her sleep, the young lady leaned over and kissed the bare shoulder of M.

"Ummm...baby, where you going? Come back to bed," she begged M, grabbing his manhood through his boxers.

"That pussy good, ma, but a nigga gotta go. I need you to get ya shit together so I can drop you off, ya heard me?" She sucked her teeth (phhft).

"Whatever, meanie-pants." She unraveled from the sheets, allowing them to fall as she headed towards the bathroom, displaying a mean ass wiggle in her butter pecan ass cheeks.

"It's ya loss, popi," she sang over her shoulder to a watching M. After M fucked mommy all crazy up against the sink while she attempted to brush her teeth, he got dressed and dropped her off. He called Shiz back while coasting the S550 to his apartment in Media, PA. The fully loaded Benz brought a warm smile to his face and a coldness to his heart. He knew big things were soon to come. The phone rang as M's thoughts deepened. All the gun play was making his blood rush. Shit ain't been this heated in a while, he thought to himself. (Still ringing)

"Yo, what's up?" Shiz picked up.

"Dis M, I'm around the corner, dawg."

"A'ight, what's up wit Dee? They let him out the hospital yet?"

"Naw, not yet. But, it's a shoulder wound. He should be out sometime this week."

"This week, huh? Niggas gotta stop shooting my youngen the fuck up. Speaking of that, we gotta tighten shit up, them 'lil niggas in the club coulda aired me out!"

"Yooo! I was just thinking the same fuckin' thang, dawg! That shit ain't ever going down like that again. That's my word on everything I love. I'ma be on that shit. I really thought niggas dropped when I saw the bullet holes through your coat. Mommy all screamin' and blood everywhere, I'm like, damn, not my man! I can't see my man in that box, and I'm not on some real shit," M spat.

"That's what's up. You know the feeling is mutual, but who were those niggas last night that cracked off? That whole thing was strange. Since when niggas start saving other niggas' lives?" Shiz said suspiciously.

"I don't know, but Bam gave the bol his number. I already told him when he calls to set up a meeting. Until then, I'ma find out what I can 'bout dude."

"A'ight, that's good money, stay on that," Shiz chimed.

"No doubt…Ay look, I'm outside. You comin' out or you want me to come up?"

"Come up, dawg," Shiz replied. "Cash Is King."

"Cash Is King." M reached Shiz's door, after signing a log in book, greeting the elder doorman, and passing two roaming muscular security guards. He entered Shiz's condo, which hosted hardwood floors, European chandeliers, and floor to ceiling windows. Even though it was only two bedrooms, the floor plan was extensive. The main foyer could swallow two bedrooms alone. Shiz's office adjoined to the living room, where M stood.

"Markell, what you doing here?" Ms. Pettiway asked while exiting the bedroom.

"Hey, what's up, mom? How you making out here?" He replied, before hugging her with a kiss.

"I'm fine, baby. You hungry? I'm 'bout to cook breakfast?"

"Nah, I'm good, mom. Where your son at?"

"He's back there. Call him…Nooddlllleeess!…M's waiting for you!"

"Yo, I'm in the office, come in," Shiz hollered back. Shiz ended his call as M walked into a warm smile of welcoming. He took a seat on Shiz's lounge, while Shiz shot hoops with the mini ball.

"Nigga, how much is you payin' for this spot?" M asked, admiring the decor on the ceiling.

"Why, whatchu trying to copp up?"

"Nah, this shit fuck around and be crib money."

"Basically," Shiz spat as he launched another shot.

"Look, I been thinking 'bout fuckin' wit that weight, man. We can pop off down North, 11th and 12th Streets are wide open, dawg. In fact, we can make a move on the project. Don't 'lil Tay and T-lo from uptown live up in there now?" M shook his head in agreement. "They can hold the weight up in there since it's the closest to the strip. Plus, niggas been wanting to get on anyway. Fuck all that nick-dime shit. Let them 'lil niggas have that money."

"That's a power move. Fuck it, let's rock out. But, what's Kev lettin' them jawns go for?"

"You know, I got the connect in Jacksonville for the fifteen, but the bol ain't never in the crib. I'ma keep trying him though. But, Kev said he'll let them go for $24,5k, if we grab four or more, but I don't really like fuckin' wit dude...Tell you what. We gonna fuck with 'em for now, but let's find another connect until I get back up with Azeez."

"Cash Is King! Let's get this money, babee," M growled, sitting up clapping his hands.

"Ay, what's up with the bitch, Tracy?"

"She chillin', calling me everyday on some nut shit. Her silly ass thinks she my bitch or something. Don't get me wrong, I fucks wit her, but the bitch want a nigga tying knots and shit. You know I copp her that Benz truck and got her the spot out Northeast?" Shiz spat.

"Yeah, that's what's up. I know the bitch happy 'bout that. When the last time you smash?"

"I ain't hit in like a month, plus the bitch be acting stupid sometimes."

"That's because you ain't fuckin' her right," M teased.

"Da fuck outta here, nigga," Shiz came back, sharing a laugh.

"You know I wanna fuck that? Ass all crazy, damn!"

"Go at her then, dawg. I don't love them hoes." Shiz began searching for his keys so he and M could get back down the way and put shit in motion. On the way out the door, Shiz told M that Chantel called and was asking about him. She said she would keep him in her prayers. M, however, showed no reaction.

CHAPTER 18

Junior : "Niggas done started something..."

I felt compelled to come back to the city after the news of my cousin's death reached me. I was one of the few he talked to last, but the only one he confided in concerning how he really felt. The whole shit got me determined to find out who did that hatin' ass shit to my peoples. I promise you, I'ma murk everything that had a hand on that shit. I still can't believe that nigga dead though. I just talked to the nigga like the other day. I mean niggas die everyday, but Butter was the type to escape death, even if he was locked in a room having no windows. That's how he got the name Butter because that nigga could slide through anything. That's the craziest thang about the streets though. It don't take much for niggas to hear about the bread you holding, the bitches you fuckin', and the whips you pushing. Big said it best in *Warning*, 'cause mutherfuckas will leave you stinking if they think they can get rich off your ass'. One thang for sure, two for certain, I don't give a fuck. If I just heard you hated on my cousin, I'm on ya ass. If you owe him money, Money, I'm on ya ass. Any reason is a good reason to jump on a nigga when it came to my mutherfuckin' people, real rap!

My agenda was full as soon as I hit the city. First stop, I got to meet Kashi out in Coatesville, so she can fill me in on everything that happened on her end when shit was going down. I just hope sis don't start trippin'. I can tell she still mourning Butter's death, but I need some info so I can put this shit on blast! I parked my Escalade outside of the townhouse, on the left side of Markease's Range Rover and Kashi's Bentley G.T. Although, I've never met Kashi before personally, the bitch had to be bad if Butter had her living way out there; pushin' hot shit like G. T.'s and shit. As I proceeded to the door, I could hear foreign voices coming from within. After a couple of rings, Kashi appeared wearing a grey Baby Phat sweatsuit with matching D&G flip flops, toes perfectly pedicured with cotton candy polish adorning her 5 ½ princess feet. Her frame was an example of regular fitness and aerobic classes, while her hair in every sense of the word complimented her flawless facial features. The bitch was bad! I saw that she was crying from the redness that tipped her nose.

"Kashi," I assumed.

"Yea, it's me, J.R.," she clarified, embracing her nose with the Kleenex.

"You a'ight, ma?"

"Yes, I'm fine. Come on in," she invited. I could see from the moment I entered, Kashi had no plans of sticking around. There were boxes filled with pictures and dishes. The furniture had been wrapped and taped up. Some of Kashi's family members had come to comfort her through the tough times. They took turns coming into the living room where we was sitting, to offer soup, aspirin, and whatever the fuck else they could think of. Kashi seen that we wasn't gonna be left alone, so she invited me upstairs to their bedroom, so I can pick her brain. Now, I ain't gonna lie, when she climbed the steps before me, her heart-shaped ass rumbled on the way up, causing my dick to jump a bit. I wouldn't disrespect Butter like that though, so I stayed focused. Kashi sat on the bed as I leaned against the dresser, admiring Butter's taste in decor.

"Kashi, I know this shit got you fucked up. But, I need you to let me know everything you know on how Butter was movin', and what you can remember on your kidnappin'," I shot.

"Junior, I don't really know what to say. 'Kease kept all his street dealings away from me. Whatever he used to do, he never brought it to the house with him or conversated with me at all concerning it."

"So, you never met any of his friends?"

"No, nobody. He didn't even mention anybody, other than Jab and you. Other than that, nothing."

"Damn!...So, this nigga that came to the crib, what he looked like?" I inquired.

"He was dark skinned, about 5'8", slim, and had brown eyes with a scar under his left eye. He said his name was ...ahh...Rrrobert Hall. After he forced his way in, he began attacking me. I tried to run, but he caught hold of me and started slamming my head against the wall. I wanted to shoot him and I tried, but it didn't fire. I don't remember much after that. When I woke up, my arms and legs were tied up." Kashi began to fight back the tears that stung her eyelids. "I thought I was dreaming, and it was over until I noticed the straps," Kashi's voice began to crack, as the tears stormed down her face. "Then... HE RAPED ME! I screamed, I cried, but he ...he wouldn't stop. Why he mak...make me do those things? Why he had to do that to me?! He wouldn't stop. I gave him the money, I gave him the money. He wouldn't stop, he just wouldn't stop!" She cried, covering her face as I began to comfort her. Just then, her family began to call in on the raised voice of Kashi, to which she reassured them of her well-being.

"Kashi, it's cool, that's over, ma. Ain't nobody gonna hurt you now. Listen, I'ma handle this shit. Ya hear me? You good, ya hear me?" I re-affirmed. So, after Kashi's crying subsided, I continued to press her for more info.

"So, where are you going, you got any money? Let me know what's up, so I can make sure you straight."

"No, that's okay, Junior. I'm moving to Atlanta after I sell the house. Plus, Markease had some money stored for me in a savings account. But, thank you, you are very kind," she said between snorts.

"Look Kashi, I'ma be real with you. I don't know what Butter coulda done to have brought this on. And, I'm sorry you had to go through that. But, if he would want you to know sumthin', then it would be his love was serious and he'll be more than happy to give his life for yours." Kashi began crying. "That nigga really felt sumthin' deep for you, shawty. And, if you need anything, get at me!" Kashi squinted her eyes, as if to recall something. She walked to the safe and encoded the combo to retrieve a black pouch that had Markease's cell and address book in it.

"I don't know what you can get out of this, but it must be important if he locked it up," she said, squeezing out a warm smile. After kissing and hugging our goodbyes, I was back on route 422 to put some heat under the grimy city that closed casket my cousin.

CHAPTER

19

Gimme Da Loot

There was a knock at the door that echoed through the hallway of the apartment complex.

"Yea, who is it?"

"Is Mikey there?" A smooth voice chimed with calmness.

"Nigga, I said who is it, not who da fuck you want!" Boo-heem hollered back, getting off the couch playing Madden with Chance. Mike laid asleep in the bedroom down the hall, hung the fuck over from the night before which just recently ended.

"Ay Heem, grab me something to drink from the kitchen when you come back," Chance demanded as Boo walked toward the door, he smiled at the paused game score, completely in his favor.

"Fuck, I look like your bitch or sumthin' nigga? Get your own fuckin' drink, dawg. You know where the box is!"

"The way I'm beating ya ass in this here game, you might as well be my bitch," Chance stated.

"Fuck you nigga...Yo! WHO IS IT?" Boo-heem asked again.

"Where Mikey at, babee?" The voice spoke as calm as the first time.

"Retarded ass nigga, da fuck is you crazy or sumthin'?" Boo-heem spat, looking out the peep hole at a slim old head, dressed like he just came from church. Seeing that he could easily smack the shit out him, he unlocked and opened the door swiftly.

"Nigga, you da fuck deaf or sumthin'?"

"Naw-mutherfucka-just crazy!" Reese replied pulling the cannon out he strategically had hidden behind him, allowing it to explode, blowing Boo onto his back. Chance attempted to reach for the chopper sitting just beneath the coffee table, but the flaming shells that Reese hurled his way ended his effort, spilling his blood across the sofa.

"Oh, you tried to kill 'lil Reese, huh? You done fucked up," he said over Chance's bitching.

"I see you's a 'lil nosy motherfucka, too. I can fix that though, babee." He placed the nozzle on the side of Chance's nose and pulled...POP! Chance could no longer feel his face, as blood fountained over the furniture adding new artistic value.

"Quit your bitching...you can still powder your nose. Now, where was I?" He said, returning to Boo.

"Oh! Where Mikey's ass at?"

"Ay, I..."

"Shhhhh...if you want to live through this shit, make your next statement the answer I'm looking for," Reese said chillingly, knelt over Boo with his hammer pressed against Boo's chest. Boo-Heem pointed to the back bedroom down the hall. The gunshots scared the shit out of Mikey, having jumped from his sleep. Words couldn't begin to describe how fearful he was. See, he played that tough shit, and that 'I ride out card', but when you aren't all highed up, the true you comes out...PUSSY! He pressed his ear firmly to the door, trying to pick up what happened. It sounded like mutherfuckas were getting the business out there.

"A'ight, tell that mutherfucka, to come see me." The door slammed and staleness combed through the apartment. He had heard it all, including Boo and Chance moaning over his own loud thumping heartbeat. He considered it could be a trick, but what option did he have? Allowing a few minutes to pass, Mikey gathered his heart and stepped into the hall with his tool. Boo and Chance came within eye view, as he proceeded down the tunneling hall. Mikey knelt down to check on him.

" 'Heem, you a'ight? Who da fuck was that nigga? Get up, dawg," he said nudging his back, but he didn't move. He could see Chance holding his face, trying his best to signal through his eyes. Mikey noticed a strange streak of blood leading to the kitchen, beginning from where Boo laid. It looked like somebody or something was dragged. He turned Boo to face him, so he could see if he was good, but what he found was Reese's cannon pressed flush against his abdomen. His eyes widened and hand twitched, but it was too late...POP.POP!!!

"What da fuck is wrong witchu, boy? We got business to handle, makin' me wait so mutherfuckin' long."

Black leaned against the door of Moet's Toyota not far from the strip. Moet stayed wearing some fly shit, coordinating her outfit to the decimal. The perfume that omitted from the new model whip coming from Moet, was intoxicating Black, as he centered in on her full lips making the gum she chewed pop, just as hard as her lip gloss. The two were becoming an item. Even though Mo didn't give him any pussy yet, she staked her claim on Black. His swag reminded her a lot of her baby father before he died. The only problem was getting his fat ass to spend more time with her.

"So, when we going out, Mo?" He shot, licking his lips.

"I guess whenever you got time. First, you need to pull yourself away from this block, acting like you gonna miss sumthin'," she replied, eyeing her reflection in the rearview.

"All you got to do is say the word."

"Umm-hmm," she responded, sucking her teeth.

"Nah, on sum real shit, I'm witchu, wherever you want to take a nigga, I'm going," he said, walking around the car to enter the passenger side, bringing warm blushes to Moet's face. He released the bucket seat to recline back, throwing his Louie's onto the dash, after venting the sunroof, "We out!" She knew Black was a hustler, and tearing a hustler from his block was less likely than banning blacks from barbequing. She refused to allow herself to get too excited at his 'We out' comment. Don't get it fucked up, she wanted him to do just that, but hustlers usually put Money, Mom, and My bad before their girl's feelings. Moet had been right before concerning hustler's unhealthy appetite to run the streets, and this time should be no different. Trig was sliding down the block in a rented 300, bumping to Camron's *Get it in Ohio*, while they continued debating Black's seriousness.

"Why you always bullshitting, boy?" She said.

"I'm not bullshitting, we out!"

"Black, I'm not playing with you, boy. If I pull this car off, I'm not turning around."

"Bitch, you trippin', I said we out."

"Oh, HELL NAH! Fuck you, Black. Who in da hell do you think you're talkin' to like that?" She said, striking him in his arm.

"Ahh!...C'mon with that bullshit," he responded, rubbing his love tap.

"Ayy, Blaaacckk!" Pierced the air, startling Black a bit.

"Fam, we gotta route. Cheese called, homeboy. He handled that business. He's waiting on us before he makes his next move," Trig said.

"Straight da fuck up?" Black asked a 'lil disbelievingly of the swiftness of Reese's movement.

"Real rap, dawg, so let's get at 'em." Black asked Moet to reschedule with a bunch of promises to make it up. Moet met that play with a firm talk-to-hand motion.

"Look, I'ma hit you in a 'lil, baby. Me & you, sis!" Black laid on, kissing a cold Moet's cheek before ejecting her car. She didn't even wait for him to close the door before peeling off, leaving him looking stupid.

"C'mon, cuz, let's get dis bread! That bitch ain't going nowhere."

"Naw, that bitch almost ran my god damn feet over. Moet gonna make me fuck her up." Trig laughed at Black's serious look he had plastered on his face, as he stared down the fleeting car. Fifteen minutes later, they pulled to the spot where they were to meet Reese Cheese. It was a vacant lot between two housing developments, sandlot style but leveled. Trig parked the 300 under the tree, shielding them from the sun rays. Black began counting out the bread that Trig brought with him for the payment of five birds and $15,000 for the hit.

"Keep it real, you didn't think old head was movin' like that?"

"We ain't get shit yet, dawg," Black spat.

"Nigga, dis shit is in the bag," Trig replied.

"Matter of fact, get that nigga on the phone and see what's taking him so long." Trig dialed Reese. He answered after a few rings with an eerie city background, over the purring V-12 engine and faint yelling.

"What up, babee?"

"Yo. Dis Trig, my nig. How long, Cheese?"

" 'Bout 5 minutes."

"You got that work on you, right?"

"Nah. But, it's not far away. Be cool, babee," Reese said, before turning a bumpy right on 8th Street.

"What he talking 'bout?" Black asked, wanting to know.

"He said we gotta go get the work, it's not far from."

"Fuck he mean? That's not what we talked about. Let me see that jack, man...Yo, Reese! Dig old head. I know we both made ourselves clear in what we expected. This shit won't cut it, dawg, and..."

"Black!" Reese interrupted. "Some niggas like to make shit hard, so I had to drag it out of him. Be cool, babee." Hearing the line go silent reassured Black that the conversation was over. A new one was beginning, when Reese's pearl white Escalade pulled up, trailing a desecrated Mikey being dragged by his legs, with his hands bound and mouth taped. Fleshy tissue hung from his body and adorned the streets for blocks to see. His torso was more devoured than an eaten wildebeest carcass. Blood stained and dripped from the remaining limbs. Black and Trig's eyes widened at the gruesome display of shredded organs that normally nested the inside of the human anatomy. Neither of them had ever seen something so malicious. They nearly painted the pavement with their own insides.

Reese hopped out of the ESCO, Newport hanging from his parted lips, as he fumbled through a mass of keys on a ring. He walked up towards the house, aside of the sandlot, ignoring Black and Trig's presence. Finding the key that gave entrance into the misused development, he shot the confused hustlers a silly look as if to say, *What the hell y'all waiting for?* before entering. As they slowly walked to join him within, they both traded glances of 'This bol da fuck crazy'. Reese quickly explained this was Mikey's stash house, and the reason they were asked to meet there. All transactions were completed, promises fulfilled, and future dealings were well on the way. Black and Trig left, feeling like Reese was a serious player in this game, a rook amongst pawns. They just knew they were sure to be a problem with a nigga like that moving for them.

CHAPTER

20

Tracy : Ms. Independent

"Oh shit, what da fuck time is it?" I said, louder than I was supposed to since I was home alone. The clock read: 9:30 am.

"Damn!" I must've overslept. I was supposed to be five minutes away from my job right now. After tearing myself from my sleigh style bed that Shiz bought for me, I managed to shower and dress all within twenty minutes grabbing a quick cup of mocha on my way out. I offer no explanation of such, because I practically run that office by myself, from opening accounts to overseeing transaction transcripts that all fell on my desk. For the last two years, I busted my ass doing exactly what my superiors asked of me. And the crazy thing is, I don't know when all of it will pay off. At the end of the day, this shit is drawing, and I ain't feeling this shit no more. I fully understand why it is that after all this time; I still haven't gotten a promotion yet…Why buy the cow, when you can get the milk for free? That's why I got every intention on resigning from that mutherfucka today! A two page resignation, typed and sealed, is in my Chanel bag, and I can't wait to give this chumpy to Mark. I already know how he gonna come off. 'Why? What's the problem? Haven't we been good to you?' And all that bullshit, like he really give a damn. See, what it is…all he want to do is smash, and always has. I can't count how many times I caught him staring at my ass, "Cracker-ass cracker!"

After parking my SUV, I sat in the lot for a minute to make sure my shit was straight. These bitches can't wait to get sumthin' on me up in here. My Mac lip gloss was poppin', hair and nails on smash. A lot of people say I look like the girl Raina off of Flavor of Love 3, but I'm definitely a lot thicker. While I was checking my appearance in the sun visor, Tammy, Joan, and Remy pulled up in Joan's red E-Class, laughing all loud and ghetto, sounding like a pack of wild bar bitches.

"Look at these hoes, knowing damn well these white folks are looking to talk about sumthin' over their lunch." If they not running around all up in everybody's damn business, then they trying to start some shit. Oh, and don't let Shiz come up in here. I don't care what they was doing before he came in, instantly they all up in his face, acting all prissy…Especially Joan and Remy ugly asses. I don't want to beat nobody's ass in here. I just want to get this day over with, so I can call Shiz's fine ass up and he can come over and beat it up. Let me go up in here…(Boob-boob-boob…car door ajar)

No sooner than I walked in the door, I heard Mark's annoying ass voice telling me to prepare drawer three for Crystal. That's not even my job. Fuck on this guy's mind? As if I ain't got nothing to do. Crystal been here for a whole month, a whole

FUCKIN' MONTH and she still can't set up her drawer yet? I did everything except prepared it, then I started cleaning my desk out. No one seemed to notice my actions, except Remy's nosy ass.

"Where you going, Tee?" she asked flat out.

"Nowhere, why?" I gave her a 'lil attitude.

" 'Cause I've been checking you out lately."

"Checking me out?!" I repeated, as if I didn't understand.

"Yea, first you start showin' up with all these cute ass bags and shit: Gucci, Chanel, and that big Fendi one you got, you know, the good shit. Then, you get rid of your Honda and jump in that new Benz and now you cleaning your desk out. What's up, bitch?" She asked, twisting her lips with a squint in her eye, like she was the chief inspector. Uh -un, I know this silly ass bitch done lost her mind now, questioning me like I fuck with her like that. Just as I was about to tear into her ass, Mark appeared.

"You know what? Let me tell ya mutherf..."

"Ms. Woods! I need to see you in my office right away," Mark interrupted.

"Alright Mark, because I need to see you as well," I snapped grabbing my purse, while my eyes shot daggers at Remy when me and Mark exited. I for sure wasn't done with her ass. That chic needed an ass whuppin', and I was just the bitch to give it to her. Talkin' 'bout 'I've been checking you out', bitch please! When we arrived at Mark's office, I noticed a few back office personnel lingering at the rear of his suite. He requested that I have a seat which I did, after pulling my letter out of my bag. He started fumbling through some e-mails, as if it was important.

"Hmmm, now where did I put it?"

"I got it, Ms. Woods."

"Mark," I whispered.

"Wait a sec, Tracy, I know it's here."

"MARK!" I repeated, raising my voice more, hoping his dumb ass would read I was about to explode.

"Ms. Woods, pardon me, what I have won't take more than a second, please," he said with his hand pressed forward. Too bad, I gave this company more than I can no longer bear. He found what he was looking for and signaled his personnel, just as I was exploding.

"You know what, Mark. I done had it the fuck up to here..."

"CONGRATULATIONS!!" They sang in unison. "MS. WOODS, YOU ARE OUR NEWEST SUPERVISOR!" I stood there dumbfounded, with my resignation letter in hand. Mark had heard my outburst and he stood before me confused, as the employees celebrated around us, spraying silly string, tooting horns, and clapping my promotion. I managed to force out a fake smile as Mark and I traded glances.

"Is that for me?" He asked, aware of what it was.

"No. No, it isn't," I whispered.

"Are you sure?" He asked with concern.

"Yes." He stared at me for a few awkward moments.

"Well, in that case, here are the keys to your new office...The old Milford suite, it's the biggest one we have and you deserved it." I was still stuck and at a loss for words, but he understood my silence as appreciation. As I left his suite, I turned to mouth the words,

"Thank you!" When I emerged from Mark's office, I heard a familiar voice out front. To my surprise, it was Shiz. And of course, Joan and Remey's ugly asses were all up in his face, all teeth and gums, key-keying at every damn word he uttered. I wasted no time making my presence known.

"Shiz, whatchu doing here?" He turned around to find me all dolled up in business girl fashion. He always liked the way I looked when I wore my business look, it made his dick hard. And, who can blame him because my skirt-suite fitted me like a glove. Instantly, I noticed his eyes combing over my protruding hips that captivated my slender waist. I loved the attention, but he still hadn't answered my question yet; and more importantly, why he got these hoes all up in his face!

"I was handling some business out this way, and I stopped by to take your sexy ass to lunch...you free?" I knew it was more to his little story as he was always up to sumthin', but I wouldn't give these hoes the satisfaction of knowing shit, feel me? Plus, his C.E.O. Muslim oil was rockin'! And, his Prada shoes was cute...his hair was cut, and ice blinging, DAMN! I love this nigga. After the reason for Shiz coming became evident once again to Joan and Remy, they both fled like the true ticks that they are, but not before I put Remy's ass in check.

"Remy!" I called out to her.

"I didn't mean to be rude when you asked me where I was going earlier," I smirked, "313, sweetie." She mashed up her face in thought of what I just said, while Shiz wrapped his arms around my slender waist.

"Isn't that the old Milford office?" Her ignorant ass spat.

"I know, hon, you can have that desk if you like." Her mouth fell three stories in saltiness, while Tammy's laughs echoed in the lobby.

I lead Shiz's sexy ass by hand, upstairs to my new office. Since I just got the promotion, I didn't have a secretary yet, so the floor was practically empty. I lowered the shades and locked the door. A suspicious Shiz stared on, somewhat confused of my actions, until I wiggled out of my panties. We had never done it here before. The risk of getting caught was far too embarrassing, but it would take more than that to stop me from twirkin' it right here on this fuckin' desk. Plus, he hadn't given me any in a while, too! Uh-un, I'm gettin' me some.

"Trase, you wild'n. Right here, though?" When I positioned myself doggy style on the desk with my skirt flipped up, he knew exactly what it was. He pushed himself into my wetness and stroked my G-spot, until I felt my insides exploding. *Umm...this dick is soo good, nothing could feel better; no thrill, no gift, no l-o-v-e, love? Do he really love me? Where is it? I know I told myself he would eventually, but will he? Shit, do he even care about me?*

"Ooh Shiz, damn baby...fuck!" I moaned. Why do he have to be so selfish? I didn't want to fuck the mood up, but I had to ask.

"Shiz."

"Yeah, baby...Fuck." He replied in ecstasy.

"Do you love me?"

"Yea bitch, I love you. What da fuck are you talkin' 'bout?"

"Ooh, oh shit. No, I'm...serious." *Yea Trase, I love you. Damn, this pussy good.*

"You do?"" I asked shockingly.

"Yeah ma, you my bitch." It was settled then, this pussy was his for ownership, along with everything else. So, I gave it to him like it was notarized, throwing my ass into his pelvic until we both fell slumped.

CHAPTER 21

C.H.E.M.E.
Cash Have Everything Murked Easily

It didn't take long for shit to fall in place, just as Shiz anticipated. The temperature was on high max in compliance with Shiz's demand. After he expanded his blocks and invaded the projects, it seemed like every goon and goblin in the area was crawling up from under their rocks and dumpsters to grab off of Shiz. The block was easy to consume, as nobody with any real money, weight, or power was holding it down, just a bunch of pack boys. So, Shiz agreed to put them on, guaranteeing whip money by the end of the closing summer, if they surrendered the block. The projects were a completely different story. M visited Tay and Tee-Io out there, and got the drop from them on what was poppin' out there. The affairs were totally an in-house thing. Niggas on the second floor were beefin' with niggas on the fifth over some baby-momma shit. The old heads that trapped 'soft' out front had problems with niggas on the ninth that pushed 'hard'. It had gotten to the point where you couldn't even walk down the hallway without ducking random gunfire. The fucked up part was nobody was getting any money with all the bullshit going on. M knew this was one of those issues that was better talked out, rather than shot out. So, he had Tee-Io set the meeting up, and Shiz made them an offer they couldn't refuse... GET DOWN OR LAY DOWN! Nobody in that room was stupid enough to go to war with Shiz and them. His money and gun power were just too strong for the .380's and 9mm's they were holding. From that meeting only, one example had to be made; some loud mouth, hard- headed nigga.

"So what, if we ain't selling your shit, we can't get no money? And, I was raised in these projects."

"That's exactly what I'm sayin'," Shiz chimed with a sinister smile.

"Fuck you, Jack!" Old head spat, wearing his 70's gorilla killa face. It was hard to determine if he even realized his brains had been blown out, since that same dumb ass look was plastered on his face, until his shell fell slumped. The smokin' .50 caliber held in Tay's grasp was enough to silence all other hopeful objectors. Bam was playing Black's old role on the blocks, held by the team. Dee was back to health and his position was right under Bam. Shiz had really beefed up security on their investment. He even had a few niggas from Germantown down there to help make shit run smooth. Nobody was left out of eating from Shiz's plate. From the look-outs to the weight holders, everybody's appetite was being nourished. That translated into less envy and a stronger team, which in turn made more $$$. Shiz had ears and eyes all over the place, his old heads schooled him well; namely his father and his left hand man Maurice, who seemed to disappear after his Pop got killed in front of him. They always used to say, 'The streets keep watch 'til the clock go stop', a saying that Shiz valued and used like the ace in a spades game. So, people knew Shiz was very generous when it came to puttin' him on. The bodies that were droppin' out D-ware created a buzz in the city out there. Black's name was in most hustlers' conversation, mainly complaining that the out-of-towners were taking over. That was a problem which eventually found its way to Shiz's lap. Baffled to say the least, how the fuck did Black manage to come up like he did boggled his mind. But the one thing he was absolutely clear on was, with his money and strength up, it wouldn't be long before he came back for the place he called home and the squad that had pushed him out. He had planned to hip Rob & M to what fell on his lap. He arranged for them to meet him at Tracy's crib out Northeast. Up until that point, he hadn't divulged any info at all to them, he wanted to make sure what he heard was correct before discussing it.

$ $ $ $ $

M and Rob awaited Shiz to pull up at Tracy's house, while they sucked down a six pack of Coronas on the front steps leading to the brick face row home. Their conversation broke by the rumbling engine speeding up the suburban block. A money green and silver GXR 1000 with an extended swing arm and lowered frame on chromed out rims flew past like a blur, circling at the end of the block. The rider had matching gear to coordinate with the sports bike. Racing back down, he wheelied the GXR, lowering it a few yards before Tracy's steps, just behind the black CLS Benz. Shiz removed his helmet and proceeded up the steps.

"Nigga, is you da fuck crazy or sumthin', ridin' that bike like that?...Where the fuck you get a bike from anyway?" M spat.

"Same place I get everything I own from, hard work and money. Let's go in the crib, I got some real rap for y'all niggas," he said walking past. When they arrived in the crib, Tracy had that piece poppin' with aromas that could've been mistaken for a five star restaurant. The rattling of pots and dishes banged from the kitchen over running sink water.

"I don't know how I let this boy talk me into this. I was in the area, Trase...I came to take you to lunch, Trase... yea right," she imitated Shiz.

"Damn, baby girl in there cooking like dhat?" Rob said to M, reclining on the sofa. Shiz came jogging down the steps wearing a wife beater and ball shorts.

"Yea nigga, my 'lil bitch know how to burn," Shiz shot, walking past them and into the kitchen. Tracy stood over the stove flicking the sizzling fried chicken, wearing a tank top and stretch pants.

"Who you referring to as 'lil bitch, Shiz? Don't show off in front of your 'lil friends," she said loud enough for them to hear, pushing Shiz to the side.

"Stop taking everything I say literally, you know how we ride, babee." Smacking her soft ass, he grabbed a handful.

"Yea, wha-t-e-ver," she hissed, as Shiz kissed her forehead. Shiz returned to the living room to his men, leaving Tracy to ponder how she had enjoyed Shiz's company over the last few days. Not only was he giving her Mr. Goodbar on a consistent basis now, she also was having the pleasure of him staying over at night. This was a huge accomplishment for Tracy and she hoped it led to more promising things. The men were called for dinner. Tracy traversed in and out with steaming plates of fried chicken, mac & cheese, candied yams, and crescent rolls for Shiz's team. Each time in, M's eyes followed her ass out. *Umm,um,um. That shit don't make no sense*, he thought lustfully. Rob hadn't noticed at first, as this was his first time meeting her. Rob could see Tracy was nice looking and he expected that from Shiz, but when he caught hold of what she was tugging; his damn eyeballs could literally be handed back to him after they fell out his head. Shiz noticed them observing, but it was nothing to him. Plus, he acknowledged her ass was really that fat ...You had to look! Tracy could feel their eyes on her ass, so she tried to hide it under her tank top, but that was useless, it was just too round. The attention would've normally been welcomed, but that was before those goodies became Shiz's. After serving the fellas, she kissed the cheek of Shiz sweetly, and then ascended the stairs with her plate in hand to her bedroom so they could rap.

"Yiz-zo, I found out some supa-dumb shit this week, cuz. That's why I asked y'all here, so I can put y'all niggas on," Shiz spieled between bites of Tracy delicious chicken.

"You know Boogie from uptown? I runs into him the other day at the gas station. You know that nigga be everywhere, right? So, while we bustin' it, he says; your man getting' it down Delaware. So, I'm like, who? He like, the nigga be running with y'all, the nigga that used to get money with y'all on Seventh Street. What's his name...Da bol? What's his name? So, I'm like, Black? He like, yea, that's his name, BLACK! He out there killin' 'em! So, Boog start telling me the nigga out there eatin' heavy and dropping mutherfuckas left and right out that jawn," Shiz informed, not showing any signs of worry while he ate. M stopped eating to digest the news Shiz was unraveling. He felt hot and on edge because he knew Black wasn't supposed to be breathing. The fact that he was not only alive, but well, was enough for M to become kettle hot. The money part was just insult to injury.

"So after my 'lil talk with Boog, I broke him a few for the G, and got on my game. Turns out Black is down D-ware gettin' it. This mutherfucka movin' bricks down there like niggas is coming to build cribs." Shiz stopped eating to wipe his hands off. "That fat greasy mutherfucka building a nice 'lil team down there...Dig this!" Shiz said tossing some photos of Trig and Black's operation onto the table.

"This his cousin, his name is Trig. And, the nigga puttin' that twirk in down there, he got a few other niggas movin' with him as well, some nigga name Cheese, old head, but vicious. We ain't got no flicks of him though," Shiz spat, as he sat back in his chair that was heading the table. "Here's the point, you know like I do M, this Black ass nigga is vindictive as a mutherfucka. This bol will make himself sick thinking about getting at us. Knowing Black as well as I do, he won't stop until he see us in the Box...I want him dead!" Shiz said, cold and straight forward. M and Rob nodded, as Shiz put the finishing touches on. "I want y'all to go down there and drop them niggas off. His cousin, old head, his team, I want all them mutherfuckas aired out! We trying to get this guap, so we don't need no nut shit hanging over our heads, dig me?" M & Rob soaked every word up, knowing what Shiz was saying was accurate. They left the trash untied and now it was starting to stink up the house.

"Cash Is King," they sang, trading looks of murder.

"Cash Is King, nigga!" Shiz returned. And, just like that, a C.H.E.M.E. was on Black's head, and he was set to die.

CHAPTER 22

I'll Be Through...

J.R. pulled in front of Markease's barbershop down on Wayne Ave. in the G-town section of Philadelphia. The city regarded this section of Germantown as 'The Hollow'. Since Markease was murdered, niggas had been swarming his forsaken treasure like flies on shit, claiming ownership of things they didn't attribute a damn dime to.

J.R. had found the address of the barbershop in Markease's phone book which Kashi had given to him, along with the name Tony right besides it. It wasn't hard to figure out this Tony character was trying to keep the shop to the face, because when Kashi called to inform them of Markease's death and that the shop will be closed for a while until she could appoint management, some man named Tony hung up on her. J.R. felt like whoever had a shiesty bone in their body was a potential suspect in his cousin's assassination, and trying to steal an entire barbershop under his grieving fiancé's nose was indeed some shiesty ass shit. He parked his black Escalade with matching 24's, grabbed his chopper from under the seat, and then exited the truck with the heat tucked in a brown paper bag. He walked past a few hustlers on the way in.

"Whatchu need done, dawg?" A braided barber asked J.R. before he had a chance to canvas the shop. He noticed other chairs were filled which indicated his barber just started.

"Just clean it up for me, pimp," J.R. requested.

"Cool," the youngen spat, caping J.R. up after seating him. No sooner had the barber begun adjusting the clippers, when a light skinned gentleman burst through the drapes covering the back portion of the shop.

"Derrick, how many times do I gotta tell you, you have to sign in all your clients for the next 30 days?" He bossed.

"A'ight, dawg," reluctantly the youngen spat, while he clipped J.R.'s waving strands.

"Fuck, you young niggas hardheaded, man," he added before entering the back.

"I'm hardheaded, this ain't even your mutherfuckin' shop and already changing shit. Main-man ain't been dead for a full month yet," the barber shot.

"Who that youngen?" J. R. asked.

"That nigga, Tony," he said, watching the edges fall from J.R. head, when Tony resurfaced with yet another complaint.

"Did you take that extra pack of cotton balls from storage yesterday?"

"Yea, I used them."

"Well best believe it will be included in this week's rent."

"Damn Tee, why you on the bol top like that?" One of the senior barbers interjected.

"Man, dis thing ain't personal, I gotta keep my bread right, dhat all," Tony clarified.

"Well, where my bread at? Since this thing ain't personal," Junior addressed, just as youngen put the finishing touches on.

"Your bread, I don't even know you family," a confused Tony fired.

"But yet, that didn't keep you from stealing from me," J.R. replied, as Derrick unfastened the cape to shake off the edges. J.R. got up and looked in the mirror, admiring youngen's work, gaining the entire shop's attention as they sensed the conversation taking a turn for the worst. J.R. passed the paper bag to Derrick, while he peeled a crisp twenty from his pocket. Derrick noticed the hard, weighty feeling from the bag before handing it back.

"Dis here a nice ass shop, Tony. How long have you owned it?"

"I don't know who you been talking to, but I do all my business on the up and up," Tony spat, with his hands stretched before him, like he was trying to prevent a train wreck. He sensed J.R.'s coldness which brought about an abnormal level of nervousness.

"So, you call brodiying a grieving woman who just lost her husband from murder, straight up business?"

"Man, I don't know what your talking 'bout. Markease left me this shop. I've been working here for over ten years, before he bought the joint. I was next in line to own it and he woulda wanted it that way."

"So, you telling me you meant more to Butter than his wife and me?" J.R. spat in a chilling manner. Tony began backing up as J.R. slowly inched forward.

"Man, I don't want no trouble. I'm a business man. Ay Na-na-nard, call the police. This mutherfucka crazy," Tony ordered stuttering, as he backed over the heels of his customers. Just as Nard picked up the shop phone to dial 9-1-1; six shells tore through his fleshy torso, painting the wall and mirror with his insides, from the begged chopper. Pop, Pop, Pop, Pop, Pop, Pop! The entire shop tried to squeeze through the door all at once, hearing the chopper purr off like that. Tony attempted to break for the back before a round of slugs took his legs from him. People gathered on the outside window, amazed at what was unfolding. Standing over Tony, swarming on his stomach, J.R. kicked him in his ass as hard as he could.

"Turn da fuck over, punk ass nigga. Your bitch ass killed my cuzzo?"

"No! Naw man, never. 'Kease was my man," he bellowed out.

"If that was your man, fuck you doing stealing from him?"

"I wasn't stealing, 'Kease gave me this joint."

"I don't believe your bitch ass, nigga. Maybe Butter will, let him know when you see him. Pop, Pop. Pop, Pop. Pop, Pop!!! His blood and brain splashed on the polished floor. J.R. left satisfied he did the world a favor by getting rid of another thieving ass nigga.

CHAPTER

23

We fly high, no lie, you know this

Shiz sat on the hood of his rented Maserati Quattroporte in Checker's fast food parking lot on Broad & Erie. M, Dee, and Rob were all there awaiting Sideeq to arrive in response to Bam's request. M was off to the side, hollering at the bitch Angie he met at the club. The crew was heavily engaged in the normal hood bullshit; who got shot, who's grabbin' what off of who, which bitch is bad, etc. Sideeq pulled into the lot in a S-type Jaguar, being driven by this bad ass white chic wearing princess cut diamond studs and Dior sunglasses, while Sideeq played the passenger trying Kelly for the fourth time. The car came to a stop and Sideeq hopped out.

"Sideeq?" Shiz asked, hopping off the hood of the Quattro.

"Yea."

"Shiz, pimp." The two shook hands firmly. He then introduced him to the rest of the clique. After making himself acquainted, Shiz told his crew to stand down while he and Sideeq go holla. Shiz could tell that Sideeq was a thoroughbred, but for who was the question? The duo leaned against the gate and began to pick one another.

"Bam tells me you from down South Philly?" Shiz jumped right in.

"Yea, Tasker."

"Okay, so you know the bol Dutch and them?"

"Yea, I know that cruddy-ass nigga. I used to fuck wit his sister, Trina."

"With da fat ass Trina?"

"Yea, that be with the bitch Mutta. They both some smiz-zut," Sideeq chimed over Shiz's chuckle.

"Yea, well you know how that shit go…Ay look, about that 'lil incident in the club. That shit was hard body, dawg. I ain't all clear on what was your motive, but a nigga can definitely appreciate anybody puttin' that twirk in. We ain't gotta get all heavy, but I come from a schooling where building bridges is always more profitable than burning them. I owe you a check or sumthin', dawg."

"Shiz, that shit was nothing. It just didn't look right, seeing y'all ball-out or whatever and some hating shit go down like that," Sideeq spilled, using his hands to illustrate his point. He continued, "Maan, these mutherfuckin' streets are filled right now with nothing but dope heads, fleas, and ratz. So, when you meet a bred, it's a collective duty to make sure the ticks don't get him. Basically, what I'm saying is; real recognize real, and real niggas do real thangs, dig me?" Sideeq rehearsed his lines well. The vibe was good. Both men could see there was something to be gained from the nearing adventure. Meeting Sideeq in person removed a lot of suspicion for Shiz. The bol had a genuine feel to him; his handshake was firm and eye contact sturdy. He was either very sincere or very dangerous.

Both are plausible traits in the heartless game that promised nothing except death.

"But, on some lighter shit, what that mutherfuckin' Quattro set you back, dawg? Them shark lookin' jawns hot ass shit," Sideeq added, as they walked toward the crew and car.

"Yea, this jawn is nice as shit. I'm thinkin' 'bout grabbin one, this right here is a rental though."

"Man, I've been tryna get my hands on one of these for the longest! Dis that boss shit, straight up!" Sideeq spat, admiring the pearl white jaw dropper. After talking shit for a while, Bam suggested they should go out to A.C. for the fight and casino. This way, they could finally put an end to who was the ultimate Gambler. Everybody agreed to meet back up in two hours. This would give everybody enough time to get fresh, and Sideeq enough time to bust shawty's ass that had been waiting ever so patiently. It was all settled before they departed.

When they arrived in Atlantic City, it was shortly after 10 pm. Everybody had that shit on. Designer labels and flawless carats were the stamp of approval for them all this night. The Mayweather fight was at the Bogota and resulted in a landslide. The drinks were complimentary with the seating Dee paid for. After the repeated shots of Patron, Henny, and Grey Goose, it seemed like everybody was ready to carry their drunk asses to the casino and play with that money. M wasted no time hitting the crap table when they touched down on the floor.

"Bet the $5000, I ain't scared of this shit, nigga. I can smell that money; let me get them dice, babee." M threw the dice after shaking them, causing the glare from his diamond watch to dance across the faces of the table betters. "Money!" He shouted.

"Seven, shooter wins!" The bookie yelled sending table betters into a frenzy.

"Ay, give me five on his shot," Shiz said quickly, before M shot again.

"I'ma show y'all how to get this paper. Ay Shiz, you better tell these niggas my number good. Watch me bring this shit back." He shook the bones. "Money!" He screamed, and sure enough, four-three displayed.

"Seven, shooter wins!"

"I told y'all niggas, I'ma hit it. They don't call me Copperfield for nothing...Bet it back," M demanded.

"M, bet it back," Rob chirped.

"You think I ain't, when I am. I keep tellin' y'all mutherfuckas, I ain't scared of these dice...Money!"

"Eleven, shooter wins!"

"God damn! That nigga buckin' da shit outta their asses," Sideeq chimed. They all started betting on M's shot, and all eventually won money. The one thing about A.C. you can count on; the bread start coming, the bitches come a-running. There was no doubt, M was the shit tonight. Not only did he win money, but complimentary suites for himself and the team for the weekend. As the night dwindled away, Shiz found himself at the casino bar downing shots with Sideeq. Dee and Bam had a gang of white bitches with them, obviously raised in the hood, as they frequently used the N-word without care.

"Shiz, you got a nice 'lil squad here," Sideeq bigged him up.

"Yea, they my peoples."

"Y'all seem to be doing well, that's a good look."

"Main-man, you ain't doing so bad yourself. A nigga can see them mutherfuckin' rocks on your hand and shit, S-type. Tasker must be treating a nigga good."

"Naw, I'm an O.T.-nigga. Reading, Dover, Paulsboro, I play out there. The money so much better and the profit margins are way sweeter."

"A mutherfuckin' dope boy, huh? That's crazy 'cause I had you pegged for the take money type shit...A nigga better be doing sumthin' out here, 'cause niggas is starving," Shiz spat. (SILENCE) Sideeq's cell phone broke the stale moment with a call from Kelly.

"Hold on, Shiz," he requested.

"Yea, where you at?" he said, after accepting the call.

"I'm in the house, where you at?" Kelly returned.

"If you in the crib, why you callin' me from your cellie, then?"

"I don't have time for this right now, Sideeq..." She huffed. "And, if it is so fuckin' important to you, then you'd have your ass here to find out. Where you at anyway?"

"A.C.," he replied.

"Figures...Who you out there with, one of them 'lil dirty project bitches?"

"Naw! But fuck all that, it's two in the morning and you just now calling me back. You gonna make me fuck you up. You better not leave that house 'til I get there," he pressed on.

"An-y-way. You ain't got to lie. I know you fuckin' on me, just admit it. And, you definitely not the only one who can stay out all night."

"A'ight, keep fuckin' with me, I'ma..." But, before Sideeq could continue with his threats, Kelly served his ass with the dial tone. Shiz heard his convo while he enjoyed the last of his drink.

"These bitches crazy, dawg," Sideeq blew out. Shiz hit him with the 'handle your biz' face.

"You know what that nigga Hov said: "If you havin' girl problems, I feel bad for you, son. I got 99 problems, but a bitch ain't one."

"HIT MAE!!" They sung in unison, breaking into a laugh.

"Yea, true that," Sideeq agreed, bearing a smirk.

"But, nah. If I found the right bitch, I'd wife her up, too. I imagine me doing the family thang on sum legit business type time at some point," Shiz reasoned.

"Yea cuz, dis shit here will definitely burn you out," Sideeq said, referring to the game, just as M walked in with a goddess. Somehow, the boy always managed to attract the baddest chics the game had to offer. This bitch was a straight up Selma Hayek type jawn; ass ridiculous.

"Yiz-zo, what's good, babee?" M asked them with shawty drippin' off his arm.

"Chillin', ain't nothing. You got all the good," Shiz replied, eyeing shawty's hips.

"Damn M, where her sister at?" Sideeq asked, hoping not far from.

"Me don't have an-nee," she took the liberty of answering for herself.

"Awww nice, she don't even speak English," Shiz chimed.

"A'ight dawg, I'm shootin' to the room. Hit me on the hitter if you need me. You good, right?" Shiz nodded.

"Naw, hit me on the hitter, if you need me," they laughed, as M faded with the bad ass Brazilian.

"That's a bad ass bitch, cuzin'!" Sideeq sang, while bowing his head with a nod of approval. The birds Dee and Bam were screaming at slid up to the suite with the crew to party, or rather get partied. Bam rolled up the Nestly, while the best of Biggie bounced off the walls. The suite view was astounding, covering the beachfront Atlantic Ocean side. The white chics were overly thrilled to be in the presence of G-Unit, or so they thought, because of the game Dee dropped on them downstairs. And, with the amount of jewelz that flooded their necks and wrists, who were they to argue otherwise.

"So, are you guys really rappers?" One of the white chics asked Shiz, as he stood on the balcony feeling like the world was at his grasp for the taking.

“Naw, we them niggas they rap about,” he said to the short Italian bubble butt who lusted the sparkle of Shiz’s diamond faced watch.

“Oh yea...fuck...yea. Fuck me, papi,” the Brazilian moaned, with M’s pipe running deep inside of her. He couldn’t ignore the way her hips and ass wiggled, crashing down on his throbbing dick. Ni’centa straddled him backwards like a true cowgirl, leaving view of her bouncing ass for M to stare at along the ride. There was no denying, the way Ni’centa’s inside went wrapping around M’s dick was a heavenly feeling in itself. He stared at her long cinnamon hair pressing against her back, as she gazed upward letting out her harmonious pants.

“Smack mae azz, papi,” she demanded.

“You want me to smack that shit?” M chimed. ‘Pap!’ echoed in the suite from M’s hands slamming into Ni’centa’s ass, leaving a red handprint before dissolving. M struck it several more times, tearing her inner freak to the surface.

“Yea popi, make a me chocha wat,” she sang, positioning herself on her feet to deepen the straddle, allowing all of M’s dick to rest within her as she switched thereto.

“Mmmmm Papi, you so muy bi’en,” she hissed, feeling his manhood seize control of her pussy. She began raising her hips to the very end of M’s dick, where it all but fell out, then allowed her weight to crash down while squeezing her vagina. That number was calling M’s milk department for delivery.

“OH! You fuckin’ dirty bitch. Dis pussy good, mommy. Yea, go hard, go in, go hard!” M grunted.

"You like it, papi?" Ni'centa spat, feeling M's hands pull from her shoulders into his pelvic, causing a fleshy-smacking sound from her ass cheeks.

"Hold up, Ma. Slow up, turn this way," M ordered, not wanting to nut yet.

"How you wanna do, papi?" She asked, before kissing him in the mouth. The soft lips that plastered M's face felt like pillows. He wanted to refuse her as he didn't usually kiss bitches who he just met in the mouth, but this brawd was downright angelic. Shit, he even pondered letting her sit on his face! As she kissed new worlds into M's soul, she stroked his dick to maintain its stiffness. He enjoyed it all, however not deterred to bust her ass literally; he swiftly positioned her on all fours and pushed it into her ass.

"Ooh papi, yea! Fuck mae like that…Fuck yea, oh yea, popi." M grabbed her hair with a firm tug, jerking her neck back with the action, where he kissed her mouth hungrily again. The pounding of M's weight into Ni'centa's ass turned her on more. His dick was sweet to her. Feeling her spine grow chilly, she wanted to cum all over his nuts while he dicked her down, then gag on the load she wanted released on her tonsils. As she began nearing her peak, she vocalized her thoughts.

"Papi, Papi…Oh Shit, Ni'centa wanna cum on ya Pinga."

"Cum on my what?! Yea, whatever ma, let that shit go." Unsure what that meant, it sounded good, so he agreed.

"Den, I want you cum in mae mouth," she said, tightening her grasp on the bed sheet. The sensation was driving them both to sheer bliss. M feeling her release on his nuts, felt free to follow suit.

"Come get it ma, come get it!" He said swiftly, unable to hold any longer. Ni'centa pulled the condom off and sucked life from M, until she tasted his seed of life. And, like a true bitch, she swallowed it while massaging his nuts under her warm chin, sending M napping away like the chump Mayweather put to sleep earlier that evening.

5:30am, Ni'centa awoke feeling a rush of urgency. She combed her eyes over M's sleeping body, then to her platinum Cartier watch stationed on the night stand. After confirming the time, she rushed into the bathroom where she briefly freshened up, as quietly as possible. Ni'centa then went in search of her clothing which was all over the place, like a savage beast tore them from her limbs. *Dammit, where my shit at? I know I had my overcoat*, she mentioned in thought. Tripping over M's Ferragamo square toes, she found the answer to her question beneath the bed. *Now, where do Ni'centa start from?* she thought. Arriving at the mini bar where M's Gucci Jacket hung from the stool, she immediately started shooting M's pockets.

"Nothing!" She tried the next one, Bingo! Ni'centa robbed plenty of men before, that claimed to be the hardest, smartest, and wealthiest guys the strip had to offer. And, each time she would fuck their lights out, then rob them blind. Ni'centa's supermodel looks made the job easier than a baby napping. No one would ever think in a million years that somebody as bad as that would ever resort to such standards, when in a heartbeat her targets would've just given her what she wanted. But, Ni'centa enjoyed the rush that accompanied the game, plus she considered herself good. No one had ever caught her, and even if they did, she would just charm her way out of it. Within a few short seconds, Ni'centa had managed to gather $83,000 from M in cash and jewelry. She had all of M's shit. The score alone would set her straight for the entire week. Ni'centa noticed M lying asleep while she cleaned him out. Nearing the door, she realized she left her Jimmy Choo's behind. She retrieved the shoes, and then focused her attention on getting out of there, and quickly, too. As she reached for the door just milliseconds away from another successful heist, M's voice shot through her spine, sending chills throughout. But most of all, the click-clacking of M's hammer was more than enough to draw stool from her.

"After all this pipe I laid on you, you wouldn't do a nigga like that, would you?" He said, standing just behind her.

"No popi, Ni'centa needed some ice so mae can feenish wat we started," she returned, batting her lashes.

"Bitch, and you gonna get it with all my shit? Da fuck outta here," M spat. He snatched the belongings in her clutch, and delivered a chilling body punch that folded her like luggage mid hallway. She melted onto the floor holding her stomach, crying. M slammed the door closed, leaving her silly ass naked and windless.

A few hours later, M walked into the suite where the fellas partied the night away. Everybody was knocked out. There were multiple champagne bottles on the table, blunt fillings, and weed bags everywhere. Ashes and take-out lay on the counters, with loose twenties on the floor. Obviously, it did some raining last night. Shiz had some white bitch sleeping across his lap. Not far from him, another laid naked with a fat ass. And, from the looks of her, she done had more dick than she could handle, with nut stains dried up on her round ass and brunette hair.

"These niggas was wild'n." M had seen enough. He turned on the television as loud as it went, scaring everybody half to death. After running the smutz away, he called room service in to get the team back right for the ride back home.

"Ay M, what da hell time is it anyway?" Shiz spat, as he departed the bathroom from his shower.

"I don't know, like ten sumthin'."

"M, Sideeq was telling me you had some bad ass bitch witchu last night?" Rob asked.

"Yea, where da fuck that bitch go at? I got five right now, right for her," Sideeq chimed, as the forgotten event climbed back into M's head.

"Awww, y'all ain't gonna believe this shit!" M bust out.

"What, don't tell me the bitch had a dick or sumthin'?" Dee interrupted. Everybody became silent, looking at Dee with the 'Fuck on ya mind' face.

"Anyway, I take the bitch back to my room, right..." M unfolded the whole story. They were very attentive, especially to the details about her fuck game. But, by the time M brought about the shocking conclusion, they didn't believe him.

"Get da fuck outta here!" Shiz rejected.

"Wal-lahi, dawg. The bitch tried to jam me."

"Nawww, that bitch ain't try no nut shit like that," Rob said hoping.

"What da bitch say when you caught her?" Bam asked.

"Some bullshit," M replied.

"So, what da fuck you do then, M?!" Shiz wanted to know.

"I took my mutherfuckin' shit back, and hit that bitch with a body shot." The crew fell out laughing. Damn near everybody was on the floor, imagining M folding that bad ass chic in the hallway. When the laughter stopped, Shiz suggested they get the fuck back before next nuns be trying to rob them.

CHAPTER 24

Kelly

I don't know why I always end up falling in love with the stupidest, most inconsiderate, self absorbed assholes the world has to offer. I could've been married by now with children to somebody who has a job that actually pays currency you can get a W-2 form and file a return with. But Noooo, I gotta have some thug ass nigga who don't respect shit I do. If it wasn't about no money or pussy, half the time there was very little to conversate about. Why is it every time you think you've found Mr. Right, it ends up so wrong? Sideeq was a charming prince that rode beautiful white horses, when this circle of madness began. Then, he would pick me up from school and take me to expensive restaurants, lacing me in high end labels. In fact, if it wasn't Louie, Gucci, or Prada, he didn't even want to see me in it. And the sex, whoo! It was incredible. He would fuck me sooo good that my pussy literally cried for him. He'd be sure to take care of me first, eating this pussy until my back stiffened. But now, he be into these really rough quickies, breathing his drunk ass breath all over me, gruntin' and shit, please! So, I be telling him go 'head with that drunk dick shit, a bitch cool. I should've just listened to my mom say, "Stay with Jay-Jay, he's such a nice boy." But, I protested, argued, and debated, thinking Jay was all wrong for me. I would give anything to just have Sideeq be a third of how Jay used to treat me. Don't get me wrong, I love the boy, I really do. But, the nigga is too god damn possessive...Acting like a sista can't go out or nothing, calling me with drama as soon as I step out. Where you at? Who you with? What took you so long to answer?... And, all that bullshit. When the truth be told, he's the one out whoring around. If I had a dollar every time I caught his slick ass running around with some bitch, a chic be paid! Phone numbers in his pockets of some trick was normal, and I always found them in the same place...The wash! He even tried storing female's numbers under guy's names in his cell, so when they call, it looked like a dude on the display screen. A bitch on that, as well. You'd think after I popped him in the head a few times he'd smarten up, but not Sideeq. That's why I be hittin' them pockets like I do. If he can go and stick his dick in every 'lil nasty bitch with a wet spot, then I can literally stay, no fuck that, live in Nieman Marcus. But, after the chinging sound of the register subsided and my fuckin-girl attitude dissolved, all I really wanted was my man to be home and not out screwing God knows who. I'm so tired of this bullshit, the games, and the lies. That's why me and this nigga 'bout to have it out. Now, who in the hell goes to Atlantic City and don't come back all night, except he stranded or spent the night in some ass. I can't wait 'til his lying ass walk up in here, so I can jump all down his shit. That's why I'm sittin' here on this mutherfuckin' couch, so the first thing he sees when he walks up in this bitch is my pissy ass face. I have my joggin' suit and track sneaks on, so I can beat up that ass with accuracy. That was like six something this morning. Since then, I've reduced myself to a tank top and a pair of boy shorts, in wait mode for him to carry his ass home.

Just as I was about to get off the couch to get something to drink from the kitchen, I heard Sideeq unlocking the door to enter. I jumped back on the sofa quickly where I'd sat in my former posture seeking the right look to plaster, so he could not be mistaken I was supa hot!

"Sideeq, where da fuck you've been at?" I knew the answer but I had to ask, plus it sounded good.

"C'mon Kel, you already know," he shot, clearly exhausted and not at all prepared to withstand my verbal assault I had planned for that ass. He closed the door, threw his Roberto Cavalli sport jacket on the sofa, and proceeded walking towards the kitchen.

"Ain't no 'you already know shit'! I see you fly as hell, who you out there tryna impress?" Acknowledging the fact that he looked good as shit, I walked behind him giving my third degree with the wiggling finger waving S's behind his head.

"I told you, go 'head wit all that," he said flat out, after facing me, not feeling my stalking presence.

"Fuck you!" I shouted in his face.

"A'ight," he replied dryly.

"So, you got some pussy last night?" I spat, tracing his footsteps into the kitchen, where he opened the refrigerator to drink from the Minute Maid container.

"Wasn't nobody out fuckin', man!" He spat fiery, between his guzzle.

"I don't believe your lying ass. Let me smell your dick?" That statement brought a choke on the juice he was drinking, as I tugged on his slacks.

"Fuck is you doing, get outta here!" He yelled, smacking my hand away.

"I ain't playing. I wanna smell your dick."

"I know you buggin' now wit all that shit," he came back with, but a bitch wasn't giving up that easy.

"If you ain't got nothing to hide, let me smell your dick then, pussy!"

"That shit ain't gon' prove nothing," he returned, with a stupid ass grin on his face...the one he always made when he thought he was gaming somebody. I tried his slacks again and he refused me.

"Bitch, you must've went da fuck crazy?" He tried to turn it around on me.

"If I did, you done it. I'm tired of your cheating and lying to me, Sideeq, like this shit is cool. You obviously been out fuckin' God knows who, then got the nerve to carry your drunk ass up in here at eleven something this morning. Your stupid ass didn't even have enough class to come in after you finished fuckin' that whore, and you gonna call me da fuck crazy. Yea, you absolutely right, crazy for fuckin' with your stupid ass!" I didn't even realize I was crying, until I felt the tears soaking my feet. I had no idea what to do next, except mug his lying ass...which I did so forcefully, it caused his head to hit the corner of the freezer. That obviously got a rise out of him, which became evident by his hands that went wrapping around my neck, squeezing air from my soul.

"Bitch, what da fuck I tell you 'bout puttin' your hands on me, you ain't the only one with trust issues. Just 'cause a nigga don't say nothing, don't think a nigga stupid and shit. Fuck you doing, coming in the crib two in the morning, not answering your phone and shit like that? Whatchu fuckin' wit, dhat nigga Jay again?!"

"I. Can't. Breath, Sideeq," I said barely, while trying to pry his hands free from around my neck. He let me go, pushing me into the cabinet where I attempted to catch my breath, watching him descend the hallway. Regaining my oxygen level, everything within my slender body screamed: GET THAT, MUTHAFUCKA! Like a bat out of hell, I flew down the hall and boarded his back, sinking my nails into his flesh like a fallen squirrel from a tree, hitting him all in his shit.

"Fuck you, Sideeq...Fuck you, fuck yooouuuu..." I screamed hysterically.

"Bitch is you crazy!" He returned, throwing me through the coffee table. Aww, I know this muthafucka done lost his mind now. He stood there with a scared expression on his face, acknowledging he might've used too much force...Until I gathered myself up armed with the flower vase that I scooped from the end table. I held it above my head, threatening to throw it.

"You throw that vase at me, and I'ma fuck you up for real, watch!" He barked seriously, right before I hummed that shit at lightening speed for his head. It shattered. His face began to bleed, as his legs and eyes became woozy. I attacked, charging him and screaming obscenities. His back hit the wall, causing the portraits of us to fall and shatter. He let out an excruciating sigh, as I began clawing his face out.

"Fuck you, muthafucka. I hatechu, nigga. I hate your muthafuckin' ass!!!" Hoping he understood every word. Next thing I remember was lying on the floor from the stomach punch he put on my ass.

"Crazy ass bitch, what da fuck is wrong witchu?!" He spat, wiping his face. I lay there with no air in my lungs again, but this time, it felt like it was vacuumed out. I was truly fucked up, but Sideeq wasn't done with my ass just yet. He began stomping and kicking me, until everything got really numb. Black and quiet.

When I finally awoke to my absolute fright, I was in the hospital. How long or when I came, I had no idea. All I really remember was us tearing the house up, and Sideeq beating my ass. I can still feel the tenderness in my body from him trashing me. I thought to call my mother, but knew she would say 'I told you so.' My old high school girlfriend came to mind, but I just got finished braggin' to her about him, and now am I to say: "oh yea, he's beating my ass now?" No, I'll pass, but I really need somebody to talk to, and the only person I really had left that would give me some honest advice regardless how he felt, or being biased was Jay. I wondered would he even accept my call? After all I did do him dirty, I guess, who knows? But, I really can use somebody to talk to...Fuck it! I tried him from the hospital phone. With every ring, my heart beat faster and harder. That's when one million thoughts invaded my mind; what to say, how to sound, should I be honest and open, or defensive and deceptive? Before I had a chance to make up my mind, the voicemail picked up. Nothing genuine came to mind, so I just hung up.

While in the bathroom, I reviewed my battle scars. Dreading how the swelling altered my jaw line and lips, it all made me question what was it all for, and how did I let myself succumb to this? Sideeq's trifling ass wasn't worth half the bullshit he was putting me through, I reminded myself. Trembling took to my lips. I tried to hold back the emotional tornado that was spinning inside of me, as sorrow swept over my body. I could no longer fight it, I needed it. It was the only way I could release my frustration. I cried. I cried while knelt in the corner of a hospital bathroom my boyfriend put me in. I cried an eternity. The ringing phone broke my release therapy session, as I rose to answer the unsuspecting caller.

"Hello."

"Yea, somebody just called Jay from this number?" He asked in his handsome voice. The same he used when he would call my name out in ecstasy. My heart froze. My tongue stiffened. And, my brain locked up.

"Helloooo, anybody there?" he asked.

CHAPTER

25

What's Beef?

M, Dee, and Tay relaxed easily in the catering cockpit of the Range Rover, being driven by Rob. Despite the classical luxurious features, the amount of fire power they had along with them could instantly be mistaken for the Hum-vee. They were undoubtedly on their way to Wilmington, DE to carry out Shiz's recent demands. Their murderous appetite felt malnourished. The flame that burned just beyond their chest cavities yearned to be ignited, as Black's existence had been widely extended for bad reason. M's blood boiled, nearing an explosion when he saw the 'Welcome to Wilmington' sign they zoomed pass, as the Range sped on. But, he was at an ease. He wasn't at all new to the murder game. In fact, he killed more than most people could ever suspect, mainly because of his pretty boy charm and handsome facial features. But, what most didn't know was murdering came natural to him. His first murder came by way of strangulation, when he was a juvenile, although it was an accident. It arose something dark within him that made the act nothing in his eyes. With the weed smoke fogging the Jeep, the blunt was in three puff rotation, as everybody began perking up for the nearing excitement.

"Ay M, Dee tell me some bitch tried to rob you a couple of days ago."

"I didn't know Dee had my shit on blast like that," M answered Tay, as he passed M the blunt over his shoulder, so he could focus his attention on loading the A-K that sat on his lap. "But nah, that shit was nothing. A bitch looking for a come-up, bitch crazy if she thought she was coming-up off of me, though," M said, as Tay inserted the clip into the assault rifle. "Bitch rob me, she won't rob nobody else, I promised you," he spat, cocking back the A-K 47, before stuffing it alongside his seat.

"Let me hit that weed," Tay chimed.

"Ay listen to this, Mo. When we get out here, it gotta go right, feel me? None of that Superman shit, Mo. The muthafuckin' police go hard out here, and I'm jive ready to go see my raise and my daughter when we get back, not them see me in the county. So, be cool while we out here, mo, and don't be fixin' to start trippin', ya hear?" Rob spat, mostly for Tay's benefit as this was the first time he rolled out with the crew. They had reached Fourth Street, where Black was serving the city from. The deadly clique parked at an unsuspecting distance, but close enough to get at good look at the activities. The plan was simple, when he poked his head up, blast that shit off. However, if for any reason problems occurred, the team was prepared to alter any strategy they had devised, and were absolutely committed to staying as long as it took to see that fat muthafucka in the box. At first, it didn't look like much was going on. A few hustlers sitting about trappin', talking shit. The rain had put a bit of a damper on the city, as the fiends dragged themselves up and down the block, observed by young hood girlz on their shielded porches. But, under it all was a well thought out system intact. There were look-outs posted on both ends of the block. Children as young as seven pack-ran while they played on the abandoned stoops of the developments. At whistle's notice, they would usher packages in empty juice containers to the corner trappers. But most of all, Black had gunmen on rooftops ready to tear anything to shreds on command. He obviously appreciated his operation and the change he was seeing off it to have guarded it like a first of the month check. Trig's 300 pulled up with the tinted window directly in front of the main development. Some of the trappers gathered around the passenger side, obviously receiving instructions. M combed the binoculars over the car thoroughly, to discover the occupants through the haze atmosphere. Trig jumped out of the driver's side, screaming obscenities as he walked towards the sidewalk, and smacked the shit out of one of the hustlers. M chuckled, seeing the hustler run out his shoes. With the door open, the second figure became a bit more visible. Kind of dark. Chunky. Obviously paid from the way the jewelz draped on his neck. He laughed and his belly jiggled. It was Black!

"Yo, Black sittin' in the fuckin' car, right now," M said heatedly.

"Let's go, let's get this nigga. Let's rock Rob, pull off, dawg!" Tay said, clacking the Mac-11 that sat thirsty on his lap.

"Slow down, Mo! I told you, we gonna tighten him up. Be cool...look," Rob said, as two Jeeps full of Black's goons swerved up beside him, while he was getting out of the car to holla at his team.

"A lot of hatin' going on out this bitch. I gotta start showin' niggas what it's hittin' for, 'til they learn how to shut their fuckin' mouths. I know everybody heard how these niggas movin' around here. So, we not even gonna act like we don't know whassup," Black spat, leaning against the passenger door, rockin' a brown Versace jogging suit with matching Created Recreations, all jeweled up like a rapper. "Muthafuckas think Black slow, let 'em keep thinking that bullshit. Anybody come through here movin' wrong, light that ass up! Niggas ain't stoppin' our flow. They can scream all that outta- town shit if they want to, but Black Ass getting' this guap!!" He growled, letting them know he wasn't going anywhere which is what they wanted to hear. As most of his team started showing weakness, thinking Black would do what the others did after they ate and the beef came. Not Black! Wilmington was a goldmine for him that he wasn't willing to give up for anybody. He would order blood on children and elders before he handed his plate over. M and them could obviously see that Black was faced with some kind of crisis. It was the only justification that could explain the high tension and heavy arms they bore.

"Yo, call Shiz. Let him know that things gonna be a 'lil longer than we expected, and we gonna stay up until we can bring this thing to a close," M ordered Dee in the back.

"You want me to tell him to send a few more niggas through or what?" Dee asked.

"Nah, not yet. Let's see what's good first. Tell him, get at me."

"Fuck man, what da fuck going on! We could've just aired this nigga out...We going to be up this jawn for like a month chasing this nut ass nigga!" M knew Tay was speaking from his emotions, so he let his comments slide. He wanted Black, too, but experience made him wait for a better opportunity.

CHAPTER

26

You Should Let Me Love You

The rain poured heavily over the Philadelphia area as the clouds coated the city, hiding the sun's splendor. Kelly closed the door of her 3-series Sideeq had bought her. She stared at the house she had only visited twice while Jay and she were together. Gathering her nerve, she proceeded up the cobblestone walk to face her troubled past. Jay was lying on the couch watching Belly on the big screen, when he heard the doorbell. Reluctantly, he carried himself to the door to answer its occupant. At first, it didn't seem like anybody was there, as the hooded, full length raincoat Kelly was wearing was white and blended in with the giant columns supporting the porch. He opened the door for a closer view.

"What's up? Can I help you?" He asked. She said nothing under the hooded coat. "Sis, you a'ight?" He spat, leaning forward to see her identity. Kelly flipped back the hood and Jay jumped back, shocked to see this was Kelly at his door. After so many unanswered phone calls, e-mails, and texts, she was standing before him, soaked in the lord's tears. He was confused. Baffled. At a loss for words. There was plenty that needed to be said, thousands of things that required an explanation, but only one that was of any real importance to him at this point.

"What happened to your face, Kelly?" He asked, ushering her in out of the rain. Again, she said nothing, as he canvassed thoroughly her injured face, while Kelly fumbled with her fingers.

"Sorry Jay. I'm…I'm sorryyy," she squeaked, as the tears began washing over her unblemished complexion.

"It's cool Kel, chill. Calm down," he said removing the tears from her face. Kelly sniffled back her emotions, pondering if she should offer the explanation behind her coming and the reason for her injuries. But, before she could find the words to put to him, he began unbuttoning her raincoat, which revealed her nudity. She had nothing on except her bra and boy shorts, which inadequately covered her chiseled body. Jay was surprised to find Kelly had no clothes on. So many unanswered questions and feelings filled the air. There was no room left to squeeze anymore in, so they did what anybody else would've done…Release. Jay began kissing Kelly's lips hungrily, as she peeled out of her raincoat. She returned his intensity, while she stripped him from his clothing, unbreaking the lip lock. He fucked Kelly so good on his parent's living room floor that she plucked patches out of the plush carpeting. In fact, it was the best sex they had ever had. She opened her legs as wide as she could to let Jay all the way in. If she could've, she would've let him into her soul, because at that moment…She needed him. She missed Jay's loving and soft touch. She almost forgot what it felt like to be loved and made love to. He pushed deeply into Kelly, exploring freely the dripping wet shot that used to be his. They kissed what seemed like an eternity, as Kelly's swollen pussy lips massaged Jay's manhood to a nearing explosion.

"Jay. Ooh baby, I missed you," she groaned, feeling his tool sliding within.

"Yea baby, I missed you, too," he replied, fighting back the nut.

"Jay," she purred. "You feel so good, cum in me, daddy. Don't stop, please..." she moaned. "It's yours, baby, it's yours to have." Jay had never heard her make such a request before. It spun him. She was where he always wanted her to be, willing to lock in with him. Kelly rolled Jay over to straddle him. Neither of them could believe they were actually fucking, and for it to be square in his Bible-quoting mother's living room, was another level in itself. Jay fondled Kelly's firm breasts while her ass cheeks slapped against his thighs. He pulled on her shoulders as his back tightened.

"Yes, Jay," she moaned. His teeth clenched.

"Ooh, it feels so good," she encouraged. His stomach tingled.

"Give it to me, Jay. It's your pussy." He came. She kissed all over Jay's face while sitting upon him, liberated from the depression of Sideeq's concentration camp she had enrolled in. Jay had helped her in more ways than he could imagine. She wondered what the hell she saw in Sideeq to have stuck around for that long. Jay was her love, her Adam, her wings, and her baby. She wanted to make the things right that she had messed up.

$ $ $ $ $

While Kelly was letting Jay shoot his seed of life in her, Sideeq was pulling up to her mother's house in West Oak Lane. He couldn't believe after all he did for her, she'd dip out on him like that. He didn't mean to put her in the hospital. Dhat shit was an accident, he thought to himself. How was he to know that she wasn't drinking enough fluids? Plus, she did hit me first, he reminded himself. Kelly's mom never liked Sideeq. She felt like the boy was too God damn possessive, demanding, and controlling. He was the kind of person that should be left where he was found…The streets. Even though Ms. Trina knew her daughter was making a mistake dealing with Sideeq and a far greater one for living with his ass, she chose to stay out of their relationship, after Kelly cursed her out for butting in. Since then, she decided not to breathe a word concerning Sideeq, as long as he stayed away from her house. If for any unjustifiable reason, he appeared, all bets were off. Sideeq dreadingly knocked on the door of Ms. Trina's 17th Street row home at the top of the block. It was just as he remembered it during his last visit months ago. The gated house's grass was clipped and steps swept, children's toys laid out in the yard by her grandchildren. The rain came to a pour, when she opened the front door to see Sideeq standing on her steps.

"How you doing, Ms. Trina? You know I hate to bother you…" he began, as she folded her arms across her chest disbelieving.

"…But, Kelly was in the hospital for some minor…"

"Hospital!" She interjected, pitching her voice.

"Nah, she cool, it's nothing to worry about. She got out today, and I was just wondering if you've seen her?"

"You her man, and you don't know where she at? Something don't sound right with that. But no, I haven't seen her. Did you call her cell phone?" She snapped.

"Well I tried, but I think she lost it. That's why she's not answering it," he gamed.

"Umm-hmmm," she chimed unconvinced. "Sound to me like she don't want to be bothered. And furthermore, didn't I tell you 'bout coming around here anyway! This ain't no-Kelly-house. So, you got no business coming around here looking for her. When she here, then it's to visit her family, not to be stalked by some street gangster."

"Ms. Trina, all I wanted..."

"It don't matter what you wanted! It's no surprise, me and you got a problem, and I done told you months ago DON'T COME PAST HERE. You deal with Kelly on your time. Now, I done my best not to interfere in y'all's relationship. I told Kelly, as long as you don't put your hands on her, I got nothing to say. I guess that wasn't good enough, huh?" Ms. Trina twisted her lips.

"Ms. Trina, I'm out here in the rain, soaking and suckin' in all your abuse, and I haven't said a word of disrespect. My whole thang is just to see if Kelly was here, or if you've seen her to let her know I'm worried. Everything else is extra."

"Well, let me tell you my whole thang. That girl follows you all over this city doing whatever it is your heart desires. You even somehow got her to drop out of school that me and my man paid for. So, that tells me, if you ain't somehow mixed up in this 'lil hospital spiel, you wouldn't have to worry about finding her. She'd be all up under your ass, where she's been for the last few months. With that being said, stay away from my God damn house! And, don't let me find out you put your hands on MY MUTHAFUCKIN' DAUGHTER. You have a good day, BYE!!" She slammed the door in his face. Sideeq shook his head, as he skipped down the steps to his S-type. "Fuckin' nut ass bitch," he slurred to himself, entering his wheel.

After two weeks, Kelly was still up under Jay in his mother's house. She told nobody about her whereabouts or her current affairs. Jay enjoyed every moment of Kelly's presence, loving her silly comments, hood demeanor, and aggressive sexual appetite. The two would stay up late watching throw-back gangster movies, as they snuggled on the sofa, snacking and trading glances of 'I love you's'. The night escapades would always end with Kelly riding Jay until his cum coated her insides. With Jay's parents out of town, Kelly was able to move freely throughout the exceptionally clean abode. She would wake before sunrise and furnish Jay a complete breakfast, to which she would serve him while in bed. They would play tag, hide 'n go seek, and charades until they ended up conversating themselves to sleep. They had successfully rekindled what they once shared. Kelly felt like Jay was the perfect person to grow old and have kids with. She knew she could trust him and he would bring his heart to her, whereas Sideeq would probably move on to whuppin' her ass regularly and bring her some kind of disease. Regardless of how happy she was playing house with Jay, she knew that it wouldn't last forever, and she would have to face Sideeq again sooner or later. The doorbell rang while Jay and Kelly laid on his bed talking about growing old.

"I'll get it, Kelly said, jumping off the bed in Jay's t-shirt, draping her like window curtains. She arrived at the door and opened it.

"Hi ma'am. U. P. S., we have a delivery. Can you sign here, please?"

"Sure. Jay, it's a package, I'ma sign for it, okay?!" She hollered in to him. The delivery guy gave her the box addressed to Jarell Mccoy. Kelly brought it in to Jay, shaking it and trying to figure out the contents.

"Whatchu got?" Jay asked.

"I don't know, it's for you."

"Well, give it to me, nosy."

"Whatever," she spat, sucking her teeth. Jay opened it, revealing his order from the web for the money mission. To Kelly, it looked like a bunch of weird shit. So, she decided not to comment, being as though nothing in the box read Gucci, Prada, or Chanel, which meant it couldn't have been for her in her mind. Kelly spun off, leaving Jay to play with his package. On the way to the kitchen, she happened to pass her cell phone sitting on a shelf in the main foyer. She had almost forgotten what it looked like, or in fact that she had it along with her. Curiosity bit Kelly's attention so she cut it on, revealing 163 missed calls and 42 voicemail alerts. She was shocked...Most of them were from Sideeq. She hesitated to replay the messages, fearing what he had left and acknowledging Sideeq wasn't to be fucked with. At first, the messages were as she expected, containing a bunch of threats, slanders, and obscenities, but then they got sweet, very sweet. He was hurt and he told her he loved her and wanted to marry her. She even thought she heard a sniffle or two. Her heart softened as the words played. He apologized, promised, and regretted it all. He wanted her to just call and say she was okay so he'd be able to finally get some rest. Kelly's eyes began to sting, as she fought back the emotion that was welling her lids. Jay's sudden grasp around her waist from behind untangled the emotions that dangled from her lash, causing it to tumble onto her mahogany cheek as she closed the flip to her cell.

"Who was that, baby?" Jay asked, hugging her from behind.

"Nobody, love, I was just checking my messages," she sang quickly, wiping her tears before he noticed.

"Anybody I know, ma?"

"Nah, a bunch of nothing." She stared off distantly, feeling confused.

"A'ight, well I got a surprise for you."

"What surprise?" She chimed.

"C'mon, I'ma show you." Jay led Kelly by hand to the third floor, a place she had never seen before. As they proceeded up the steps, it got darker. Kelly had to stick her hand out to make sure she wouldn't walk into Jay accidently, while they traversed the hallway. He pushed opened the door, and a heavenly glow burst into the hall. The room was all white, with handsome Italian sculptures affixed to the wall, and deep red rose petals leading within. It was a luxurious bathroom. Jay had filled the jacuzzi with warm milk and pink chocolate kisses. The soft glow came from the multiple candles lighted around the quarters, giving off a therapeutic apple cinnamon aroma. Jay turned towards her, and then backed in causing Kelly to inch forward, enjoying her expression while holding her hand, as if they were performing the waltz. Kelly was breathless. Jay had outdone himself and she couldn't believe it was she who had the honor of the spoilage.

"Jay, how did…" He shhhh'ed her. "But, when did you have…" Jay placed his finger over her succulent lips, then undressed her. After pulling her from his t-shirt, he stared inching over her perfect frame. She blushed. Knowing Jay was combing her thoroughly struck her nervousness. Overlooking her mango sized suckable breasts, chiseled stomach, unblemished hips, thighs that defined her perfect figure, sculpted legs, and shaven sugar gate, his eyes went back and forth until they met hers again, pleased and satisfied. He entered Kelly into the Jacuzzi, after stripping from his clothes to join her. Jay took his place behind her in the warm milk, as the sweetened fluids danced about their skin. He began sensually massaging Kelly's shoulder, as her wet hair went wrapping alongside of her slender neck. Jay inserted his tongue slowly into Kelly's ear, then ran it down her nape. She moaned. Kelly leaned forward so her ass stuck right in Jay's face; round, chocolaty, and dripping. Jay smushed his face into Kelly's pussy as she gasped. His tongue spun circles in her sugar walls, hitting Kelly's clit in a sexual motion.

"Ooh Jay, yea, eat my pussy up, daddy," Kelly groaned. Jay's tongue slivered around Kelly's insides, until his face was covered in her juices. She didn't have the fattest ass, but she knew how to arch her back correctly to create the illusion. Gently he pulled her lips apart with his fingers, then lightly flickered his tongue across her clit. Feeling it give back, he did it again, but this time faster.

"Ooh shit, Jay! I'm 'bout to cum," she screamed. He began jabbing his two fingers in and out of Kelly's love until she let out his name, "Jay". She was nearing an explosion and Jay knew it, so he sucked and licked her spot until she released her own supply of dairy. Jay watched Kelly step from the shower. He helped robe her up, then she took a seat on his lap in the scented bathroom, smearing Cucumber Melon lotion over her legs. Jay eyed the bruises still visible on her face and neck.

"Kelly."

"Yes."

"I'm still waiting for an explanation."

"Concerning?" She played dumb.

"You know what I'm talkin about." She closed the cap to the lotion agitated, exposing that this conversation was one she wanted to avoid. But, she knew Jay wouldn't let it go, and she felt she owed him at least the truth after all the kindness he had displayed in their relationship.

"Jay. I don't even know where to start from," she chimed, eyes becoming watery.

"How 'bout you start with your face," he laid out. She paused.

"The guy you were fighting back at Cheyney punched me." Jay became upset instantly.

"That's why your face looks like that?'

"Yes Jay. He put me in the hospital."

"And, that's the kind of shit you want for your life?" He questioned heatedly.

"No, not at all. I didn't think he'd do that to me. He's not the same person he was, Jay...I'm scared. I don't know what he might do next," she cried, tucking her head into Jay's neck while he wrapped his arms around her to console.

"Damn Kelly, you gotta stop fucking with those type dudes. Niggas like that ain't no good for you," he spat.

"I know, I know Jay. I love you, baby."

"I love you, too," he chimed, kissing her forehead.

"These bitches is crazy, dawg. You take them in, clothe them, make sure they got money, a name, good dick, and they still be on that bullshit, feel me?" Sideeq said to Spank, coasting his dark green Infinity truck down Snyder Ave., while Sideeq puffed on the blunt, elevating his mind.

"That's why I don't take these bitches personal, Deeq," Spank replied.

"I feel you, but I'ma be real; I expected a lot more from this 'lil bitch. I raised her. She know this some bullshit," he said, lowering the window to knock the ashes from the blunt. Spank knew his man was hurt regardless of how much he down-played it. He knew how much Sideeq loved her and to what extent he invested in her. So, he decided to drop a little game he'd learned from his stalking days. Plus, they were in the middle of pulling off the biggest stick of their lives and everybody's minds needed to stay clear.

" 'Deeq, do you think Kelly got her cell phone on her?"

"I'm not sure, but yea, she probably got that shit on her."

"Then, all you gotta do is track her GPS. Call the company and say you lost your horn 'n shit, and you trying to find it. It's in your name, right? So, they gonna move right out on it."

"Straight up?" Sideeq asked.

"Straight up, 'Deeq. That's what it is...So, whassup wit the Shiz thang? I know that nigga gotta be open by now."

"Shit goin' right, niggas is feelin' me. I'm just waiting on the right moment to make a move. It's coming though, it's definitely coming. I gotta keep my eyes on his left hand man, M. This nigga a problem, dawg. Somehow, someway, I gotta get this lame out the way. The rest of them..." (sigh) Sideeq waved them off.

"...It ain't shit, for real. Whassup wit Pig, he get that info yet? We need Coop on point, and who da fuck is Black?!"

"I don't know, but I'ma check on it," Spank chimed.

"GPS, huh?" Sideeq asked, eyeing his man.

"Yea, GPS," he said turning on Broad Street.

"Jay, I don't want none of that corny ass Chinese food from up this way. You don't feel like driving up Ogontz? They got some banging ass wings up there," Kelly asked while Jay shuffled through the armoire in search of the iron his cousin left there.

"A'ight, I'll go there, but I want some head when I get back," he spat, as Kelly slid off the bed and up Jay's back.

"If you go get my food, I'll give you some thing better than that," she sang, re-climbing the bed so Jay could get a good view of her ass she tooted up.

"Word?" Jay asked lustfully.

"Umm-hmm," she shook her head while licking her lips. On the ride over, Jay thought about Kelly. He realized that she did play him out back at school with Sideeq, but he loved her. They had four years together and she knew she had made a huge mistake leaving him for Sideeq. At the end of the day, his math was: she was a bad ass jawn with good sex and the woman he planned to marry. On another level, he was heated that Sideeq put his hands on her like that, let alone stole her from him. And, to top it all off, the ass whuppin' he served Jay was still very fresh in his mind.

"This muthafucka is crazy, running around here doing whatever the fuck he wanna do. These city niggas think too much of themselves. They got guns, we got guns, too. Niggas gonna stop acting like 'I'm a bitch, Straight up!" After getting Kelly's food on Ogontz Ave., Jay proceeded back to the car where he was approached by three highschoolers. They asked him for the time, which Jay obliged them not sensing anything wrong. When he turned to get into the car, one of the three snatched the bag of Chinese food, as the other waved the .38 special in his face.

"Go ahead, I dare you to make a move, pussy. I'll blow your muthafuckin' face off with this jawn," the youngen spat, as Jay stared on from behind the barrel.

"Shoot dis nigga pockets, dawg," the gunman ordered. Jay was motionless, while the youngens rummaged through his pockets taking him for a few hundreds and much of his manhood.

"You even think about movin', dawg, I'ma air you da fuck out!" The gunman spat, as the trio ran off. Jay was piping hot watching them run off with not only his money and Kelly's food, but his pride as well. A wave of coldness brushed over him. Jay pulled the .50 caliber from his waist which the crooks neglected to check, and let the heavy cannon off, bringing the Fourth a little sooner this year. The deadly rain tumbled the crook onto the walk. Jay ran up on them and kicked the gunman in the ass thunderously. Then, in a fit of rage and resentment, shot him at point blank range, CRACK, CRACK, CRACK, CRACK, POP!!! He hadn't heard nor seen anything around him until a little girl screamed at the bloody massacre. He panicked. At that point, he realized what he'd done, how far out of character he was, and life in prison without the possibility of parole. He broke for the car, leaving shorty's co-conspirators moaning in agony. He ran damn near every light until he reached his house. His heart beat a million times per second. Nervously locking the door behind him, he gathered his thoughts for a millisecond before Kelly's voice broke his mathematics.

"C'mon Jay. Hurry up, I'm hungry...and I hope you ordered your own," she bellowed from the bedroom. Jay came darting in, slamming the door behind him. His breathing was heavy and face sweaty. Kelly almost jumped out of her skin at the sound of the closing door. She breathed his name for reassurance, but Jay was sitting propped against the door with hands draped over his face.

"Jay, what happened? Where's the food?" She came to his aid, kneeling just inches from him. She could tell he was weeping. A siren aired passed causing him to tense up. Kelly looked on puzzled, wondering what could've happened.

"Jay, talk to me. What da hell is going on?" She questioned. He looked up at her and she began cleansing his face. Kelly inattentively looked at her hands and noticed blood smeared on them. Jay, this is blood on your face. Why is there blood on your face? You scaring me."

"You don't understand, Kelly. I fucked up. I fucked up; I went too far, ma. I wasn't thinking. It just happened." It was clear to Kelly he was hysterical, and it scared her seeing him like that. She needed to calm him down so they could think things through. It was awkward and weird, but she didn't know what else to do. So, she did what any bad chic with a sex game on one thousand would do, she swallowed him whole until his toes curled up, sending him napping away. Three in the morning, Kelly woke up and noticed Jay had gotten up. She found him in the basement typing fiercely on the computer. She circled the chair to massage his back.

"Hey baby," she purred.

"Whassup?" He replied overlooking news reports from the local broadcasters, trying to see what was the buzz.

"Jay...What's this all about?" She wanted to know the truth and he knew that. He inhaled deeply, then let Kelly in on his dark secret, fearing she'd think he was some kind of monster. But Kelly was way tougher than Jay knew of. She sucked her teeth.

"Is that what happened? That's what those 'lil niggas get then. They ain't have no business tryna rob you anyway. You shoulda shot their asses. Muthafuckas always trying some nut shit." Jay smiled, relieved that Kelly was so hood. Moreso than that, she helped him see this street shit wasn't really about nothing. Actually, it was quite simple; You violate, you get popped!

It took a week for Sideeq to get around to it, but finally he had a location on Kelly's cell phone. And, today was free enough for him to go get his chic back. He had no idea the location he was heading to was Jay's. Kelly and Jay were dressed to kill when they exited the house to catch dinner and a movie. The past few weeks had been so life changing for the both of them. Kelly finally had her head on straight, acknowledging Jay was her man for life and she was willing to devote to him. Jay, on the other hand, discovered what Kelly liked in the bedroom, and the type of man you needed to be in order for Kelly to feel safe on your arm. They were in love. When Jay pulled off, he could've sworn he had seen that G.S. Lexus sitting on the corner before, but he brushed it off as 'buggin' while he proceeded down the suburban street. Kelly played with the radio until she found her jam by Jodeci:

> *"You look so sexy, you really turn me on, blow my mind everytime, I see your face girl."*

"Ooh Jay, remember this at the school dance?" She chimed.

"How can I not? You gave me some of them drawers that night," he teased. She sucked her teeth.

"What-ever," she chuckled. "I only gave you some because you promised to do my history report."

"Then that will make you a book hoe," he joked.

"Ohh, ya know you 'bout to get hurt, punk," she countered.

Sideeq was kettled hot seeing Kelly with Jay.

"Not that nigga." The absolute last nigga Sideeq wanted to see Kelly with was that sucka ass Jay. He waited for the most opportune time to make his move. Kelly thought about when she went to get her clothes from her mother's house. Mom informed her that Sideeq had come past there looking for her, and she got cussed out.

For Sideeq to go by there, he must've been in bad shape and that couldn't be good at all.

"Whatchu thinking about, baby?" Jay asked as they stopped at the light.

"Nothing. I don't know why it keeps raining so much. I swear it's been raining all week long," she returned, eluding his question. The screeching G.S. pulled up diagonally in front of them blocking the intersection. Kelly's throat dropped into her belly. It was Sideeq. She and Jay watched the rain fall on him as it glistened from the blinding headlights of Jay's Jeep Cherokee, while he walked towards the passenger side with his gun out. Jay began shuffling items around on the floor in search of his .50 caliber that he had placed under the seat. Sideeq tried the door, but it was locked.

"You better open this muthafuckin' door!"

"What, Sideeq?! Leave me alone. I don't wanna fuck wit you no more!"

"I'ma say it one more time. Open this muthafuckin' door before I shoot this bitch open," his voice boomed. Kelly glanced over at Jay who was reaching under the seat. She loved him and didn't want to see him get hurt, so she had no other choice but to open the door. Sideeq snatched her by one hand and slammed her against the car.

"What the fuck is wrong witchu, running around here wit this nigga?!"

"Damn that, Sideeq. You don't know how to treat me, puttin' your muthafuckin' hands on me like some rag doll!"

"Kelly, you hit me first. What was I supposed to do? This some bullshit and you know it."

"Ain't no fuckin' bullshit, you hurt me!!!"

"I'm sorry, damn! What da fuck do you want me to do? And, why are we standing out here arguing in the rain. I love you, bitch. Let's go home."

"Uhn-unh, I ain't going nowhere with you. You don't know how to treat me and I'm tired of your bullshit."

"And, this nigga do? I betchu if I pop his ass, you'll cool da fuck out." Sideeq raised the gun as if to shoot Jay. Kelly screamed.

"Nooo. Don't hurt him!" and began crying.

"Well, get da fuck in the car," he yelled. He had won. Being ushered by her arm to the G.S., Jay began kicking himself in the ass for not having the tool ready while he continued to search over the front seat onto the rear floor. He found it and chambered the first round, as Kelly was being stuffed into the whip. She stopped to have one last look at Jay. But, what she found was a demonic frown on a figure as he hung out the window pointing the .50 caliber at Sideeq, while the raindrops beaded down his chiseled line-up. He fired. CLICK! She jumped.

"What? I told you, that's my word. I won't ever hitchu again," Sideeq spat, unaware of the real reason that caused her to flinch. Jay sat back in his seat eyeing the bullet that jammed in the chamber. Kelly stared on intensely from the car. She loved Jay but knew he was out of his league. What was he trying to do? she questioned herself, knowing that had Sideeq seen him, he would've killed Jay. Sideeq passed in front of Jay's Jeep, hurling pussy's & sucka ass nigga's at him. He entered the Lexus and peeled with Kelly for the second time. But, this time Jay didn't loose everything. In fact, he found something...His heart! If that cannon hadn't jammed, without fear, Jay would've popped Sideeq and he knew that.

CHAPTER

27

What It's Hittin' For

Shiz watched his dick slide in and out of Mona as she rode him backwards on his king size bed. He smacked her bodacious ass and squeezed it deeply. Mona was Shiz's lawyer for as long as he could remember, and he'd been wanting to fuck her for an equal duration. The craziest thing is, after all the waiting, chasing, and gaming for this very moment, the pussy was trash to him. She, however, enjoyed every inch of Shiz's manhood.

"Ooh, Sean! Fuck me harder, baby. Fuck me, Sean," she moaned slapping her ass cheeks against his thighs. Shiz reached for the lit spliff on the nightstand and inhaled deeply while Mona was nearing her climax. It really didn't matter to Shiz if the pussy was good or not. He just wanted to lock her in, in case something serious began brewing against him from the Feds. As Shiz observed her pussy lips stretch around his wet dick, his mind drifted to sewing shit up in the city and then opening up a production company. He pondered what it might mean to lock the city down. The blood loss could be unmeasureable. Niggas had been eating in the city forever; more importantly, had been killing muthafuckas for talking like they wanted to expand. At this time, he only had a side portion of North Philadelphia. He knew in order to pull off some shit like that, he first needed a nice ass connect and a sick ass team that was able to move buildings. After some more thought, he realized he was high and talking out of his ass. Greedy shit like that was the thing to get niggas killed in the city. "Fuck it," he dismissed the idea, blowing the weed smoke on Mona's ass.

"I'm cumming, baby. Daddy, fuck me. Fuck me, daddy!" She let out, feeling Shiz wrap his hands around her wavy hair causing her to lean back for more friction to her clit from his drilling cock. The poles of Shiz's king size bed were surround sound that not only aired the TV, radio, and intercom, but also the telephone, which was ringing now. The TV displayed the number boldly, but Shiz didn't recognize it.

"Salaamu Alaykum, Shiz. This is Aziz. Call me when you get in at this number," the messenger bellowed bearing an Arabic accent. The sound of Aziz's voice instantly registered with Shiz. He damn near pushed Mona onto the floor in chase of the receiver.

"Yo, yo, yo," Shiz spat quickly before he hung up.

"Shiz! Salaamu Alaykum." He sounded energetic.

"Wa Alaykum Salaam, what's up, man?" He said sitting up.

"Not much. Did I catch you at a bad time?" Aziz asked.

"Nah, not at all," he said, eyeing an upset Mona scrambling for her clothes. "Why da fuck you ain't hit me back all them times I was calling your phone?" Shiz asked heatedly.

"Shiz my man, I was out of the country. But, that's water under the bridge. I got something big for you and I mean big. But, you're gonna have to fly down to discuss it."

"How soon?"

"This week. The plans are already made. All you gotta do is come. Don't blow it, my friend. This could be life changing," Aziz chimed as a beautiful maiden brought him a cold drink. "Look, I got some affairs to attend to, so I'll catch you when you fly down. Take care, my friend."

"A'ight, I'll get up," Shiz replied. That was the phone call Shiz would've died to receive. Aziz was his connect from Jacksonville that used to serve him at fifteen a bird. Now that he was popping weight, that price was even more needed. But, he couldn't put a finger on why Aziz wanted him to fly down to discuss something they were already in bed with. His daydream was broken by hearing the door slam.

"Shit!" He ran to the hall to catch a flaming hot Mona who was waiting for the elevator, amazed how Shiz had played her. She reminded him of Ashanti when she was upset.

"Mona, my bad. Don't rollout on me, ma," he sang allowing his plea to marinate.

"Answer one question for me," she shot coldly with a tight face. "You've been chasing me for years. I finally decided to spend some time with you and you treat me like this? I really think I may have made a mistake, Sean."

"Don't say that, Mona. You know how I feel about you and how important you are to me. That phone call, I've been waiting for it for three months! I promise if you come back in, no interruptions until morning, and I'll..." Shiz whispered in her ear some freaky shit that caused Mona to blush and push out a chuckle.

"Boy, you too much," she smiled. "I'm serious, Sean. I'm not going to have you playing with my emotions." Her voice became firm and her eyes intense.

"I promise," Shiz said, pledging his hand over his heart. They returned where the two went at it like horny highschoolers until the wee hours of the morning, fucking and sucking until their depleted bodies fell slumped onto the bed.

Shiz's CLS 500 pulled up to the Cumberland Street projects. He grabbed the iron from beneath his seat and ejected the whip. Business was good in the projects. The fiends poured in to copp up.

"We ain't gotta put it on blast, y'all know where da butter at!" rang off as he passed the scramblers. He had a full agenda today. Shit had to be right in the city before he left to meet up with the connect. And, since M was out on business and he planned to take Bam with him O.T., he had to personally see to it his investments were on point before he peeled. He entered Apt. 403 on the fourth floor, finding a few chics bagging up, T-lo, and his man, Keem in the kitchen busting a grub.

"Shizzy Wiz, whassup nigga?" T-lo asked partaking his meal.

"Shit...You got that bread ready, pimp?" T-lo gave Keem the nod to go get the money from the back room.

"What's up with them 'lil niggas out front trappin'?"

"Who, Diz and them? You gotta be talking about them, they the only niggas Tay put out there."

"Listen, tell them 'lil niggas to pipe that down, we don't need no more attention on these projects that ain't already on it. So, keep these bols cool, dawg."

"A'ight, I'll let them know when I go down," T-lo spat.

"And, hit Bam to tell him to meet me out front in a half hour." Keem re-entered the kitchen with two shopping bags full of money. Shiz sat at the table and began loading the counter with the dope money. T-lo ushered the girls into the back, so Shiz could handle business without the birds stalking his count.

"Better yet, make that an hour and a half," Shiz chimed overlooking the huge stacks of currency.

"Seven hundred nineteen thousand, four hundred and fifty two!" Shiz sang; one blunt, three wine coolers, and 120 minutes later. He bagged the bread up, made sure T-lo was good, and then exited the building to the awaiting Bam posted out front with the Mac-90. The two entered Shiz's CLS and slid towards Broad Street, watching the rearview camera Shiz had installed. Safety was always a question to them in this business, and you could never be too safe when you were flipping the kind of bread dreams are built on.

"Bam, whassup wit your 'lil ass?" Shiz spat accelerating the CLS engine.

"Ain't nothing Shiz, tryna keep these niggas in line," Bam replied.

"How the block doing?"

"We doin' our number, but to be honest, I'm tryna see more," Bam said, hoping Shiz was ready to give.

"Youngen, ya 'lil ass only twenty. What da hell is the rush?! You seeing more dough then niggas twice your age. You can't say that you didn't get hit off sumthin' nice from that Markease shit. And, don't think I didn't see that muthafuckin' cranberry Range Rover you just copped." Bam started laughing knowing that Shiz wouldn't stop putting his success on blast until he realized he was good.

"Fuck all this street shit, dawg. Get yourself a 'lil bitch and fall back. I don't wantchu really lovin' these streets like that anyway. Love the money nigga, not what comes with it."

"I got a 'lil chic, Shiz. She hard-headed but I fucks wit her."

"See, that's the fly shit I be talkin bout. You gotta have a balance. Get money but live life, and never forget to give back, ya heard me?

But, as them bitches is concerned, never let them know how you movin'. Bitches are made to be in the crib doing what chics do in the house. So don't ever bring your street shit to the crib or her lap. Pussy get niggas locked and murked, dawg." Bam soaked up the wisdom his old head was dropping. He really appreciated the game Shiz had been dropping over the years, and the position of block lieutenant was definitely a bump up. So, if Shiz said be patient, then he was willing to be patient.

"So, who this 'lil chic you fuckin' wit? What's her name?"

"Some 'lil jawn named Shontay, back East Oak Lane."

"She ain't got no kids?"

"Yea, one. Matter of fact, I just had to smack her baby daddy for sum nut shit the other week. It ain't nothing though; next time it happens I'ma air 'em out…"

> *"But on the strength of you and that's your kid daddy, I ain't gon' send 'em on his way, put 'em up in that big Caddy, but let 'em know."*

Bam rapped the lyrics of DMX and Shiz laughed noticing the words.

"Yeah, you better make sure that chic ain't around if it go down like that, ya heard?" Shiz spat, cutting the A.C. off while Bam channel surfed on Shiz's in-dash TV, satisfied nobody was following them.

"Dig, the only reason I scooped you from the block is I got a major trip coming up with a connect, and I want you to fly down with me." Bam had been around Shiz since sixteen and he had yet to meet one of his connects. So, the invitation was an honor that he wasn't willing to pass up for anything. Shiz knew the youngen would be feeling the invite and this was a another opportunity to sharpen his game by seeing how business is orchestrated; because at the end of the day shiz could see Bam running his own shit and dealing with connects was the type of shit a nigga needed to be seasoned on.

"That's what it is. When we leaving, dawg?" Bam said excitedly.

"In three days. So, for the next couple of days, I want you to get those other six birds cooked up and all the money out from 11th Street, and bring it to my crib up Media. As for that shit on 7th Street, that stay down there, a'ight?"

"No doubt, yo." Shiz pulled the CLS over in front of the Chinese store so Bam could grab something to drink before they hopped on the freeway. Bam jumped out to purchase their sodas. On the way back out, he brushed past three males coming in and one gave him a bitter stare-down before he entered the CLS.

"Yo, where that muthafuckin' chopper at?" Bam spat, searching for the Mac-90 he had left on the floor.

"Why, whassup youngen?"

"Remember the nigga I was tellin' you I had to smack? This nigga acting like he wants some trouble. Where that jawn at?!"

"I put it in the back ..." Shiz spat as Bam scrambled to find the chopper over the seat. "That's crazy, 'lil niggas don't even do homework no more; just runnin' all up in shit, not knowing who they fucking wit or nothing," Shiz said coolly, loading Jay Z's Blueprint into the player as Bam cocked back the Mac-90, gearing to launch his assault. Fortunately for them, a squad car pulled to the corner, parked, and began enjoying lunch there.

"Woe, woe, woe, dawg. This gonna have to wait for another time," Shiz shot, seeing the police on sight. Bam observed what Shiz saw and reluctantly packed the Mac-90 back up.

"Dhat pussy lucky! God must love that nigga," he spat. Shiz pulled off, pondering the low value life carries, and as if nothing happened, he asked,

"Whassup with Dee? How my 'lil nigga movin'?"

"He good, holdin' shit down. He called me last night talkin' 'bout some hoe he met out Delaware," Bam chimed looking out the side view mirror.

"That's how he doing his?" Shiz chimed, switching the monitor back to rearview camera as they floated down Old York Road.

"Yea, that's how he doing his," he parroted.

"Well, when he get back, I wanna take y'all 'lil niggas out Miami and show y'all sumthin'. You ain't seen no bitches until you seen some Miami bitches, dawg." Shiz had noticed a few lights back a grey Bonneville picked up its tail as he swerved in and out of lanes.

"I know I ain't trippin'. Look at this shit," sang Shiz, pointing to the car on the monitor at a three-car distance. Bam stared at the vehicle mimicking their motion on the monitor.

"What da fuck is these niggas following us?" He asked picking the Mac from the floor. Shiz maneuvered the Benz to allow a few cars to pass them, so the Bonneville was directly behind them. This way, they could get a clearer look at the figures within.

"Bam, look and see who da fuck is this followin' us," Shiz chimed. Bam studied the monitor at the four figures trailing them. Unable to make out who they were, he zoomed the camera in revealing Shontay's baby daddy and his goons that were rolling with him at the store were the tags. He was hot!

"Shiz, I don't believe this dawg. This nut ass bol Dink, the one following us!"

"Dink! Who da fuck is that?"

"The bitch baby father, dawg. I'ma air this nigga out, yo!" Bam said heatedly, cocking back the Mac-90, with intentions to jump out and swiss cheese the following goons.

"Nah, chill Bam. I got these 'lil niggas. Wait 'til I tell you to come through the roof.'

"Shiz, you gonna let these nigga squeeze on us??" Bam asked shockingly.

"Fuck I look like, slow down youngen," he chimed. Shiz turned off of Old York onto Rockland Street and they followed, just as he expected. He double-parked on the quiet residential block, and they swerved up, just as he expected. They opened fire on the tinted CLS. Bam ducked down in the seat while a barrage of bullets ping-panged off the bulletproof Benz. Shiz looked at Bam with a silly look.

"Get up youngen...You trippin'," he sang with a chuckle. Bam saw that Shiz wasn't even blinking as the cracking gun fire ranged off. So, he realized the CLS had been padded with teflon. Shiz opened the sunroof as he swigged off the Pepsi. Bam came poking through, firing the Mac-90 onto the amazed hitters, drenching them in blood as the deadly fire danced their bodies about like the Harlem shake. Shiz sped off, sippin' the Pepsi that brought murder, while Bam's heart pumped speedily watching the smoke rise off the Mac-90.

"See what I mean about pussy? That shit be having niggas trippin'...Ain't nothing though, let's get focused," Shiz mentioned, turning onto the E-way in ear's reach of screaming sirens.

"That was a bad ass bitch!" Shiz sang to Bam exiting the first class flight on the 747. The duo were finally in Jacksonville, Florida, and they had flirted with the flight attendants every step of the way. Bam toted the carryon Louis Vuitton over his shoulder as they made their way through the crowded airport. Shiz was definitely dressed for the occasion, wearing a black Cavalli button up, matching Versace shoes, and cream slacks. He had no heavy jewelry, except a five carat pinky ring and a diamond faced Movado. Bam's Sean John cocoa brown two piece went well with his peanut butter complexion and iced out belt buckle. There was a white Maybach '62 and suited chauffeur standing before the polished vehicle, holding a huge sign reading 'S. Pettiway'. At an eye wink, the chauffeur approached and placed their luggage in the trunk, after showing them inside the vehicle. Despite Shiz never having been in a Maybach before, he showed no signs of amazement as his eyes danced around its interior. He was collected enough to know when shit changed over legally, he'd have one sitting in front of his own estate. Every gangster, thug, and hustler watched movies like Scarface, Godfather, and Carlito's Way growing up, pondering would they ever make it to the level where they could enjoy the spoils of mega success. The cribs featured on them were always the most elegant land structures around. It was shit like that, that made the game alluring and worth the risk. Shiz was no different. And, the fact that this was his first time ever in Jacksonville, his mind wondered on the long scenic ride over to Aziz's, was he in fact living like the villains he idolized on the classic movies. The long swervy roads began to dwindle down, as the hilltop horizons soon sizzled from the scene. Four vineyards that stretched across three acres became visible. A passing Lamborghini and F-430 Ferrari blurred by them speedily, as they neared their destination. Lust instantly filled the hustlers' eyes when the enormous estate coated their pupils. It was now impossible for Shiz to return to his $250,000 condo like it was anything except a fucking hovel, in comparison to the luxurious landmark he and Bam were witnessing.

After traversing the iron gates of the 23 bedroom and 16 ½ bathroom palace, the Maybach pulled under the forty foot alabaster, being supported by giant crystal columns that hosted ruby fixtures from the base on up. The stairs leading to the castle style doors were made out of elephant tusk and 14k gold trimming. Shiz knew

Aziz's shit would be tuff, but this was unimaginable. They were escorted by two Egyptian belly dancing type females who led them into a massive indoor swimming pool area where countless amounts of people with unblemished skin and perfect teeth intermingled. It looked as if some type of party was going on. Shiz spotted Aziz approaching them through the topless girls that randomly jumped into the pool, onlooked by Saudi Sheikhs with darkened shades.

"Shiz, Salaamu Alaykum my friend. How was the trip, pleasurable I hope?" Aziz asked, shaking the hand of Shiz wearing a smile.

"Walaykum salaam, Zeez. I'm good, and yes the trip was straight...Check it, though. Dis my youngen, Bam... Bam, Aziz," Shiz introduced the two and Bam nodded.

"As you know, Shiz, any friend of yours is a friend of mine." His eyes read over Bam.

"That's whassup..." Shiz looked around at the firm breasted cuties."

"Aziz, you really got a crazy nice crib here. This shit is real major, dawg. I didn't even think sumthin' like this was possible."

"Shiz, that's what's wrong with the world today. We dare not to dream. Your compliment was appreciated, but undeserved. This isn't my home; it's my uncle's, Marwaan Al-Yemenee."

"Al Yemenee?' He asked shocked.

"Yes, why do you know of him?" Shiz instantly recognized the name from the CNN and 60 Minutes coverage of the international mogul, related to the Bin Ladens. He had been rumored to have his connect to the international drug trade, but nothing concrete could make those accusations stick. His diplomatic ties made it pretty much impossible to ostracize him from the U.S. He was seldom actually here in the states, but when he came, media flocked to him like Beyonce sightings.

"Ye-Yea," Shiz fumbled, while Bam and Aziz eyed his troublesome expression.

"Let me guess, you saw the broadcast, right?" Shiz nodded.

"Well, let me say this. That ain't nothing but bullshit and TV propaganda," Aziz protested. Shiz was still confused as to why they were in Jacksonville and in Marwaan's home. His wrinkle faced stare told it all.

"Zeez, you my man, but what's this all about. What's really good? I don't do the in the dark thing, and you got a lot of surprises and new twists for the old business you and I are accustomed to. So, I need you to clarify what's this really about?" Shiz spat flat out, noticing the confused look that Bam wore. Shiz flashed his sinister smile, alerting Bam to the trap he was laying.

"Shiz, I understand your concern. But, as I stated, there's an opportunity of a lifetime here to gain," he chimed.

"With all respect, Zeez, you been telling me this same thang for a week! Listen, I saw, I heard, and I'm good, dawg. I'ma go ahead home," Shiz attempted to bait Aziz to reveal what was really going on. Shiz and Bam attempted to spin off when Aziz firmly grasped Shiz's forearm. Bringing him within inches, he leaned in, "700 kilograms at eight grand a pop," he said tight-lipped. Shiz's eyes met his thirstily, as Bam paused his exit.

"Do I have your attention now?" Aziz asked. Three suited gentlemen appeared behind him with ear pieces and darkened Aviators.

"Mr. Aziz, you and your party are being asked for. Follow me, please," one of the suits instructed.

"Very well. Shall we go?" Aziz asked Shiz, before they inched off behind the muscular escorts. They were led down a hall with fifty foot ceilings adorned in Turkish decor, while gold plated Arabic calligraphy coated the marble floor. The hall ended at two huge pearl French style doors that also had solid gold door handles. Before they entered, Aziz shot Shiz a look indicating how serious this was. He could also feel what was nearing was enormous. They took their seats in the classical style study and awaited their host. A suited

Marwaan and twelve henchmen wearing traditional Saudi garments and head wraps entered and surrounded the room, while Marwaan took his seat next to his nephew, Aziz, on the leather sofa. Shiz could see the family resemblance of the handsome Middle Eastern men. They were offered drinks and cigars before anything was discussed. A few of his men relayed messages to him secretly that he would only respond to with a nod or an eye blink. Any fool could see Marwaan was a man of status and business. A grace coated his motion, while determination set in his eyes. But, he wanted for nothing because everything was at his fingertips since he was a man of little words, but great actions. All of these were what Shiz desired to be.

"Ammu, this is my associate, Mr. Pettiway from Philadelphia, who I've been speaking of, and he has come to join us here today for the purpose of this meeting along with his protégé," Aziz sang.

"Aziz, introductions are wasteful to my time because, as you know, he wouldn't be here if I didn't know everything I needed to know about Mr. Pettiway and his associate. So, shall we discuss the meat of the matter?" Marwaan straightened out. Aziz swallowed deeply, acknowledging his error while Shiz pondered what exactly did Marwaan know about him.

"Shiz, my family is looking to expand our cocaine distribution well into the East Coast. We control 65% of the cocaine that exists in America today. The other 35% is controlled by the Mexicans, who ultimately are distributing in the East Coast. Now, there are five focal points for us that are of interest; Philadelphia not being one of them. Because of the recent increase in crime, the F.B.I. is swarming the city trying to resolve the new epidemic of violence, and particularly, coke and gun based crimes. However, what I believe is, if we can get Philadelphia, we own a huge piece of the market which would give us a threshold to steal their other points. So, I managed to convince my uncle to take a shot on the city, despite the current crisis there, and he has agreed… Somewhat," Aziz spat glancing at his uncle who sat motionless, while Shiz listened attentively to every syllable that rolled off of Aziz's tongue. Bam sat wondering how all this was relevant to them, but mostly in awe of Marwaan's king pin status.

"This is where you come in at, Shiz. After overlooking many of the candidates in your city, I felt like you were our guy, and we want you to be our host from Philadelphia."

"Damn Zeez, I appreciate the fact that you have confidence in me, but what exactly are we talking about here?" Shiz questioned.

"Ahh, about urrr, five to one thousan…" Aziz attempted, bobbing his head.

"TWENTY-FIVE HUNDRED KILOGRAMS!" Marwaan interrupted firmly in a rich nasal Arabic accent. Aziz looked puzzled at his uncle.

"Twenty-five hunnit?" Shiz parroted, shockingly.

"Yes. Is that a problem?" Marwaan countered with a sly grin.

"That's a heavy number for…"

"Eighty days!" Marwaan interjected. Bam looked at Shiz, reflecting on the mere 100 units they were struggling to overturn monthly. Aziz lowered his head while his uncle took over.

"You have eighty days to remit payment of 2,500 kilograms, then increase distribution by at least 50% in the following three months. Any failure in these conditions will be deemed as aggression, which will be met with force. Am I making myself clear?" He sang smoothly. Shiz reluctantly nodded, pondering how hard he'd have to bang in the paint to get this one off, if he accepted. Bam saw this as a once-in-a-lifetime opportunity that had to be accepted. And, if for any reason it didn't go right, then they'd just burn the shit out of the connect for the whole stash and product.

"Personally, Mr. Pettiway, I don't think you can pull it off, you barely muster over a hundred units monthly. You have rival forces moving on your turf as we speak, and you seem to focus your attention on old vendettas, rather than protecting new interests. To be quite frank, had not your cousin, Chantel, had that ugly run-in, this conversation wouldn't be taking place now. However, my nephew seems to believe you have it in you to carry the entire city on your back. Why? I don't know, but to your credit, your apparent desire to be wealthy is much stronger than your resolve to quit." Shiz stared into the cold eyes of Marwaan, wanting to tell him '*Fuck you, pussy!*' but he held his tongue in check, realizing his odds.

"Nonetheless, you have been summoned. And, your time will be rewarded with an opportunity to prove me wrong at the price of your blood, and a three million dollar deposit that will be returned to you at the end of our dealings. You have until the end of the year to inform us of your decision," Marwaan spat as he stood to exit the side door he had entered through. He turned to add, "Gentlemen, enjoy the rest of the weekend and my home I invited you to. I prepared quarters for the both of you in the west wing of the mansion. Spare no expense, and please enjoy it all, how do you say...'Homie'." He clapped his hands and the French doors flew opened, tons of butt-naked, voluptuous, beautiful women poured in flocking to Bam and Shiz, itching to serve them as Marwaan exited the study. This was truly what the game was all about...???

- THE END -

C.E.O.
2

"Oh, oh, ooh shit. It feels so good, daddy. I'm cummin'," Moet spieled in pleasure.

"Get that money, freaky bitch," Black chimed, spreading her butt cheeks. He licked his thumb and stuck it in her asshole. She squealed in pleasure, causing her pussy to drench Black's lap, along with the nut he coated her insides with. She leaned back and gyrated her fat ass against his oozing dick while he played in her hair.

"After…we..get out the shower…we out..A'ight?" Black huffed, clearly out of breath.

"Well c'mon then, get your fat ass up," she said, helping him off the couch.

The team Shiz had deployed suited up in the hotel located in downtown Wilmington. It had been three long weeks since they set up to wipe out Black's empire. After being reinforced with scoped M-16's and beamed Mac-90's, they had devised another plan that was sure to bring Black's shit crumbling. While most of the crew sat back chillin' and waiting for nightfall, Tay was up pacing the floor, repeatedly checking the window for daylight.

"Dawg! Sit da fuck down somewhere, man," M screamed on Tay.

"Nigga, I'm ready to rock da fuck out, you need to be telling these niggas to get on their toes," Tay fired back.

"You muthafuckas is crazy," M spat. Tay said nothing, rather concentrated on his eight step pace from wall to wall. Rob looked at M and shook his head. He knew Tay was a loose cannon who thought he had it all figured out. Dee disconnected the call with Shiz and Bam, looking upbeat and alive as he re-entered the suite.

"Yo! Shiz said he and Bam down Jacksonville fuckin' wit some major niggas, and we have to have a meeting as soon as he get back.

Nigga talkin' like we got some serious shit to consider. OH! M, he said don't let this nigga get off this time, and to watch Tay because the 'lil nigga be speedin' sometimes." Rob laughed at the last of Dee's comments. M began loading the weapons at the table as he eyed the time on the clock.

"Major niggas, huh? Who da fuck this nigga done met now way down Jacksonville?" M shot. "You know Mo stay runnin' into money. That's the only muthafucka I know that keep coming up heavy," Rob shot, lying on the bed flipping through channels.

$ $ $ $ $

Black's seven series pulled into Saks Fifth Avenue being chauffeured by Moet. His two goons parked beside him and walked at a ten step distance behind him and his chic. Since the beef started, he took out several precautions to assure his life, while he wiped theirs out; all night look-outs, bullet proof windows and doors on the whip, and mothafuckas that looked like him wearing his clothes parading around. Moet dangled from Black's arm as they browsed the aisles, with two sales reps tagging along. He sat down when Moet went into the fitting room to try on some Racheal Roy fall dresses.

"How many can I get, baby?" She bellowed from the dressing area.

"Whatever you want, Mo, go 'head," he said eyeing his diamond faced Breitling.

"This shit is hot, Black. You gonna love me in this 'lil muthafucka, watch!" She sang stepping from the closet.

"You like it?" She asked, twirling around in the mirror looking into his reflection.

"Yea, that's fly. Let me see, turn around." She did what he asked, noticing his goons staring as well.

"Ahem!" She cleared her throat, shooting Black a look to alert him of the outta pocket help. He looked over to them, but they acted like they were browsing as well.

"What these dresses runnin', man?" He asked, glancing over his cell phone.

"The V-neck is $7,500 and the strapless is $5,900. We have matching shoes, would you like to see them as well?" The rep asked him, while he attempted Trig from his cell.

"Yea whatever, sis, just get it out here." Trig didn't pick up so Black left a message to call back. Moet already had a mean shoe game from Jimmy Choo to Monolo, but she would rather miss her wedding than an opportunity to add to her vicious shoe collection. Black could care less. He just wanted to go after not reaching Trig.

"Get whatchu gonna get 'cause I'm out after this."

"Alright Black! Why you gettin' an attitude, baby?" She wanted to know, but he ignored her as he played with his Blackberry. The reps began wrapping Moet's purchases up while she took a seat on Black's lap.

"Thank you, baby. I love you," she chimed, kissing him on the cheek, happier than a homo in boys' town.

"And?" Black sang with a distant look. She sighed rolling her eyes.

"And, I appreciate you taking time out to shop with me."

"And?" She giggled.

"And, I'ma be a good girl," she sang, wondering where the dark skinned sister had gotten her bag from.

"And?"

"What, Black?!" She hissed. He answered with a pelvic thrust that jerked her frame.

"Ill...You are soo nasty. Ain't nobody fuckin' with you, Black," she chimed, admiring the gold buckle and silver stitched Gucci bag shorty had her hands tucked in, as she proceeded towards them behind over sized Chanel shades.

"Dropp that shit N roll wit it," Black chanted, imitating the Ying-Yang twins' voice on his bug-out. Moet laughed at the lyrics and Black's silly sense of humor. She loved his persona.

"I don't know why I love your stupid ass," she teased before shorty pulled the .40 caliber out of the purse she was drooling over. No one seemed to notice shorty advancing the well lighted department store with the toaster out. Black's goons were on lookout for strange looking males. A chic took everybody for a spin, as the entire scene played chopped and screwed for Moet.

"I love you, too, Mo," he said unknowingly.

"No God, no, not Blaaaacckkk!" Moet's horrific scream pierced the stale department store....

(SILENCE BEFORE THE ERUPTION)

CASH IS KING PUBLISHING

Shaahir
Author & C.E.O.

As a youngin', I knew I wanted to do big things. From the penny candy store, I coached my brothers to run, while I played freely, to the crack deals I negotiated between periods in middle school. It was clear I would go places, but I wanted to do so, receiving more for less. Unfortunately, that attitude landed me in S.C.I. Albion with a 20 year max. It was during a recommit period (i.e. parole violation) from a three year run, in which I managed to build an empire and lifestyle loaded with high end luxury whips, trips, and my very best, Zaahid & Asheyaanah. This was considered my defining moment, but yet again, I was stripped of it all in exchange for the "box".

So, with the walls closing in, everybody and everything that was supposed to be forever began fleeing. I realized that it's not how great you build your empire that matters; it's what you build it on that's essential. From that moment on, I was determined not to be a victim of systematic fatality ever again. All of my funds and assets had to be founded on lawful businesses that were more than my 'get rich quick' schemes.

I knew at that time, I had the ability to write inspiring works from love to hood novels, but I really wanted my voice heard as I spoke it. So, I founded Cash Is King Publishing, along with my man Brian Holt who has a tremendous eye for business, and released my first urban fiction title C.E.O.

I had always heard as a child from my Umm (mother) "you can obtain what your mind desires." And, that statement was never believable until this hustler became the C.E.O. based on sincere efforts and sheer determination to succeed. Somebody once asked me, "Why y'all name the company Cash Is King?" Life's experiences have taught me something - people are subservient to C.R.E.A.M. How many relationships, family, and partnerships have been destroyed or built on dough? Undoubtedly, those who are 'up' get the red carpet treatment. So, I named it Cash Is King because 'we demand royalty through paper'.

It is my hope that others realize that dreams are meant to be fulfilled, regardless of what situation and circumstances life thrusts at you. The bare butt naked truth is, if you want to pop off, success is at your fingertips and opportunity is what you make it.... Dare to dream!

Sincerely yours,
Shaun Pettiway

CASH IS KING PUBLISHING

Brian 'B-Easy' Holt

Co-Founder

For me, Cash Is King was an opportunity of a lifetime. Financially, I was in the position to enrich the industry with quality material. Never in my wildest dreams did I ever imagine teaming up with my man, and establishing a company in literary art. Being raised in the inner city, I experienced a lot of heartbreak and setbacks. A single parent household has many disadvantages, but the saying holds true, 'It gets greater later' and I'm bearing the fruit of that now. This publication is a testification that tough times always pass; it's the people that remain. So, here I am, Cash Is King!

Always much love and blessing to my mom, Kim Brown, and my beautiful sister, Nakisha Brown, my wonderful neice, Dasiyah, and my loving grandmom, Thelma Holt...My best days are ahead of me, this is just the beginning!

Major love to my gone but not forgotten people. R.I.P. to my grandfathers, Jody and Hitler. Also, my loving aunts: Gigi, Libby, Jackie, and Delores. R.I.P. to those folks who treated your boy like family: Ms. Yvonne Harvey, Ms. Olga Hartwell, Ms. Rosie Queen, Uncle Pete, Danny Rumpf, Khalif, Bleek, Big Rell, Lil Reefie, Hanif, Doc, Ahjere, Billy Nole, Moo Bennett, T. Sheaff, Q. Rainer, D. Pelle, Aaron Young, Bonita Young, Shawn and Shannon Wiggins, J. Halles, LA...

SPECIAL THANKS to those that stood tall with your boy through the whole fight. Without y'all there wouldn't be no me. Let major love and blessing be upon you: My aunts: Joe, Bootsie, Adella, Sarah, Rashida, Fran, Pat, Mo, Lorna, Phyllis. My uncles: Hope, Meaty, Larry, Fess, Mark, Kirk Love, Big Shot, Bozo. My cousins: Tanya, Toni, Kim, Steph, Ife, Fela, Tia, Chandra, Sabria, Mya, Lesha, Jj, Anitra, Lori, Danielle, Val, Adia, Charity, Elaine, Mickey, Nicole, Ashley, Khalilah, Steve, Kev, Porky, Squalky, Harv, Zay, Chris, Shank, Jelani, Chioke, Tahid, Fred, Khalil. My extended family: Ms. Jean, Main-ski, Reem, Sweets, Dub, Zeus, Ret, Coosa, Shanks, Banks, Meat, Miz, Reese, Baby Don, Butter, Bub, Beasley, Cheeks, Mel, Shiz, T-mac, Epps, Ant Green, Oatmeal, 007(Q), Leon, Rome, Milk, Dust, Nicky, D-nice, Tiff, Keisha, Kim Smith, Nydira, Shadiyah, Cherie, Joy, Sherell, Shiny, Shanell, the Pettiway's, the Queen's, the Harris', the Ford's, Haines Street, Pastorius Street, BWL, the Alkies, the Jungle, and last but not least GOD. No disrespect, I'm sure I left a few good people out, but I got y'all for sure on the next go around, 'cuz it's more bangers on the way!

Wow, I almost forgot! A very special thank you to the few lames who hated ya boy out or tried to. I would bust back and air y'all out, but you won't get no free press here. Plus, to hate y'all out is beneath me and the negative energy would kill this whole super-cool calm swag I got going on with me, and oh boy how would y'all love that, but you know I can't let y'all win. Look, ya boy ain't hard to find so reach for me. Maybe we can straighten out this mess y'all created, then I might let y'all jump back in the car before it pull off again without you. Until then, I'm too busy doing me, cranking out these hitz. Just remember, ain't no hard feeling with this, Easy still loves you.

Sincerely yours,
Brian Holt
'Demanding royalty through paper'

'S KING PRESENTS...

CASH IS KING PUBLISHING

Quantity	Book Info	Cost Each	Cost Total
	Copies of C . E . O .	$15.00	
	Special Note-Inmate Discount $2.00 off the cover price for all orders from or on behalf of inmates at state and federal institutions	$13.00	
	Shipping Charges Add $2.00 for the first copy Add $1.00 for any additional copies	$2.00 $1.00	
TOTAL PAYMENT ☐ **CASH/MONEY ORDER** ☐ **CHECK** ☐ **CREDIT CARD**			

☐ **VISA**
☐ **MASTERCARD**
☐ **DISCOVER**

***ORDERS ARE PROCESSED WITH* PAYPAL NETWORK**

CARD NUMBER	EXPIRATION DATE
CARDHOLDER NAME	SECURITY CODE
SIGNATURE	AMOUNT

SEND ORDERS TO:
Cash Is King Publishing
P.O. Box #44434
Philadelphia, PA 19144
www.cashiskingpub.com